Eat What You Kill

Introducing Arlon Grey

Book 1

Josef Peeters

DEDICATION

To my adventurous brother and sister-in-law for laying it all on the line to make a silk purse from a sow's ear. Were it not for their generosity and good intentions this author may never have had the opportunity to visit their town, experience the excitement or participate in some small way in its transformation.

Books by the author

Fiction:

Dumped (action/adventure)
Daintree Denizens (thriller)
Mt. Moulamein (sci-fi)
Transience (magic realism)
Black Heart (psych. thriller)
Endure (dystopian) Out soon

Horror Series:

Eat What You Kill (Book 1)
B.A.M. (Book 2)
Eye For An Eye (Book 3)
The Guardians (Book 4) Out soon

Non-Fiction:

Wood Whisperer Volume 1
Wood Whisperer Volume 2
Wood Whisperer Volume 3
Giving Up (Short, autobiographical)

Visit Josef's web page for all purchase links and book descriptions;
http://lakesidecaravanpark.wixsite.com/josef

AUTHOR'S NOTE

Authors are often asked about the source of their inspiration for story ideas. In the case of this novel, it is an easy question for me to answer. My brother bought a town! Rarely can someone make that sort of extraordinary proclamation but in my case it is true. My brother and his wife purchased the town of Allies Creek in 2019 for a sum that would normally be associated with a single home in many of the cities in Australia and gained some notoriety in the media as a result.

While performing a little research on the town, my wife came across a short fictional story on Reddit. My story was inspired by a combination of that item and the town purchase. I tried to contact the author of the Reddit piece to gain his or her blessing for my story but I was unsuccessful. I thank the author of that short story for inspiring me.

My story is completely fictional and the characters in no way represent my brother, sister-in-law or anyone else associated with the town of Allies Creek. That said, it will be interesting to witness their reaction to the tale. I hope you, the reader, will enjoy my story.

ONE

"Do not go there, do not buy this town," announced the article-cum-fictional melodrama being read by Arlon Grey as he sipped his first coffee of the morning. It was some internet thing, something he should take note of Clarice had said as he entered the office earlier. Arlon didn't go for all the internet social media nonsense as, it seemed, did ninety-nine per cent of the population.

He used the internet sparingly for research only. For that reason he had all the latest in computers and high-speed access installed in his office the moment he signed the lease. It was imperative for his line of work, one that had adopted him when he left the police department. It seemed a natural progression for the tall, lanky Australian with handsome, chiselled features and olive complexion, betraying his Mediterranean heritage on his great-grandfather's side.

Born and bred Queensland, Arlon had a broad Australian accent which seemed incongruent with his clipped speech and pompous mannerisms, as well as a swarthy buccaneer image of dark wavy hair and lustrous cobalt-blue eyes that weakened the knees of most females when they came under their spell. The image of an enigmatic charm was, however, short-lived. After only the briefest time in the man's company, people were more likely to describe Arlon Grey as 'a cold fish'.

His secretary, Clarice Manning, had experienced that conflicting image-versus-reality adjustment during her first interview with him. It was disconcerting in the extreme to separate the romantic vision of the man with the actuality facing her over the large desk. The soft-spoken voice devoid of all human emotion clashed so violently with the charismatic countenance that it left her struggling to find a voice that first day. Over a year in his employ she had grown to accept his indescribably soulless demeanour as the falseness he professed it to be, yet never ceased to be amazed at its presence.

"Ms Manning?" asked the disembodied monotone voice over her intercom in the outer office.

"Yes, Arlon?"

"Why do you believe that it's important for me to read through campfire ghost stories?"

"The woman was hospitalised after she wrote that; complete mental breakdown," explained Clarice in her most cheerful voice, hoping, however impossibly, that her ebullience might somehow rub off on her boss.

"I see. So I should pay attention to the mad scribblings of some demented sheila rather than employ good sense and judgement after a thorough investigation?" asked Arlon rhetorically, knowing his secretary would answer nonetheless.

"Don't you think it's very mysterious, Arlon?"

"No, Ms Manning, I don't. I haven't been engaged by Mr Granger to undertake investigations into flights of fancy or be influenced by internet stories, regardless of how intriguing you deem them to be. We have a job to do regarding due diligence for our client acting on behalf of the potential purchasers, the Henderson couple, that concentrates more on the quality of the water table and its possible contamination by the sawmilling operation..."

"What about the reports of missing persons and all the talk of the strange noises?"

"Come in here, please, Ms Manning."

"Sure thing, Arlon," she replied with her usual unassuming grace.

When Clarice went through the half-glass door into Arlon's office, she sighed at the sight of the most handsome man she had ever laid eyes on. *If only he never spoke a word it would be so easy to love him*, she thought. She pushed back her ringlets of gold falling about her cherubic face, looking amazingly like an adult version of Shirley Temple, including the dimples, albeit with a slightly darker complexion. A full figure, clad in a bright floral-print dress ending at the knees, bespoke of her inability to decline an eclair or two yet did not take away from a certain voluptuous appeal...to anyone but Arlon.

"Yes, Arlon?" she asked upon entering his office, pen and pad in hand should he wish her to take dictation.

"Ms Manning, when was the last time you recall hearing of me attending the cinema?"

"Um...never?"

"Theatre production?"

"No," she admitted quietly, knowing what would transpire.

"Fiction book?"

"Not ever, Arlon."

"No forays into fiction or entertainments of any description?"

"No," she said flatly.

"Why is that?"

"Your condition?"

"Precisely. My condition. No, I'm not interested in reports of missing persons or strange noises or mental patients with delusional paranoia. I'm interested, primarily, in attaining test results for the subterranean water table to ensure its potable nature, as requested by our client, and anything else the purchasers require to enable them to make an informed decision on the property, Allies Creek. That's where our responsibilities ends and also our interest. Clear?"

"As a bell, Mr Grey," she replied, reverting to a more formal tone as she felt thoroughly chastised.

"Have you heard back from Mr Henderson regarding the second inspection?"

"Emailed a few moments ago. He and his wife will be staying over for the weekend. The owner will be away and invited them to house-sit. Sort of gives them free run of the place without her being there. Mrs McAllen said she'll be back early Monday to answer any questions they might have. Knowing those two, it will be a bloody long list," she said with an infectious smile that did not affect Arlon.

"Excellent. I'll meet them there on Saturday morning with the building inspector and the water bloke. What's his name?"

"Which one?"

"The water bloke. I can never remember his name."

"Oh, he is a queer one, isn't he? Gloom and doom. Never smiles...shit. Sorry."

"Always apologising for no good reason. The name?" he asked pointedly.

"Oh, right. Gavin Gaze, and boy, doesn't he? Gazes at you like a blooming zombie, all dark under the eyes and..."

"Are you finished?"

"Sorry."

"Again?"

"Sorry."

"Stop it. Stop being sorry. I know I never smile and I have no feelings that you can hurt, so stop being sorry all the time. It's impossible to insult me. If you end up saying something a bit stupid, which is pretty regular, then just accept it and move on, would you?"

"You've never once in your whole life been hurt or insulted?"

"I can be hurt in the physical sense only. No, never insulted. Can't happen."

"Must be a blessing and a curse all at the same time for you, that?"

"Hardly either. Now, if you've finished trying to psychoanalyse me maybe you can send that email informing the Hendersons that I will join them at Allies Creek by, say...ten o'clock Saturday morning if that suits them. If they agree, tee it up with Mr Gaze and the building inspector, Bill Rogers."

"Sure thing, Arlon. Sorry if I'm a bit nosey. I...I said sorry again, didn't I?"

Arlon ignored his secretary, turning to face the computer screen again. He retreated from whichever website had housed the silly horror story about the goings-on at Allies Creek. Robert Granger, the solicitor acting on behalf of the Hendersons, had hired Arlon to do some of the due diligence involved in purchasing the property about three hours west of Brisbane. Arlon's purview ended with securing the building inspector to report on the status of the cottages and other structures, and attaining a water evaluation. Mr Gaze would be taking samples from the large dam on the property as well as samples from any wells or bore water, which might include some drilling.

The solicitor had been instrumental in Arlon's success to date, favouring him with substantial investigative contracts on a range of matters concerning his clients' needs. Arlon had operated his current business for only twelve months and might have faltered had it not been for the generous nature of Mr Robert Granger. Arlon's choice of clients remained slim because of his unique qualities that disturbed most people he met.

Were it not for the fact that Arlon had saved Robert's reputation and his livelihood a few years earlier in his capacity as a policeman, Robert may not have been disposed to deal with Arlon either. His condition, quite rare, quite annoying...if he could feel annoyance…was the reason he was no longer in the force. Doctors pronounced his condition when he was approaching his teenage years. While his parents felt a modicum of relief that the problem had been identified and gave them possible absolution for any involvement in their son's condition, it continued to cause great concern.

Commonly affiliated with autism, alexithymia is the inability to identify and describe emotions. On the Toronto Alexithymia Scale, Arlon registered in the top percentile, the more acute end, rendering him incapable of displaying emotions or understanding them. Naturally, this leads to an inability to empathise or sympathise with others.

Arlon was finally given his marching orders from the force when he answered a question truthfully. The question was being asked by the mother of a five-year-old girl found raped, sodomised and then tortured to death over a year. Arlon explained in graphic detail what had occurred to her little girl based on the forensic evidence, while the mother shook with grief in wide-eyed horror.

It was the final straw for Arlon's career. His chief told him to resign then and there or be arrested, or be taken out the back of the station by the biggest and meanest of his detectives or...something. His chief did not know what to do with his underling. Arlon resigned that day. The rest of the agency silently cheered.

"Ms Manning?" Arlon asked through the intercom.

"Yes, Arlon?"

"I've changed my mind. I think I'll venture up to Allies Creek on Friday night with my new caravan. Time for its shakedown cruise, I think."

"Arlon...do you...do you think I might come along?"

"Why on earth would you want to come along?"

"Oh, I'm super-interested. It would be fun. Don't you think?"

"No."

"Are you saying 'no', it wouldn't be fun, or 'no', I may not come?"

"It's your free time and you may ride along if you wish. It won't be fun. It's never fun. I don't know what fun is. You will stay in one of the...*other* accommodations?"

"Of course, silly. I wouldn't dream of asking to stay with you...unless you asked me to...?" Hearing no reply and not expecting one, she clicked off.

Arlon believed he had just made an error in judgement. He had the distinct impression that his secretary harboured certain notions about him and her: impossible notions. He understood that she was attractive according to almost any man that had contact with her, despite her largish proportions. 'Big-boned' is how she sometimes put it when Arlon had the tactlessness to ask. She knew about his condition, yet strived at every opportunity to inveigle herself into Arlon's good graces. Flirting, he believed it was called.

Men somehow reacted to a woman displaying this trite, inane behaviour aimed at them. Arlon had read about it, experienced it from time to time, yet could not conceive of a reality in which such odd behaviour succeeded. It had to work, he surmised, as women and men found one another somehow and ended up marrying and making babies a lot of the time. It was a foreign concept to Arlon, one he felt sure he had explained at one time or another to his secretary.

"Are you there, Arlon?" came the plaintive tone from the desktop speaker.

"Is there someplace else I might've gone in the last few seconds?"

"Yes, I mean, no... Sorry..."

"I think we've covered that by now, surely?"

"Yes, yes, I suppose we have."

"Ms Manning?" asked Arlon after a long silence.

"Yes, Arlon?"

"Was there a question in there somewhere?"

"Oh, oh, goodness, silly me, yes."

"Yes, any time now?"

"I wanted to know...what you think I should wear."

"Asking a bloke what a woman should wear is open to any number of fallacies and vagaries, Ms Manning. If you're asking me what you should wear and expect any accuracy or honesty, it might be helpful to know a time and location for the enquiry."

"Well, to Allies Creek, of course. I thought a smart detective like you might have figured that one out."

"I'm probably the last man on earth to have deduced the machinations of a woman's mind, especially yours, Ms Manning. As to Allies Creek; it's not a nudist colony to the best of my recollections, therefore 'clothes' might be the appropriate answer."

"Well, DUH! I knew that much, Arlon. I was asking if there was anything specific I might wear or bring along in your opinion."

"Ms Manning, while it's certainly true that I am out of the office and often at different country locations, hence the need for my new caravan, I'm hardly an outdoors person and have few ideas regarding *my* wardrobe, much less yours. If it helps you at all, I intend to bring along a set of khaki work clobber and stout walking boots for when I have to accompany the water tester to the property perimeter, and for when I am asked to inspect any of the houses and buildings. It's necessary to wear the appropriate footwear in case of snakes..."

"Snakes!"

"Certainly, snakes, red back spiders and any other creepy-crawlies thereabouts. A good sun hat would also be recommended. If you choose to go bathing with the eels and whatever else may occupy the dam, then a swimsuit may be in order. I suggest light nightwear of a non-flimsy or transparent quality. Practical wear is the term that comes to mind. I'm not venturing into any town to sample nightlife or food as I'll be providing for myself, mainly barbeque fare. If you wish to chip in with me to share my meals, I'm happy to do so, otherwise, you'll need to bring your own. I believe the houses have all the basics for short-term accommodation."

"Snakes?"

"Absolutely. All country areas have snakes, both poisonous and non-poisonous, though mostly the former. Still wish to accompany me?"

"Arlon?"

"Yes, Ms Manning?"

"You sure don't sugar-coat anything, do you?"

"Most assuredly not. I'll be leaving Brisbane from my residence in Indooroopilly about four-thirty I reckon. Do you wish to meet me there or should I pick you up?"

"It would be better for you if I met you there, Arlon. I assume you're going up through Toowoomba?"

"Correct. You have my address?"

"Sure. See you around a quarter past four then."

"If you're certain that's how you want to spend your weekend off. Have you filled in your time card for the week?"

"Sent it through five minutes ago. No overtime, so standard week."

"Ms Manning?"

"Yes, I am still here!" remarking in much the same tone as he had employed moments ago.

"I know for a fact that you've come early to the office at least twice this week, why would you not put down for overtime?"

"Well, Arlon. The way I see it is this. If you ask me to stay longer or come in early, that is overtime. If I decide to come in early I class that as my decision and on my own time."

"I appreciate that, however, either claim the overtime in future or come in on time. I prefer it to be that way."

"If you say so," she said with a sigh.

"I do."

TWO

As they turned left into the road for Allies Creek, Clarice became nervous about the possibility of snakes. Then, out of her peripheral vision, she spotted a large bird wandering in front of Arlon's Toyota Prado 4WD. It was a tall bird with a curious little tuft of black feathers or hair atop its white head. The bush curlew continued to march in front of the slow-moving vehicle without concern for its safety, peering back occasionally to ascertain the distance of the strange object.

Clarice smiled at the charming bird while Arlon simply kept his distance, not wishing to alarm the creature in any way. Eventually, the curlew decided it had had enough of the road for the time being and veered off into the scrubland. Over the distance of just a few kilometres from the town, they witnessed a variety of Australia's fauna dashing over the road or bounding along beside the slow-moving vehicle towing Arlon's brand new 16-foot Jayco pop-top camper.

"What the heck is that?" asked Clarice suddenly.

"I believe that's a goanna."

"Oh, that's right. I've seen them before in the zoo. Dangerous?"

"Only if bitten."

"Great!"

"I think you'll find that most animals will leave you alone if you do the same, Ms Manning."

"Arlon, would it hurt you to use my name while we're out of the office?"

"Didn't I just use your name?"

"I meant my first name, Arlon."

"Why would it make a difference?"

"A bit less formality out of office hours would be nice. Don't you like my name?"

"I have no feelings on the matter, as you know. It's impossible for me to like or dislike your name. If you prefer me to use your first name during the weekend, I'll do my best to remember. I hope you'll understand if I lapse at times."

"That's okay. You don't have to use my first name if it makes you feel uncomfortable."

"I don't feel comfort. I don't feel anything at all in the emotional sense, nothing. I know no other way. It's not like I did at some point and then magically lost it. I was born with the condition. Rare as it is, especially being in the high range, leaving me incapable of normal emotions, I have it and therefore I must live with it. I can't feel bad about it or guilty or anything else. It makes no difference to me."

"That is so...sad."

"Not for me. I'm beyond such things as sadness."

"And happiness."

"Naturally."

"Nothing natural about it, Arlon. No one should have to suffer the non-existence of emotions."

"I don't know. I see a lot of what people go through and what they are capable of because of those emotions and I conclude that I am probably better off without them."

"No, that can't be true. I admit that a lot of bad things come from emotions, but I still believe the good outweighs the bad by a long shot."

"You wouldn't say that if you'd seen what I've seen as a policeman and detective."

"Arlon, you've experienced only the worst. Unfortunately, you'll never share the good side because you have no interest in love, laughter or happiness. I've only just realised that now for the first time. You'll never marry or love another human, and that's very, very sad, Arlon."

"I'll also forgo any heart-break, arguments or divorce as a result of my condition. I'll never be swayed by emotions to do the wrong thing by me or someone else. I had to learn self-defence early on. Children are especially cruel and incapable of understanding what they consider to be a freak sharing their classroom.

"My father taught me the rudiments of self-defence, utilising the martial arts. It's a discipline I maintain to this day. It's served me well in many situations when confronted with persons of limited imagination and an oversupply of brawn.

"Some might view my circumstances as less than ideal. I don't care one way or the other. I deal with what or who I am in the only way I know how, abstractly, as though I am viewing myself from an exterior point of view."

"I still find it sad for you, Arlon. Emotions are the stuff of life, for better or worse. Sure there are always the extreme examples, but mostly, folks get to experience the joys of living and you can never know that joy or experience the love of another."

Arlon stole a sidewise glance at Clarice to discover tears in her eyes. He was puzzled by the sight. He could not begin to understand the depths of emotions required to weep silent tears of compassion for another human being she hardly knew. He supposed Clarice was just that type of person, or perhaps it was true of most females. He could never be sure.

The road ahead was bare earth with runnels and ruts formed by the last heavy rains several years before. Arlon proceeded at a sedate pace, keeping his vehicle to the centre of the road. The scenery was of a drab scrubland variety seen on most inland Australian journeys: mainly eucalypts, acacias and wattles. Sturdy ironbark and red gums, of the general timbers useful for milling purposes, were to be found only further inland of their position, in the section now classed as a state forest once the timber concessions expired or were denied.

Arlon peered sceptically at the parched surrounds, doubtful of the purchaser's plans for the township when the fire hazards and lack of water were considered. To Arlon's understanding, the dam on the property was at ten per cent capacity with forecasts of only minor rains in the coming months. It was not within his purview to make comments or observations on that score, so he would keep his opinions to himself unless specifically asked.

Clarice remained silent, watching the monotonous scenery pass by the slow-moving vehicle. She absently monitored the verges for signs of animal life. She had long been an admirer of Australian native fauna, frequenting zoos whenever possible. Her favourite was Steve Irwin's wildlife park on the north coast with all the reptiles housed safely behind enclosures. She had mourned with the rest of the country and the world at his passing from such an unlikely cause.

Anyone who had seen any of Steve Irwin's nature documentaries would have placed a bet on him being taken by an enormous saltwater crocodile or bitten by any one of the venomous snakes he handled so brazenly, even flippantly, some might say. It shocked the nation to hear of his passing when he was stabbed in the chest by a stingray's lethal barb. The odds on such a rare death would have been astronomical. The world grieved with his well-known family and paid homage to the likeable Australian larrikin.

When the forest finally cleared as they approached the entrance to the town of Allies Creek, Clarice was overcome with a sudden and inexplicable feeling of pure horror coupled with an overwhelming sadness. The feeling was fleeting, yet indelibly inked in her recollections thereafter. From the small rise on which Arlon paused the vehicle, the desolate town descended to meet the bush again at its boundaries. In the centre of all that scrub was the small town consisting of thirteen period homes, circa the early 1900s, one church of no particular denomination, and two very large sawmilling sheds next to a large dam with only a minimum of water.

To say that the homes were run-down would be understating the matter. The place had a queer ambience of desolation and desperation. The term 'ghost town' did not do it justice. But Arlon didn't share in Clarice's foreboding. He inspected the town with the clinical eye of his profession. His condition allowed him the convenience of dispassionate appraisal in all things, without the hindrance of emotions colouring the result.

He looked for an overall impression of suitability for the end-users' projected plans. The Hendersons were hoping to make something of a country resort out of the derelict township, an enormous undertaking if they decided to refurbish the present infrastructure. It was up to their solicitor, and Arlon's agency, to help determine the best course of action and suitability for the Hendersons to pursue their goals for the town. Arlon would be meeting Bill Rogers, the building inspector, later that evening, who would share accommodations with Gavin Gaze.

The Hendersons would be occupying the present owner's home, the first on the left upon entry to the town. The house opposite, on the right side of the main street, would accommodate the two inspectors, while Clarice would take the home next in line after the church, two down on the left. Though Arlon and Clarice had both attempted to contact Mrs McAllen to ask her advice on where Arlon might park his caravan, there had been no reply to either phone messages or emails. They were not overly concerned because they knew that Mrs McAllen would receive telecommunications only once she left the area, closer to Mundubbera, where there was a cell tower.

Arlon figured that Mrs McAllen had left early and was driving to her destination, despite the presence of a vehicle in the McAllen carport: an old, worn and dusty Toyota Landcruiser ute. Arlon concluded that perhaps the dilapidated, old ute was only used as a paddock-basher and was not her main mode of transport. He was unsure if there was a *Mr* McAllen in the picture, whose car it might have been if that was the case. He hadn't heard of a husband or partner in his communications with Robert Granger, the solicitor.

Arlon assumed the area to the immediate right of the main residence would suffice for his caravan, as long as there was a power-point he could plug into. He had equipped his van with solar panels in case he worked in truly isolated locations, and even included a back-up generator. However, it was always preferable to use power if it was readily available. The owner had an electric golf buggy she used around the town for general purposes of transport and haulage. They had been instructed that the buggy could be utilised by them during their inspections. It also meant that an exterior power-point would be available.

No sooner had Arlon parked his caravan in the small clearing to the right of the McAllen residence, when he and Clarice were visited by numerous wallabies and a plethora of birdlife, including a flock of vociferous drongos, of the family Dicruridae. Arlon imagined that the animals were used to being fed by the owner. Clarice fawned, fussed and cooed over the animals, while Arlon looked on unimpressed, especially when he spied the large ticks hanging in grape-like bunches from the wallabies' backs and ears.

He would be sure to check all exposed areas of himself whenever he returned to his caravan each evening. He hoped that the ticks he observed were not of the paralysis variety, one of the commonest ticks, found mainly on Australia's eastern seaboard. A family of currawongs began warbling in the hope of inducing the humans to feed them.

Arlon turned away to tend to the task of readying his van for occupation, retrieving his extension lead to plug into the power-point he had located nearby, on the outside of the house under the veranda. Afterwards, he ushered Clarice back into the Toyota Prado to deliver her and her impressive array of luggage to her cosy, albeit run-down, cottage one hundred metres down the road.

Before Arlon returned to his van, Mrs Henderson arrived in her Lexus SUV with its plush leather interior and sophisticated styling. She turned directly into the carport of the owner's home, parking next to the battered, yellow ute. She emerged from the driver's side with an air of confidence and assumed authority. She was greatly disappointed to find no welcoming reception. Her stature almost crumbled as she peered about her frantically, relieved when she spied her husband's underling approaching.

Arlon saw the lady standing just inside the carport next to her late model vehicle, now covered in the ubiquitous red dust of the outback. She appeared to be concerned about something. Though he had not yet been introduced to either Mr or Mrs Henderson, he assumed that the lady had to be Mr Henderson's wife. He could not see any sign of the husband as he drove up to the side of his van.

"My luggage is in the back," said the lady.

"Good to know. You're Mrs Henderson?"

"I am."

"Has your husband gone inside already?"

"Mr Henderson will be arriving tomorrow morning. He had a last-minute meeting to attend in the city and was unable to accompany me. Who are you?"

"I beg your pardon: I assumed you knew. My name is Arlon Grey, your solicitor's contractor for certain evaluations and inspections to be made tomorrow. I have my assistant with me, Clarice Manning, whom I have just settled into the cottage beyond the church. If you will excuse me I have some..."

"Mr Grey, fetch my luggage if you would be so kind, so that I may get *myself* settled," said Gloria Henderson with a look that brooked no challenge.

Arlon peered at the woman in front of him with her ramrod straight posture and an air of superiority exuding from every pore. A voluminous shock of pure black hair, obviously not her natural colour, topped off the odd-shaped head. Her face had seen more than her share of the surgeon's 'artistry'. Her eyebrows, highly arched and almost touching her hairline, were stretched incredibly taut, giving her a permanent look of inquisitiveness or surprise. Her nose had been shaved down to a mere sliver, while her lips had the appearance of having been given a proper belting or two over time.

Arlon's gaze slowly swept down the figure before him, taking in the enormous, implanted breasts attempting to break free from the designer blouse, down to her waist held firmly in place by a wide cowgirl belt studded with rhinestones, and a huge buckle that glinted gold in the waning afternoon light. The spray-painted jeans showed every contour and dimple her aging body had to offer, including an unflattering camel-toe in the crotch. The jeans ended in a pair of Cuban-heeled riding boots that had never seen a horse.

"Mrs Henderson, I'm not contracted to you or your husband. I'm in the employ of your solicitor, Mr Robert Granger. I would not, however, be attending to his luggage either if he demanded it of me. I have certain tasks to perform here for Mr Granger and neither I nor my secretary will be at your disposal for any other duties you feel inclined to request. If you'll excuse me, I'll now see to my dinner."

"I beg your pardon?"

"Didn't you hear me? Must be all that hair, I reckon. Be difficult to hear anything through that lot. Just so you can hear me this time; see to your own luggage, Mrs Henderson," he said in the loudest voice he could muster above his usual whisper.

Arlon turned away immediately to unlock and enter his van, leaving a bewildered and frustrated Mrs Henderson staring after him, open-mouthed.

He saw her again only after he had cooked and eaten his frugal fare, sitting outside in a camp chair, viewing the evening sky full of stars. She had changed into a flouncy, red-and-white patterned skirt that was way too short for someone of her age, showing a considerable amount of overly-tanned flesh ending in the most inappropriate pair of heels Arlon could ever imagine for their current location. A tight white T-shirt bulged with the Dolly Parton breasts. The enormous hair had been replaced with a long blonde number that hung straight to her waist. Her blowfish lips had been liberally coated with extremely bright red lipstick.

Arlon watched as she sauntered over to him carrying a bottle of what he assumed to be expensive champagne and two long-stemmed crystal flutes. Unfortunately, Arlon had placed a spare camp chair beside his own in case his assistant had wanted to join him after her dinner.

"I think we may have got off on the wrong foot, Arlon, was it? Allow me to make up for that, would you?" she asked as she plonked herself down in the vacant camp chair. Without waiting to ask if

Arlon wanted a drink, she filled a flute and handed it to him, filling a second one for herself.

"Mrs Henderson..."

"Gloria, please. As I said, I think we got off on the wrong foot. I'm Gloria Henderson, pleased to make your acquaintance, Arlon Grey. Here's to a lovely weekend, I hope?" Gloria clinked her flute against his with a huge smile that made her lips look even bigger if that were possible.

"I hope you weren't offended by my earlier request?"

"Impossible," replied Arlon.

"Oh, well, that is kind of you to say..."

"I didn't mean you couldn't be offensive, because that's clearly not the case. Only that it's impossible to offend *me*."

"Not quite sure how to take that. Do you always say anything that's on your mind?"

"Mostly, yes."

"Well, I can't understand how your girlfriend would cope with that..."

"I do not have a friend of any gender, Mrs Henderson."

"Gloria. Come now, Arlon. That can't be true. A wonderful specimen of a man like you, with eyes that scream at women to throw themselves at you?"

"I wouldn't know about that."

"Modest, too. Very rare and equally attractive, I must say. Do have a drink, won't you? It is a Dom after all. Wouldn't do to forsake the monk's heavenly elixir."

"I don't drink."

"Oh, it isn't drinking when we're talking of Dom Perignon. It is an ascent into divine bliss. Nothing else quite like it."

"I don't need anything of a blissful nature. I'm unable to experience any sensation."

"What on earth do you mean? Are you saying you have no taste buds?"

"Oh, I can differentiate tastes and flavours readily enough:

however, I gain no enjoyment from anything I eat or drink. It's an emotion, one I'm incapable of."

"My dear man, I have had my fair share of soulless men, and you cannot possibly expect me to believe you are devoid of all emotions? That just isn't possible."

"Oh, it is. I have a condition. I'm on the spectrum. Autism. It doesn't show in any way other than a complete lack of emotions. They have a name for it, alexithymia. I can't display emotions, empathise or sympathise with others, nothing."

"You mean to tell me you have never known a day of happiness or sadness in your entire life? You are what...thirty-ish?"

"Closer to forty. That's right. No happiness, no sadness, no anger, nothing."

"That's truly horrible. I feel so... Wait, what? No sexual gratification either?"

"I hardly think that's an appropriate thing to ask a gentleman you've just met, Mrs Henderson," said Clarice in a proprietary tone, as she walked into the halo of light provided by the external fixture on Arlon's van.

"Mrs Henderson, may I introduce my assistant, Clarice Manning?"

"My, my, aren't you a dear thing in that old dress. Wherever did you pick up such a classic ensemble? One of the Op shops, perhaps?"

Picking up the clear challenge and the intended insult, Clarice said: "Well, we can't all afford to purchase designer label outfits that are too young for us. Are you drinking champagne, Arlon?" she asked casually while casting her eyes about for another chair. Arlon was quick to recognise her need, rising to retrieve another camp chair from the storage unit on the front A-frame of the van.

"Thank you, Arlon," said Clarice self-consciously patting down the front of her floral-patterned dress. On her feet, she wore the sensible walking boots Arlon had recommended. She wrapped the lightweight green cardigan about her shoulders as Arlon offered her his flute of champagne.

"Thank you. I don't think I've ever tasted Dom Perignon before. Heard of it, of course, but never tried it. Ooh, it's wonderful. The bubbles tickle my nose."

"Do try not to expel this divine elixir through your nose," requested Gloria with undisguised disdain.

"No, that wouldn't go down well with the toffs at all, would it? We mere folk have no understanding of fine wines and champagnes. Totally lost on us poor schleps," agreed Clarice with a cheeky grin. "I'm sorry if I was interrupting something? I saw the light on and thought I would..."

"Barge right in?" suggested Gloria.

"Oh? Was there something personal going on? Is that the reason for the expensive champagne? That *was* a waste, wasn't it? My boss never drinks, do you, Arlon?" she asked sweetly.

"No, no," replied Arlon uncertainly, suspecting more to the conversation than he could interpret.

"Well...I guess I'll have to speak to my husband tomorrow morning about whom he allows onto his property in future."

"Oh, has he purchased Allies Creek already? I wasn't aware."

"Good night, Ms Manning. Arlon, I'll be in the house should you need...*anything*?"

"I have everything I need in the van, thank you," said Arlon innocently.

"Well..."

"Good night, Mrs Henderson. Enjoy your bubbly," said Clarice with a cheeky little wave.

"What just happened? Did I miss something?" asked Arlon, looking perplexed.

"Yep, you sure did. Over the top like a jumbo jet, boss," said Clarice, passing her hand over the top of her head.

"I had the distinct impression that I wasn't talking the same lingo as you two."

"You weren't, Arlon. That was pure woman talk in all its catty wonder. Started the moment she insulted my dress."

"Did she? I thought she was complimenting you on being thrifty."

"Men!" said Clarice, rolling her eyes. "She was coming onto you like a dog in heat, Arlon, and I came in between."

"What are you saying?"

"Sheesh! For someone with above-average intelligence, you sure can say some dumb things. She was flirting with you, Arlon. 'I'll be in the house if you need *anything*?'" said Clarice mimicking the husky voice of Gloria Henderson.

"That can't be right. I think I offended her earlier when I refused to carry her bags inside."

"Did you?"

"Yes."

"Well, bully for you. Didn't think you had it in you."

"I have no idea what you're on about, Clarice."

"Stepping up to the knobs of this world who think they can lord it over everyone with less money than them. I'm proud of you, Mr Grey, damn proud."

"Mr Grey?"

"Just slipped out. Don't take that as a sign to go all formal on me, okay?"

"If you say so."

"There you go again."

"What?"

"That's what I was talking about. You're always so compliant when it comes to clients and women. That's why I was proud that you stood up for yourself with the high and mighty Gloria Henderson, who should be ashamed of herself for coming onto you like that as a married woman."

"I really think you're mistaken, Clarice. Why would she be interested in the likes of me when her husband obviously has more money than I am ever likely to see?"

"You don't know, do you? You have no self-awareness at all.

No idea how utterly dashing you are...until you speak, that is," attested Clarice who would have swooned then and there if she knew how. Somehow the art of swooning had never been passed on to her by her knowledgeable mother.

"I think you may be exaggerating, Clarice. I haven't got any sort of physique like those actors in the movies, no deep timbre in my voice. In short, nothing that I would assume a woman could want."

"Oh my, your eyes alone are worth walking over flaming coals for. I've never seen such depth and hypnotic appeal in a pair of eyes in the flesh or on the big screen in all my life. I guarantee that your eyes could attract any woman you'd want. As long as you didn't open your mouth to say anything, they would fight to the death to be in your arms and in your bed."

"That would be the end of it if we ended up in bed."

"Truly? Not to be impolite, and at the risk of asking the same question I was admonishing Gloria Henderson for, have you ever experienced being with a woman...that way?"

"Nothing would happen if I were in bed with a woman, so, no, never."

"Are you... I mean, can you...?"

"Engage in the physical act?"

"Yes."

"No, not really. As I understand it, while the physical instincts to procreate are quite strong and fairly natural in humans, we require the emotional impetus to succeed. There must be desire on an emotional level to perform the physical act. Or so I am told, at any rate. Think of what it must be like for someone wishing to make love to an anthill, for lack of a better example. No feelings there, no desire, no real possibility of sex."

A sudden sound emanating from the nearby bushland broke the spell encompassing the pair. Harsh, eerie, semi-human, the sound seemed to come from everywhere and nowhere, enveloping the township in its thrall. Trees and grasses on the perimeter began to shudder with the vibrations of trampling and stampeding animals.

Snorting, whining, grunting sounds displaced the previous banshee wails. Then everything stopped at once.

Not a breath of air, not a squeak nor a sigh, disturbed the returning silence. The quiet was greater than before because no crickets, cicadas or any other normal bush sounds could be heard. Clarice quaked with fear, while Arlon peered about the dark area beyond the halo of light surrounding them in a calm and studied manner.

"Th-there. What did I tell you? That piece was telling the truth, Arlon," whispered Clarice.

"We heard some sounds. Strange? Yes. Strange to me, at least, because I've never been to this type of bushland before. Nothing mystical or evil about it, just different to the city or the beach where I *have* been. You're allowing your over-active imagination to run away with you. You almost want to believe the nonsense you read in that story, and would have me believe it as well."

"They weren't normal bush sounds, Arlon. Far from it."

"Oh? When was the last time you stayed in the outback?"

"Nothing normal about them sounds. I don't need to have been anywhere to recognise abnormality when I hear or see it."

"Calm down, Clarice. You are getting yourself all worked up over nothing."

"Listen to that, Arlon."

"What?"

"Exactly. Nothing. What happened to all the insects we heard before, and the night birds? Where have all the wallabies gone? They were all around us before that unearthly caterwauling."

As the pair listened intently, Clarice desperately hoping for a return of the normal sounds associated with the bush, a new sound made itself known. Distant, though distinct, it was hard to miss the familiar sound of an approaching vehicle, most likely a diesel four-wheel drive.

The early model Nissan Patrol roared out of the night with its headlights and LED light bars blazing, illuminating the entire area and blinding the pair who were staring directly into the mesmerising beams. Spots swam before the eyes of Arlon and Clarice once the high beams and lighting bars were killed, with the only sound coming from the motor ticking as it began to cool down after its thrashing through the bush.

When the interior light came on, they saw the two passengers. Gavin Gaze and Bill Rogers alighted from the vehicle at the same time. Gavin, the driver, ambled over to where Arlon and Clarice were sitting. He had the air of a gloomy Gus at the best of times, and the stature of the butler from the fictional TV show, The Addams Family. His gaunt expression gave away nothing of the emotion lurking behind the exterior. His complete opposite, Bill Rogers, short, dumpy and incessantly jovial, beamed at the pair as if he had just enjoyed the experience of a lifetime.

"I expected you a little later, Mr Gaze," suggested Arlon.

"Oh, Gavin is a superb driver, Arlon. It was an exhilarating ride through the bush at a breakneck speed. He has nerves of steel. I would never be game enough to drive like that, at night through such dense scrubland. Kangaroos and even an emu or two hurtled out of the bush heading straight for our car, but Gavin here simply altered the wheel to left or right and whizzed straight past," gushed a florid-faced Bill.

"Did you take the forestry road, Mr Gaze?"

Gavin merely nodded his head solemnly.

"No fallen trees or any other obstructions then?"

"All clear," Gavin said in a sonorous voice, adding to the mental image of the fictional TV character.

"I have you two bunking together in the little cottage across the road there. I believe they refer to it as the witch's cottage, according to Mr Granger."

"Will Robert be joining us this trip?" asked Bill.

"No. Only the Hendersons, with Mr Henderson due in tomorrow morning. Her ladyship is in the McAllen residence enjoying some very expensive champagne by herself."

Bill looked askance at the offhand comment.

"And you must be the delightful Clarice Manning? I have spoken to you often on the phone, but we have never met in person. I must say, I am pleasantly surprised. You are looking ravishing, if I may say so?"

"You may," agreed Clarice, a bright flush suffusing her features.

"Well, I suppose we should get ourselves squared away then. What do you say, Gavin? Then we can come back and have a nightcap with these good folks."

"I was planning on an early start, say six o'clock, if that's okay? That way we miss the heat of the afternoon" said Arlon.

"Earlier if you like, Arlon. I keep tradesman's hours most often to keep in with the builders who need early inspections before a cement pour or such."

"I don't think any earlier will be necessary, Mr Rogers. I estimate that we should need only around four or five hours to complete our inspections?"

"Sounds about right," agreed Bill.

"How about you, Mr Gaze?"

"Barring unforeseen problems."

"That's settled then. Yes, why don't you two get yourselves squared away in the witch's cottage and we'll see you back here for whatever you are drinking? I'll be having some cold water."

"Well, that doesn't sound very exciting. Sure you wouldn't like something with some punch to it? I have a fine Scotch with me."

"I don't drink," explained Arlon.

"Well, doesn't that make you the dull boy? I hope you won't be offended if we have a tipple or two?"

"I wish everyone would stop asking me if I get offended. I cannot be offended...ever. You can tipple to your heart's content, I have no control over your own time. Just be sure to be bright-eyed and bushy-tailed come morning. Fail to be at your peak and it will be the last time I use your services," warned Arlon in a flat tone.

"Here, no need to be like that."

"Like what?"

"Well, I mean, threatening-like. No need for that, Mr Grey. No need for that at all. I don't drink as a rule, but..."

"Mr Rogers! I cannot be offended and therefore am incapable of being deliberately offensive to others. Ergo, anything you're feeling is of your own making. I speak plainly because I know no other way. You're more than welcome to join us and have your drink. As long as you and Mr Gaze are one hundred per cent tomorrow morning, then there is nothing more that need be said."

"Righto, then. We'll be off," said Bill uncertainly.

"Um, Mr Rogers?" Clarice halted him in his tracks.

"Call me Bill, love."

"All right, Bill. Did you hear any noises as you were driving in tonight?" asked Clarice with a look of grave concern.

"Couldn't hear much over Creedence, I'm afraid."

"Creedence?"

"Oh, I suppose you're a bit young for them. Creedence Clearwater Revival. A rock band with more than a touch of bluegrass in them, who got quite big in the sixties and seventies. Gavin and I were enjoying their concert in the car all the way from Brisbane. Cheerio, then. We'll see you in a bit."

The pair left them to unload their gear in the cottage opposite. Clarice peered about her in a worried fashion, imagining all sorts of perils and monsters attached to the eerie sounds they heard. Arlon entered his van for a short time to prepare a brew for himself. He was not looking forward to an evening of conversation where he would have to explain himself yet again.

His awkwardness in any group of people always led to the inevitable questions about his total lack of emotions. Though he had grown accustomed to it over his thirty-eight years of life, the never-ending questions took their toll on him. Some believed him and either pitied or attempted to take advantage of him. Others wanted to make a career out of his condition. The worst ones were those who didn't believe him, who thought he was a smug and obnoxious individual, someone who delighted in stating things bluntly for the effect.

He did not get upset over it, because that was impossible, yet it gradually became more and more tiring in a physical sense. He couldn't quite explain it, even to himself. After an hour of receiving a grilling by a group of people, no matter how well-intentioned, he always came away exhausted, as though he had endured an interrogation session as a POW. He was never impatient or obtuse during those sessions, but he did build up some defence mechanisms over the years. He learned how to occasionally hold his tongue instead of saying whatever came to mind.

He emerged from his van with a mug of steaming brew in one hand and a stainless steel thermos in the other. He extended the little table attached to his camp chair and placed both items on it. The regular night sounds were returning gradually as he regained his seat with the brew in his hands. He used coffee as a means of staying sharp. He assumed it was the caffeine that accomplished that task. It was not that he enjoyed the flavour, as with anything else he ate or drank. It was a ritual he performed most evenings when he knew a barrage of questions awaited him.

Clarice watched Arlon as he made his way back to her side. His dashing appearance melted her heart once more. *If only,* she thought for the umpteenth time. *Was it possible to be in love with someone incapable of returning that love?* She supposed so. There were many stories, fictional and otherwise, about unrequited love. She had read a ton of romance novels about such themes. It was such a shame, such a waste of a beautiful man, she thought.

Clarice had grown up with five brothers and one sister, all of whom were older, meaner and more rambunctious than her. She had learned how to hold her own when scrapping with them, but she lacked the brute strength they developed as they grew older and more athletic. She had often wondered about and hoped for less animosity between her and her siblings, had often prayed for a surcease to their endless outrage at all things, imaginary or otherwise. Men, it seemed to her, knew only two things in their lives, or, at least, were ruled by them: lust and anger.

Arlon was the polar opposite of her brothers in that regard. Where they were loud and obnoxious a lot of the time, he was quiet, reserved, yet powerful in that brooding intensity. He was highly intelligent, which she also found alluring. His lack of emotions was, in many ways, a blessing to her. She'd had enough of the arguments and raw emotions displayed by her family to last her a lifetime. He claimed he could fight, yet Clarice had not observed him demonstrating that particular talent during her short year of employment with him.

She knew it was hopeless to love a man like Arlon, yet she was unable to prevent herself from doing so. The only time it became painfully obvious that no such union was ever possible, was when he began talking. His tone had a monotone quality to it, devoid of the essentials for life. When Arlon told a story of any length, when he asked Clarice to take dictation, it was like listening to a robot. In fact, she had heard synthesised voices sound far more entertaining and lively.

It was not his fault; she understood that. He was born with the condition, and his parents were relieved to find that out, believing that they, somehow, had been responsible for it before the revelation, by not lavishing enough love and attention on the boy as he grew. According to Arlon, on the rare occasions he discussed it, his parents were on the brink of a breakdown before his diagnosis. They despaired about eliciting any kind of emotion from their only child. Everything they tried only made matters worse for them.

Clarice wondered, if she and Arlon worked at it, could they make it work? Would it be possible? Was sex something they could achieve, albeit a one-sided affair? She did not think that was fair, however. If making love was beneficial and enjoyable only for one party, then it seemed cruel to subject the other person to it, if it could be accomplished at all. Arlon was right, she thought, it would need a sense of desire to attain and maintain an erection through to climax. If there was no passion, no desire, no lust or other emotion spurring on the male, then the act became perfunctory at best. Knowing that would also make it unenjoyable for her.

Her musings were interrupted by the approach of the other two from across the road. Clarice was shocked when she checked her watch to see that thirty minutes had passed between her and Arlon in total silence. Arlon was neither perturbed nor aware of the lack of communication that transpired. He simply kept his eyes glued to the firmament, thinking his silent thoughts and keeping them to himself. Clarice sighed and envied the man his natural independence and his comfort with himself.

"So, Clarice, what was this sound you heard?" asked Bill, as they strode into the light.

THREE

Before Clarice wandered up to the main house at eight o'clock the next morning, Arlon and the two inspectors were hard at work in and around the houses. Clarice had hardly slept because of the weird sounds erupting frequently around the town during the evening. With the amphitheatre effect caused by the topography, it was impossible to pinpoint a location of the unearthly sounds. Several times Clarice woke with a start when she heard something skulking around the cottage in which she dozed.

Every so often she picked out an individual grunt or snort from the group sounds all melding into one another. Trampling, running, shuffling noises accompanied the other sounds to make the night very uncomfortable and worrying. The distinct and wholly terrifying shriek that heralded the start of the other sounds much earlier made Clarice's blood curdle. She had no idea what creature could have made it.

She was immensely grateful to see the first rays of sunshine pouring through her bedroom window and to hear a blessed reduction of the horrible cacophony. Exhausted from her night's restlessness, she dozed far later than she would have liked. She had hoped to make breakfast for Arlon and the other men. She knew she was somewhat of a third leg to the project headed by Arlon, and so hoped to make herself indispensable in other areas. It was not a fortuitous start to the day.

She stood up straight, after exiting the cottage and approaching the main residence, at the sound of an approaching vehicle roaring in from the road at a ridiculous speed. It skidded to a halt only metres in front of Clarice, showering her with a cloud of dust and small debris. The Lexus SUV, an exact clone of the one already under the carport, she assumed belonged to the male half of the Henderson couple.

Mr Travis Henderson stepped out of the driver's side door, squinting in the morning sun, despite his Ray Bans. His fake tan almost glowed as he approached, wearing a very colourful tropical shirt, white linen trousers and loafers with no socks, an outfit more suited to Hawaii than the Aussie outback. When he beamed at Clarice, it was all she could do not to hold her hand in front of her face to shield her from the unnatural brilliance of his enormous choppers.

"G'day, there, sweetheart. Name's Travis Henderson. You can call me...anytime," he said with a wink and another flash of his horse-like teeth.

"Um, hello, Mr Henderson. My name is Clarice Manning. I'm Arlon Grey's assistant."

"I'm sure you are. I wouldn't mind being *assisted* by you myself. Maybe we can talk a little later. Now, where is my wife?"

"Yes, maybe you should be talking to your wife now, and later on as well? She should be in the main house there."

"That where you're staying as well?"

"No, I am in the first cottage down that way, after the church."

"How about you get my bags and bring them in the house for me..."

"How about you get your own bloody bags and put them where the sun don't shine? Jeez, first the old broad, now this git," said Clarice under her breath as she walked back in the direction of her temporary abode, shaking her head.

Travis Henderson just smiled and assured himself that the weekend had only started as far as that little distraction was concerned. For the moment, he seemed unsure of himself in the alien environment. He supposed he might as well get his only lightweight suitcase from the car and go search for his ghastly-looking wife.

He sighed as he thought of the horror awaiting him. She had needled and wheedled him so often about getting 'a little bit of work done' that he had finally relented. Many operations later, he was horrified with the way his trophy wife of earlier years turned out.

That she had no idea about beauty became abundantly clear when she returned from her ops looking far worse than when she went in. Travis told her time and again to leave well enough alone. She reminded him of a Dolly Parton mannequin. It was just one of the reasons he had been straying over the last few years.

Travis entered the main house through the unlocked front door, expecting to see his wife either still in bed or lounging around watching her soaps. He didn't know how she could stomach that tripe. When he saw no sign of her, he sighed with relief. He plonked his case on the made-up bed in the main bedroom, presuming that his wife had arisen earlier and made the bed for once in her life. At their palatial residence in Sydney, it was the housekeeper's duty to attend to that chore.

Travis helped himself, reluctantly, from the instant coffee on the kitchen bench, after turning the kettle on to boil. He would seriously miss his cappuccino in the morning. He wondered again at his impulsiveness concerning Allies Creek. Gloria had been appalled at the suggestion.

Travis' initial response had been one of amusement when he saw a whole town advertised for sale, with the listing going semi-viral on the internet. As he sat in his recliner after leaving the office early, he began to entertain the idea of owning an entire township which he could rename: Hendersonville, perhaps, or Travistown. He started to see the potential for the property as a corporate training centre, a conference destination or team-building location with war games and the like.

He contacted a few designers and architects, inviting them to offer their opinions on the prospect and to give very rough guidelines of the costs involved to bring the infrastructure up to code and make the houses attractive. Several ideas were swimming around his head as usual when he sought an investment. He had no plans to run the centre or even stay there for any amount of time other than the present weekend. He hoped to find it a viable venue to make a profit-heavy turnaround once the refurbishment was completed and a clientele established.

More than once he had heard the CEOs of large corporations complaining about the lack of decent facilities for weekend meetings or team-building exercises outside the cities: somewhere secluded enough not to attract the media, and close enough to major cities to be practical. Though a great distance from Sydney, Allies Creek was only a short plane ride or a long bus trip from Brisbane. Travis foresaw building a landing strip for light aircraft to bring in the upper echelon of Australian business, while the plebs made it by road.

He had already secured initial interest from several companies he approached. The price tag on the town would have to be negotiated even further. The original selling price of over two million dollars was just laughable. Then the price dropped dramatically. It stood at a mere $750,000 when Travis first showed interest in the property. He believed he could knock that down to around $500,000 if he offered an immediate cash settlement.

At Allies Creek, Travis settled himself onto a comfortable chair on the covered veranda at the rear of the house, overlooking the enormous sheds and the dam from its slightly elevated position. Many wallabies and birds were gathered around the house expectantly, voicing their protests at having to wait longer than usual for their feed. It surprised Travis to hear the grunts and growls coming from the male wallabies as they objected to lesser males attempting to usurp their position.

It was a dog-eat-dog world wherever you were on the planet. As in nature, so was it in business. The same rules applied: to the victor go the spoils. And Travis saw himself as a victor when it came to business. He had crossed the million-dollar threshold in his late twenties. He had his fingers in many pies by the time he reached his forties and was close to becoming a multi-millionaire, at least on paper. Stock market speculation had hampered his progress at times, though, and depleted his working capital of late.

He needed something like the current project to pan out for him and his bleeding empire. His financiers were nipping at his heels for him to repay his excessive loans. The interest on those loans was crushing him. If Allies Creek turned out to be half as profitable as he imagined, he would make good on those enormous debts.

He figured he had one to two years in which to make the turn-around. After the initial outlay of half-a-million to purchase the place, then an injection of around two million to make all the refurbishments required, followed by an extensive ad campaign which he estimated would cost around another half-million, he saw the eventual sale going through at around the ten million mark. This would start him on the road to economic recovery, stock market crashes notwithstanding. He was still heavily invested in many shares he was unable to offload.

He held a palm to his brow when he saw some movement near the sawmilling sheds. Unable to make out exactly who it was, he thought it might have been the investigator hired by his solicitor, driving the golf buggy in his direction. He stood up to wave at the occupant, hoping to have a conversation with him to garner preliminary information about the property. The driver of the buggy gave him a perfunctory salute to indicate he had seen the gesture. Travis went back through the house to meet the man at the front, where the charging station for the buggy was situated.

"Mr Henderson?"

"Travis, or Trav, if you like. You are...?"

"Arlon Grey. Mr Granger hired my services to carry out the inspections you ordered."

"Pleased to meet you, Arlon," said Travis, shaking Arlon's hand with an iron grip. "How's it coming?"

"Fine."

"No, I meant have you come across any major problems yet?"

"Mr Rogers has inspected only three of the thirteen houses and the results of Mr Gaze's findings will not be known for many weeks after they are sent to the labs."

"Yes, yes, that's all well and good, but have you found anything that will seriously impact the purchase yet?"

"Hardly."

"That's not a very satisfactory answer, Grey."

"Well, *Henderson*, that's only to be expected a few hours into our inspections."

"You taking the piss out of me?"

"Not sure I follow."

"Are you making fun of me?"

"Not possible, I'm afraid. I simply have nothing to report at this early juncture, either in the negative or positive. Mr Rogers will probably be able to give you a detailed conclusion at the end of the day. I wouldn't like you to interrupt him during his inspections."

"I will bloody-well interrupt him all I like."

"Mr Henderson, neither the inspectors nor I am directly in your employ. We're not answerable to you. If I say you're not to pester them during their inspections, then you'll obey that directive. If you are dissatisfied with my services in any way, then feel free to inform Mr Granger of those objections. I'll be sure to leave immediately if that's the case."

"Now, now, no need to get your back up like that. It's just..., well, I guess I am a little impatient with this one."

"I don't have my back up, whatever that means. I assume it has something to do with my taking umbrage at something you said? I don't."

"Whatever. Have you seen my missus, by any chance?"

"I have not seen Mrs Henderson since last night when she left our group to drink champagne by herself in the house. Perhaps she's taken a morning stroll?"

"My wife does not...stroll. She exercises on our thousand-dollar treadmill or has a game of squash occasionally, but never takes a stroll in any weather. Hates outdoors, hates the country. I have no idea why she decided to accompany me at all."

"To spend some time with her husband...perhaps?"

"What's that supposed to mean?"

"That Mrs Henderson wanted to spend time with you."

"Yeah, what are you implying?"

"You mustn't try to read between the lines with me, Mr Henderson. I have nothing to say that I don't state clearly, often to my detriment. But I am who I am, and there is nothing to be done about it."

"You're a bit of a queer duck, aren't you? You sound like a bloody robot or something. With a deadpan face like that, you could be king of the comedy circuit."

"I don't think I can recall ever having been called a duck before, queer or otherwise. As for my deadpan voice, it goes with the personality. I haven't seen Mrs Henderson. If you like I'll ask the rest of them if they've seen her or know of her whereabouts?"

"Never mind. I'll find her myself. She can't have gone far, that's for damn sure."

By lunchtime, with everyone back at the main house on the veranda partaking of individual foodstuffs, no one had seen Mrs Henderson. She was last seen the night before trudging off to the house with her champagne. No one had seen or heard from her that morning. Travis Henderson was impatiently pacing back and forth, attempting to get a signal on his mobile phone.

"Anyone else got a signal on their phones?" Travis asked the gathering. They all retrieved their mobiles, and shook their heads in response.

"I don't get it. Her car is here. You saw her last night, but none of you has seen her this morning?"

"We've already stated that several times now, Mr Henderson. I don't know what else to tell you."

"Ooh, you don't suppose that thing we heard had something to do with her disappearance?" asked Clarice, conspiratorially.

"What thing?" demanded Travis.

"Pay no mind to my assistant, Mr Henderson. She has a very overactive imagination."

"How can you say that, Arlon? You heard it, same as me, last night."

"Heard what, woman? Make sense."

"Horrible sounds, they were. Turned the blood to ice in the veins, it did. Never heard anything like it in my life. Not likely to again, I don't reckon."

"That's quite enough, Ms Manning. We don't need your fantasies conjuring up impossible scenarios for Mr Henderson. I'm sure there's a perfectly logical explanation for her not being here. She may well have wandered down the road to get a signal on her phone, as you're trying to do, Mr Henderson. I take it she is no different to everyone else in the world who is simply lost without that electronic umbilical to the ether?"

"Yeah, she practically lives on the bloody thing. Only, her mobile is on her dresser next to the bed along with her iPad, her laptop and her organiser. I can't even get onto them without her password to see if she's communicated with any of our friends. Look, I'm afraid something has happened to her. She wouldn't just go off by herself, especially not out here in the bush. I'd call the police, only I can't. One of us will have to go by car to the nearest town, Mundubbera, is it?"

"To do what, exactly?" asked Arlon.

"To report her missing, of course, while the rest of us form a search party," answered Travis, with an edge of annoyance creeping into his voice.

"You can't possibly expect us to search this hostile terrain, Mr Henderson after your wife has not been seen for only a few hours," said Bill Rogers.

"My wife has not been seen since last night and the bed doesn't appear to have been slept in," Travis added.

"If you're that concerned, perhaps you should be the one to go to the police, Mr Henderson? She is your wife."

"I gotta stay here to organise the search, Bill. What about you, Gaze, isn't it? Could you go to Mundubbera for me to alert the police?"

"Arlon could just as easily do it," said Bill, before Gavin could answer.

"No, I need him here to begin searching, tracking her."

"Why do you suppose I could be of any assistance to you?" asked Arlon with a raised brow.

"Well, you are a detective, aren't you?"

"A former detective, yes. Not some native tracker hot on the spoor, I assure you."

"You're the best we have at hand, unfortunately. I'll get you to scout around, see what you can come up with."

"No, I don't think I will be doing any...scouting around, or following the spoor, tracking or anything like it. If you want to form a search party, you're on your own."

"That's bloody cold, that is. Don't you care that my wife is missing?"

A loud hiss could be heard escaping Clarice's lips: she suspected she knew the answer her boss would give to that unfortunate question.

"No, I don't."

"I beg your pardon?"

"No, I don't care. I..."

"Why you..."

"STOP," cried Clarice, halting Travis mid-stride with a fist raised. "He has no emotions, so he isn't capable of caring...for anyone," she explained.

"You expect me to believe that?"

"It's true. I have a condition that prevents it," said Arlon.

"So, the straight-faced comedian is more like a freak show?"

"If you choose to see it that way."

"Mr Henderson, that was uncalled for," said Clarice.

"Hear, hear. Not good form at all. No need to be putting anything onto Mr Grey. He isn't to blame for your wife running off," argued Bill Rogers.

"Who said anything about my wife running off? You know

nothing about my wife to be making that sort of remark," Travis stated.

"Quite right. I don't know anything about her, or you. I wasn't suggesting anything. I simply assume she has wandered off somewhere. She may have gotten lost."

"Probably," muttered Gavin Gaze, who had remained neutral until then.

"Look, I agree. I think, despite my better judgement that she's gone for a walk and gotten lost. It seems the only explanation. In which case, we need to mount a search and have a look around the area to see if we can pick up her footprints or something. If she hasn't taken water with her she may be suffering from dehydration already in that heat out there. Maybe you should be the one to go to Mundubbera, love?"

"I don't have a car and you won't get me going anywhere on my own, not for all the tea in China...*sweetheart*!" harking back to his earlier name for her.

"Well, we're back to you then, Gaze?"

"Something tells me you won't get very far, Mr Gaze. Unless my eyesight is not what it used to be, I detect a severe listing of your vehicle, indicating one or both of your driver's-side tyres are flat," observed Arlon.

"Just my luck, that is. Don't even have one spare, let alone two."

"Well, it seems there may be more to it than that. Maybe more to Mrs Henderson simply wandering off, as well."

"What do you mean, Arlon?" asked Clarice, in a guarded tone.

"Well, I just had a look at my Prado and it also appears to be listing. That would suggest a purpose in my opinion and not just some random occurrence. One flat tyre I could accept readily enough. Two, possibly, but not three or..."

"Or?" prompted Travis, when Arlon would not elaborate.

"Well, have a look at Mrs McAllen's old ute and Mrs Henderson's car."

All heads rotated. It was clear to everyone that both tyres on the drivers' sides of the old ute and the Lexus had been slashed as well.

"Now try to tell me there isn't something strange happening here?" asked Clarice, of no one in particular. "Arlon, no way can you tell me that four cars with slashed tyres are natural."

"No, I can't. Something is definitely off-key. Mr Henderson, it would appear that yours is the only vehicle that is drivable at present. This certainly supports your concerns for your wife's whereabouts and safety. I now agree that it would be prudent for someone to drive into the nearest town to report this to the police, while the rest of us attempt to use what daylight we have to begin a search."

"About time. Now I suggest we..." began Travis.

"I thought you wanted me to head the search?"

"Thought you said you weren't suited?"

"Will you two kindly cut out all the alpha male bullshit and start doing something more productive?" demanded Clarice.

Arlon and Travis merely turned to stare at Clarice.

"I think I should go to the police," suggested Gavin Gaze.

"I disagree. It should be the sheila that goes, not a bloke who may come in useful if we need strength at some point against an opposition," declared Travis.

"I tell you I'm not going anywhere on my own. Besides, if your car is the same as your wife's, you both have manuals, and I can only drive an automatic. Your car wouldn't be worth spit after I drove it. Wouldn't make it out of town, I reckon."

"I'd say I might be the best person because of my heart condition. Had a triple bypass a few years ago and I never fully recovered. Makes me quite ill at times and it's all I can do to keep breathing some days. You may have noticed that I have a bit of a gaunt appearance?"

"I am so sorry to hear that, Gavin," offered Bill.

"Yes, we thought you looked like that naturally. Clarice here described you as a bit of a gloomy Gus, didn't you, Clarice?"

"Arlon!!!" cried Clarice, in reddening horror.

"It's okay, Clarice. My wife calls me that as well sometimes. I have to remain kinda calm, my doctor says. So I try not to get excited or animated if I can help it. It would be impossible for me to join your search party, folks. Much as I want to help out, I think it best I go and notify the authorities. If you permit me to drive your car, that is, Mr Henderson?"

"Yes, of course. Leave straight away, please. The sooner we get the word out, the sooner we may find her. Arlon? If you want to take the lead on this, I'll step back. My wife and I haven't exactly had a harmonious marriage of late, but she's all I've got."

"I suggest everyone go and change into practical clothes for trekking through the bush. Long-sleeved shirts if you have them, long trousers of a durable kind. Stout shoes or boots are a must, as well as hats and sunglasses. Bring along as much water as you can comfortably carry, as well as some basic rations such as sandwiches and boiled eggs..."

"We don't have time for all that. We need to get going, now!" said Travis, with an edge of panic.

"I can appreciate that you're anxious to get going but we don't want to become casualties ourselves out there, Mr Henderson. We must leave prepared. Who knows how long we'll be? I envisage at least twelve to twenty-four hours. We'll use what's left of the day until we pull up for the night. No way can we follow anything or traipse blindly through the Australian bush at night. I don't know about you, but I don't possess night vision capabilities. So some basic bedrolls will be required as well, and torches, plenty of torches. Go now, all of you. Mr Henderson, a word before you go?"

Arlon pulled Travis aside as the others left the veranda to see to their preparations.

"What's up?" asked Travis.

"Guns."

"Sorry?"

"I predict that we will require a weapon at some point. Do you or Mrs Henderson own a gun?" asked Arlon in hushed tones.

"No, I don't, and neither does Gloria."

"Perhaps you can look around in there to see what you can find while we get ourselves ready?"

"You're starting to worry me. I wasn't really scared for Gloria until you mentioned needing guns. Just what do you suspect?"

"It's obvious, isn't it? We're dealing with a human element here. A person or persons has taken the time to slash our tyres, making sure we'd be unable to use our vehicles in a search. They may have miscalculated with you coming into town, leaving us with one good vehicle, but it was human interference that took care of the rest. I believe now that Mrs Henderson was abducted by whomever disabled our cars."

"Who?"

"I can't answer that. Go get ready. I'll do the same. Give us all, say, half an hour to get things ready. You look for a possible weapon in the house as well as preparing yourself. Have you brought along anything of a practical nature to wear, especially better shoes?"

"Yeah, yeah, I got things," Travis said dismissively.

FOUR

"I'll be fucked! Doctor Livingstone, I presume?" asked Travis with a sneer, upon seeing Arlon dressed in a khaki safari suit complete with pith helmet and flynet over the top. A canvas rucksack on his back, and a utility belt Batman would have envied, completed his outfit.

"I may look a little silly, but I'll be more comfortable than you in an hour. Tight jeans are not exactly the best trekking items, and those gold Nike runners are never going to stand the test. You'll be limping within a few hours when the soles on those things begin to deteriorate. They're not designed for bush-walking. And I specifically asked everyone to wear long sleeves and you turn up in a T-shirt. Have you seen all the ticks on these wallabies bouncing around here?"

"Listen, Livingstone, you can make all the suggestions you want, but don't expect me to fall into line. I'm my own man and no one tells me what to do or how to bloody dress, especially not someone dressed like a Pommy ponce about to go on a jolly jaunt down the fucking Nile. Besides, your theory of a human hand in this has been disproved by Roger, who found this," said Travis, holding the object under Arlon's nose.

"What is it?"

"A tusk, most likely."

"A tusk? What, like a boar's tusk?"

"That would be my guess as well. It's about the only animal I know of in Australia that grows tusks. There are probably feral pigs all through this bush," explained Travis.

"Where did Roger find it?"

"Wedged tight between the wheel rim and the tyre on the Patrol. No human can slash a tyre holding a tusk, so that blows your theory."

"Unlikely. Feral pigs or not, they would not deliberately slash tyres of their own accord. None of this adds up. The noises we heard could have been made by a sounder of wild hogs, at a stretch. I've discovered some odd tracks behind the house, some of which could be attributed to pigs. One heavy set of prints has me baffled, though."

"Show me," said Travis.

"By the way, did you find anything we can use as a weapon in the house?" asked Arlon,

"Don't know how much use it'll be, but, yeah," came the cryptic reply from Travis.

"Is it a gun or not?" asked Arlon.

"It's a .303, I think?"

"Nothing wrong with a Lee-Enfield .303 rifle if that's what you're alluding to," said Arlon.

"Bloody thing is ancient. Probably doesn't work."

"Bullets?"

"Found a box of them next to the rifle in a locked cupboard."

"Locked?"

Travis shrugged his shoulders, "Not anymore."

"I have a feeling it'll work just fine. If we're dealing with feral pigs, they're extremely dangerous when cornered or protecting young."

The other two turned up before they left the front veranda. Clarice wore loose jeans and a long-sleeved cotton blouse in pure white. A sunshade did little to protect the top of her head, but at least it shaded the eyes. She had a small bag of provisions slung over one shoulder. Bill Rogers had on a pair of tradesman's trousers with many pockets, stuffed to the brim with his gatherings. A long-sleeved, hi-vis shirt adorned his upper half. On his head, he wore a safety helmet.

"Christ, now we have someone from The Village People," remarked Travis, staring straight at Bill's helmet.

"I don't have a hat. Next best thing, I thought," confessed Bill.

"The helmet is fine," said Arlon. "The flask of liquor isn't, and the fact you've had a tot already is not acceptable at all."

Bill turned beet red as he gasped out loud.

"Now, now. Nothing like a bit of a shot to steady the nerves, mate," argued Travis on Bill's behalf. "I'd have one myself if I had any."

Bill quickly withdrew the hip flask from one of his many pockets, offering it to Travis. Travis accepted with a look of defiance toward Arlon, daring him to voice a challenge or rebuke. He handed it back after wiping his mouth with the back of his hand.

"Good to know there'll be some real men going along, Bill," Travis said with a wink. "Why don't you show us these strange tracks you found?" he motioned toward Arlon.

Arlon led the entire party behind the house, where he bent over a confusing assortment of tracks and indentations in the dusty earth.

"See these here? They're most likely pig tracks. Similar to deer, however, not as pointed."

"How the fuck would you know that if you say you aren't a tracker?" asked Travis.

"I read, Mr Henderson: a lot. I read everything non-fiction I can lay my hands on. From an early age, I learned to keep mainly to myself, when it was clear that I wasn't like the other boys in my class. Rather than getting involved in fights all the time, I retreated to my room, where I devoured books. I've read journals about wild boar hunts in Australia and how to recognise the signs. I think we'll probably find wallows and nesting signs as well as favourite rubbing trees or posts," explained Arlon calmly. "Now, I expect you to keep down your foul language while in the company of my assistant, otherwise I'll be forced to act on her behalf."

"Really, and just what would you be able to do to me, pray..."

Travis was unable to finish the sentence, finding himself in the dirt at Arlon's feet, with his left arm twisted painfully behind him, and his wrist forced into an unnatural position.

"Does this satisfy your curiosity, Mr Henderson? Would you

like further demonstrations?"

"Wait 'til..."

Arlon twisted his arm more while applying so much pressure against the wrist that Travis was firmly convinced it would snap off at any moment.

"Okay, okay, I give. I believe you," conceded Travis with acrimony.

Arlon released his grip. Travis lifted himself from the ground, massaging his arm with a grimace. Travis shot Arlon a glance of pure hatred, before placing an enormous fake smile on his face, a smile reserved exclusively for his business dealings. Arlon watched silently as the man seemed to caress the firearm he retrieved from the ground after dropping it. It seemed quite likely that he would not hesitate to use it against anyone disagreeing with him, Arlon in particular.

Arlon's affliction became a handy tool in the situation he faced with Travis Henderson; namely, he was unable to feel fear. He knew to be cautious around the man, would possibly have to hold his tongue in future, and would have to watch his back but he did not fear the man. It was that lack of any fear that caused him the most problems growing up. Until he learned to defend himself with the tough discipline of martial arts, he had to endure the hostility of his peers, who misinterpreted his lack of fear as a challenge to their superiority.

"If you 'gentlemen' have finally finished with your pissing contest?" suggested Clarice.

The sun was at its zenith, with the hottest part of the day two or more hours away. They followed as Arlon led the way behind the strange spoor. While Arlon had shown the group the clear tracks left by wild boar, he had not had the opportunity to discuss the unusual prints he had discovered. They made no sense to Arlon, nor could he recall any such print or track being discussed in all the books he'd read.

If he had to describe the weird print, he would start by saying the rear part of the foot closely resembled a human heel print, then a small gap was followed by what appeared to be a fist imprint. The overall print was quite large, if indeed the entire impression was of one foot, measuring almost four hundred millimetres long by about two hundred millimetres at its widest, with another set of two fist-like imprints in front of that.

It was not an animal track like any he had ever seen or read about, and he could not conjure up an animal, or human, capable of leaving the impressions. He thought through all the literature he had perused over the years and could come up with only one creature that might make a similar print; a gorilla. It would have to be an extremely large gorilla, making impressions at the rear with his feet and knuckle-like prints at the front where the fists punched the ground.

Of course, that theory didn't entirely explain the rear prints Arlon had discovered, nor gained any feasibility when he considered that they were in Australia, and not the deepest, darkest Congo. It was impossible to arrive at any firm conclusions. Arlon decided it would be prudent to keep wild speculation away from public scrutiny for the time being.

The group was heading in a southerly direction, down past the town's sawmilling sheds and dam. Before they crossed the town's boundary fence line, Arlon turned to Clarice.

"Are you sure you wouldn't prefer to stay behind, Clarice? I don't see it as being an easy trip, and someone should stay behind to update the police when they arrive."

"Arlon, there's no way I am going to stay in that spooky place by myself. What's to stop whatever it is from going back there? I might end up being the next one on the missing persons list. I'm coming with you lot, end of story."

"All right, then. Tuck the bottoms of your jeans into your socks. Move that bag from your shoulder onto your back, more or less. Bill, you need to do the same with your trouser legs."

"What will that do, Arlon?" asked Bill tentatively, still feeling the sting of his last rebuke.

"It'll prevent ticks from crawling up your legs. I also have two extra fly nets, if anyone is interested?"

"I'll take one of those," said Clarice enthusiastically.

"I guess, I'll take the other," said Bill.

"Christ, what a bunch of namby-pambies. Can't even handle a few flies. Worried about a couple of little ticks on your legs. Want your hands held as well? Let's get a move on, for Christ's sake!" declared Travis impatiently.

Half an hour later, with the dense bushland pressing in on them from every side; with the oppressive heat causing rivulets of sweat to pour down their faces; with the flies coating them in a shroud of shimmering black and iridescent blue; Arlon reminded them all to take regular small sips of water to keep up their hydration. Travis, he noted, was nearing the point of exasperation with the number of flies attacking his face, syphoning off the salty sweat. Arlon had another fly net tucked away in his rucksack, but he wouldn't let on until Mr Henderson either asked for it or seemed about to lose it.

Several times throughout the afternoon, the group was forced to wait in the sweltering heat while Arlon cast a wide radius to pick up the spoor again after losing it in the rough, rocky terrain. Arlon knew the principles involved with tracking but had no practical experience, and so was flying by the seat of his pants, never one hundred per cent confident in his abilities.

Towards evening, they came across a grisly scene that few of them would be able to un-see in their lifetimes. Arlon approached the small clearing with great caution, advising the others to remain behind by several metres. The same odd tracks that the group had been following since noon entered the clearing ahead of Arlon. From his position at the perimeter, he could make out the continuation of the prints through the clearing and out the other side.

In the centre of the clearing, however, he witnessed the macabre remains of feasting. Bits of bone and flesh that were covered in blowflies buzzing noisily and lifting off as one entity whenever a small disturbance occurred, only to settle back as soon as the interruption had abated. As Arlon crept into the clearing he became aware of the putrescence associated with rotting flesh. He halted his instinctual gagging reflex to refrain from puking into his fly net.

Wallows and depressions in the bare earth provided proof of his assumptions that they were following a sounder of hogs, accompanied by one very large...whatever. Poking at the fleshy remains with a leafy switch he picked up from nearby, Arlon saw a cloud of flies rise and scatter, momentarily revealing the true nature of the meal.

Although Arlon could not be certain, he believed he was witnessing human remains. One small digit left whole among the carnage convinced him that the remains were female, though at first there appeared to be too many bones for just one person. Arlon did not hold out much hope for the return of Mrs Henderson...alive. He turned in time to see Mr Henderson advancing into the clearing, despite being asked to remain behind.

"Fuck! Is this what I think it is? Have you... I mean..."

"Yes, I think they're human remains. No, I don't think it's your wife, as they're too far gone. If you take a look at that little finger there, I think you'll agree that we're looking at female remains."

"What do you mean, 'too far gone' to be my wife?"

"I'd estimate these remains to be at least a couple of day's old, going by the rate of deterioration and the putrefaction. Far too advanced to be that of your wife, who has been missing only since last night."

"You saying that a bunch of pigs ate some other person here?"

"Exactly."

"Who?"

"My guess?"

"Sure."

"Considering everything we know, and the fact that her car is still at the house, I think we may be looking at what's left of Mrs McAllen. I'll bag up the finger for the police to take a fingerprint."

"Are you off your rocker? Leave it the fuck alone for the police to do their job when they get here."

"By that time other animals and insects will have possibly destroyed what's left here to identify. I don't even think this is just one person. I know the human body has over two hundred-odd bones, but this seems a lot more."

"Why would pigs be eating humans? How could they possibly have abducted my wife? This is bullshit. You have no idea what you're talking about."

"I'm making a few guesses, yes, based on what's evident. It's clear to me that this area was used by wild pigs a few days ago to consume a meal. It was a feeding frenzy by the way the bones have been scattered about. There have been tussles and fights over certain portions between competing males, while the leftovers were apportioned to the rest in order of their hierarchal rank in the family unit."

"How could you possibly know this shit? I don't believe a word you say. You're making all this up," Travis accused, getting louder and louder with each statement.

Clarice nearly fainted as she entered the clearing to see what the shouting was about. She was caught and steadied by Bill bringing up the rear. Once he recognised the ghastly scene for what it was and the stench finally pierced through the denial, he turned aside and threw up his lunch, thankfully, after raising his fly net.

"What, what sort of an animal is that, Arlon? What's been eaten here?" asked Clarice cautiously.

"Not animal," replied Arlon.

"Not... What? Oh..." Bill was quick to ensure he was able to support Clarice again from behind as she went weak in the knees.

"Arlon, I think we'd better move on, don't you think?" suggested Bill timidly, attempting to hold Clarice up.

"Yes, I think we should all move upwind of here while I do what needs to be done. That way," said Arlon, when no one seemed to know which way upwind was. "Go about one hundred metres that way and stop for a drink. I'll catch up to you. Mr Henderson?"

"Hmm?"

"Keep that rifle at the ready, won't you?"

"You think the pigs are still around here?"

"No, I think they've moved on from here, but you never know. They might just as easily circle back and strike us from the rear."

"We're talking fucking pigs here, Livingstone. Get real."

"Yes, well, those 'pigs' are possibly responsible for one human death already and, ostensibly, they have your wife. So before you carry on insulting me, as if that has any effect whatsoever, you may want to start taking notice of what I'm saying if you ever want to see your wife alive again. I'm under no obligation to conduct this search for you and have no personal interest in your wife's safety. I'm unable to care about anyone or anything, so there's no point in this display of animosity and machismo. It has no effect."

"I could so easily shoot you right now, and I don't think anyone would mourn your passing. I may get a medal for it."

"I can't ever be frightened, Mr Henderson, by anything. Your threats are meaningless to me. Do or don't. Just don't bother threatening, and make sure that if you do, you're prepared to defend yourself and make your first shot count. If you fire and fail to kill me, I assure you that I won't fail."

"That sounds like a threat to me."

"Then you obviously can't tell the difference between a threat and a promise. I don't make threats or bluff, as you found out just recently. Paraphrasing the words of the immortal Jack Palance in a movie I haven't seen; I've dealt with men who shit bigger than you, Mr Henderson."

"You better watch yourself, Livingstone."

"I don't have to watch myself, Mr Henderson. If you had the balls to carry out your threats, you would have done it already. Now, off you go before I stop being a nice person," said Arlon dismissively.

Travis lingered a moment longer, seething inside with contempt and hatred for the repugnant man insulting him so casually. He toyed with the idea of ending the twerp's existence there and then, only to shrug and follow after the others. Arlon remained only long enough to bag the digit in a sealable plastic sandwich bag he took from his rucksack. Giving the area one last glance to make sure he missed nothing, something he was able to do efficiently, he then left the clearing to meet up with the rest.

"We have about three or four hours of daylight left. I suggest we use every bit of that before we decide to settle somewhere for the evening," suggested Arlon when he caught up with them.

"What...what exactly are we doing, Arlon? What do we hope to achieve, I mean?" asked Bill anxiously.

"We are GOING, to rescue my wife, you sad and sorry sack of lard. That's what we hope to achieve. You trying to beg off, coward?" warned Travis through gritted teeth.

"Okay then, let's say we do catch up to this pack of pigs, then what, smart-arse?" asked Bill, feeling slighted by the insult.

"We shoot the mongrels, that's what. What the fuck do you think we're going to do? Sit down for a meal with them? Maybe you can be the next course. Enough bloody meat on your bones, that's for sure."

"I don't think it'll be as easy or all that safe but we intend to locate and liberate Mrs Henderson before they have a chance to...do anything, Mr Rogers," said Arlon.

"But we're talking about pigs. How can they have abducted his wife, and how are they moving with her?"

"Both very good questions without any real answers for the time being. I don't know how pigs, wild or not, go about abducting or moving a female...hostage. What I do know is that the tracks we're following began outside the house where Mrs Henderson disappeared. It's too coincidental for it not to be connected. Besides, what other choice do we have? I think we can all agree that Mrs Henderson was not the type of person to go for a casual stroll around the property at night or in the early morning, then get lost? The where and the how of it will have to wait to be answered. Right now, all we can do, seeing as we started this, is to follow the signs to see where they lead, hopefully in time to save her."

"Yeah, so shut your trap and move," warned Travis.

"Mr Henderson, you do realise that we're volunteers in this pursuit? If you continue to harass, insult and insinuate, I sincerely doubt anyone will want to assist you," said Arlon.

"Mr Henderson? I think we can understand how you must be feeling, and you have our deepest sympathies, but it doesn't help to be so antagonistic to everyone. We *are* trying our best, after all," offered Clarice.

"You're wrong about that. None of you has the slightest idea what I'm going through, especially this cold-hearted bastard. He admitted he didn't care a jot for my wife's safety."

"Well, of course, he doesn't. He told you he has a condition that prevents it. All this arguing and blaming and puffing out of chests won't bring your wife back, Mr Henderson. We want to help you, and if you will just accept that, we all might get along better."

SCREEEEEEEEEEEEEE-YAHHHHHH

The supernatural sound bounced off the surrounding terrain, with a piercing effect that had the group holding their ears.

SCREEEEEE, SCREEEEEEE, SCREEEE-YAHHHH

Frantic movement seemed to explode from everywhere at once, as a dust cloud announced the trampling of many feet, circling the group, without revealing the perpetrators. There was a glimpse of a fleeting black shape, an impression of something large and outraged. Other animal sounds, snorts and grunts, accompanied the unearthly whistling, screeching, possibly from the leader, causing a self-perpetuating frenzy.

Above the din, Arlon attempted to inform everyone to remain perfectly still, as they all coughed with the amount of dust being stirred up by the mêlée. Suddenly shots rang out. Arlon looked about to see Travis blindly and ineffectually firing the old weapon into the cloud of dust. Unable to be heard above the insane noises, he moved over to Travis's side, where he placed his hand on the barrel of the .303 and forced it down, shaking his head to indicate that he should not waste his time. They were unable to make out any definitive targets in the maelstrom.

It seemed like an age that the commotion continued, circling them, inundating them with a melange of auditory assaults. It truly lasted only five minutes or so before the dust gradually settled and the noises abated, becoming distant and quieter until utter silence befell the group of stunned humans. Bill had made his way to Clarice's side to provide a modicum of comfort, something she dearly wished Arlon had done instead.

Everyone, bar Arlon, had been shaken by the bizarre experience. Nothing in their wildest imaginations could have conjured up anything quite so fantastic and terrifying. Travis was beside himself with fury at having been prevented from killing something. He drew himself up to his full height and began to bear down on Arlon, the target of his fury, with all the strength he could muster.

Once more, he ended up in the dust, his arm being painfully twisted behind him, with Arlon's boot placed squarely on the side of his face, exerting enough pressure to ensure his captive's complete submission.

"Mr Henderson, this is getting tiresome. I give you fair warning; I'm a black-belt in many forms of martial arts as well as a few other disciplines. I'm quite capable of hurting you very badly without too much effort at all. I stopped you from firing wildly into that mass because you were achieving nothing and giving away any advantage we possessed. The enemy now knows we have a weapon, a solitary weapon. They may well have been testing us for that exact information. You fell for that test because you allowed your fear to overrule your common sense," explained Arlon in an even tone.

"I'll kill you, you fucking coward. I'll kill you..."

"I don't think you'll get the chance now. I believe we'll all be killed by these things long before you make good with your hollow threats. You don't get it, do you? *We're* being hunted, not the other way around. They've been observing us all along. They're playing with us, causing unrest within this group. Fortunately, they have found an easy target in you to accomplish that task. What better way to reduce an enemy's numbers than by making them turn on one another? There's an intelligence at play here. Perhaps a greater intelligence than we have afforded it to date. We'll all be dead by nightfall unless we work together," warned Arlon.

"Bullshit!" spat Travis through the dust below his mouth, causing him to nearly choke while Arlon kept up the pressure with his boot.

"You're foolishly allowing your undeserved hatred for me to colour your thoughts, Mr Henderson. I'm not the enemy here. I've not taken your wife, and it's you endangering her safety and ours at this moment. I firmly believe she's still alive, however, that may not last for long. If you had managed to kill or injure one of those animals, I assure you, we'd find the remains of your wife soon thereafter."

"He's right. What the hell do you think you were doing shooting into that lot? You may have shot one of us, you were shooting so wildly. I, for one, refuse to continue with this madness. I propose that we return to Allies Creek at once and let the authorities deal with this," Bill stated.

"I have to agree that we're out of our depths here. I can just about guarantee you that I won't be able to find a trail to follow anymore. That lot will have effectively, and I dare say purposely, wiped out the tracks we were following. I agree that we should attempt to return, however, I don't think we'll be permitted to do so," said Arlon.

"Permitted?"

"You think it was a coincidence that they just happened upon us? You don't think they've been intentionally leading us away from the town on a rather circuitous route to lure us on to their home ground, to make us lose our bearings? Can anyone say with absolute confidence which way is back?"

"Ha! Bloody Livingstone got us all lost! So much for his leadership," harped Travis. "Let me up, arsehole," he demanded.

"Not until you've calmed down enough to be sensible. I didn't say I was lost. I know the general direction we have to take to get us back close to the town, give or take a kilometre. I asked if any of *you* know the direction if I'm harmed or incapacitated by you, as unlikely as that may be."

"I could get us back,"

"Somehow, Mr Henderson, I find that very difficult to believe," said Bill.

"I think it's laughable," added Clarice. "I wouldn't follow you around your back yard. Did you even begin to think you might have shot your wife while you were firing away? Then it would all be, 'Oh God, what have I done?' and shit. You wouldn't take responsibility for it, though, you'd try to push the blame on to Arlon, most likely. Why did we ever agree to help this horrible man? Oh wait, that's right, for his *wife's* sake. You get that, do you, dimwit? We're only doing this to help your wife, though God only knows why we would do that, either. She practically jumped Arlon's bones the moment she got the chance, and you came onto me like a beast in musk the moment you arrived. You both make me sick, and I don't want to be a part of this anymore."

"I think we should all take a moment to calm ourselves. Bill? Would you kindly pick up the rifle so Mr Henderson is unable to reach it once I let him go?" asked Arlon. "Thank you. Now, Mr Henderson, are you going to behave yourself or must I render you unconscious, then tie you up?"

"Fuck you!"

"Wrong answer."

Arlon dealt a swift but stunning blow to the side of his head that turned the lights out for him. He then retrieved some twine from his rucksack with which to bind and neutralise the man. Once that was done, the remainder stood about uncertainly.

"What now?" asked Bill.

"I think it's intended that we remain here, so I suggest we settle in for the evening as best we can. I'll gather some wood for us to make a fire if you and Clarice would gather some decent-sized rocks to form a firebreak?"

"Sure, Arlon, we can do that, but what then? And what about him?" asked Clarice.

"I'll tie him to a tree so that he can't endanger himself or us when he comes to. As to what else we can do, very little at this juncture. We wouldn't make it back to Allies Creek before dark. If nothing untoward occurs tonight, we'll decide our best course of action in the morning.

FIVE

By the time the fire had been lit and the group had formed into a rough circle to eat, the evening had settled about them. Disturbingly, not a single sound from the surrounding bush accompanied the forlorn group. Travis Henderson had finally contained his temper long enough for Arlon to agree to set him free. He sat apart from the others, nursing his strained arm and injured pride. He had to endure watching the others partake of a simple meal while he went hungry and thirsty, having disregarded Arlon's advice about preparing for their search.

Arlon had taken control of the weapon, which he kept close to him as he eyed his antagonist closely for signs of further unrest. He also kept a watchful eye on the other members of their little group as they huddled close to the fire, more for the security than for its warmth. The deathly silence played on their nerves. Clarice especially had shown indications of panicked fear. Bill sat by her, attempting to placate her with his proximity alone. He was quite scared himself and did not trust his voice to be able to talk to her confidently.

Arlon had an idea that they would not be in for a pleasant evening. He had already submitted to the notion that sleep would not be possible for him. Quite apart from the external threat, was the ever-present danger of the man who brooded menacingly a short distance from him. Arlon sighed inwardly, knowing he had not heard the last from Mr Henderson. He'd had to deal with that type most of his life: usually, the confrontations ended in conflict.

He reflected on his need to use force on so many occasions during his life. He was thankful for his father's careful and concentrated instruction in self-defence that started him on the road to several black belts but regretted its necessity. No one had ever been able to fully understand his condition, what it meant to be utterly devoid of all emotion. Without the ability to feel emotion, he couldn't comprehend it or appreciate it in others. He supposed he could take some basic tuition in acting, thereby affecting an outward appearance of someone who...gave a shit?

He didn't think he would succeed, no matter how well he applied himself. It neither interested him nor weighed heavily enough on his mind to make the effort, just to comfort others around him. That may or may not denote laziness in him, he couldn't be sure. It just didn't seem worth the effort to produce false emotions for the sake of keeping some sort of harmony. There would always be those who saw through his ruse, who would take offence no matter what he did.

The smallest flicker of movement in his peripheral vision caused Arlon to pause in his reflections. Something at the extreme edge of the firelight had caught his attention, yet, when he concentrated on the area, he saw nothing but darkness.

Then it seemed as though the darkness moved: black on black, moving ever so slightly, revealing a patch of light bark behind it. Arlon followed the blackness up to a pair of shiny white specks. It took some time before Arlon recognised the white specks as eyes, shining out of the darkness of a black face, an Aboriginal face, blending entirely with the evening and the background.

"Hello," said Arlon softly, startling the others. "Care to share our fire and a little food?" he asked.

"Are you seeing things now, Livingstone?" sneered Travis.

"I'm talking to the Aboriginal who's standing right next to you, Mr Henderson. I suggest that you don't move too suddenly. Wouldn't pay to upset them."

"Them?" asked Clarice in hushed tones.

"I would imagine so, yes. More than one at any rate."

As Arlon spoke, a shape peeled itself out of the darkness like wallpaper drifting from a wall after losing its adhesion. A tall, incredibly thin, old man with the blackest skin Arlon had ever seen slunk into the circle of light cast by the small fire. Though he appeared to be ancient, he had not a single grey hair on his head or long beard. With one quiet word from him, several members of his tribe emerged from the darkness around them.

One of the younger bucks approached the fire carrying something substantial over his muscled shoulders. He unloaded the enormous goanna unto the fire, sending embers high into the darkness. The old man came to sit beside Arlon and began to prattle in his language.

To the old man's and everyone else's consternation and obvious surprise, Arlon began to answer him haltingly in the same language. This repartee carried on between the old man and Arlon for ages, while the other members of the tribe began to munch on the goanna once it had cooked enough for their liking. Once they had eaten their fill and thrown the bones into a heap on the fire, one by one, silent as ghosts, the tribe merged with the blackness.

Only the old man remained, talking quietly and respectfully to Arlon, who nodded politely while taking in every word, asking the occasional question when something required clarification. The others looked on in total fascination, not saying a word until well after midnight, when the old man finally rose on creaky knees to bid farewell, then suddenly disappear as if by magic.

"Arlon, could you understand all that?" asked Clarice eventually, while stifling a yawn.

"With a little difficulty, yes. I haven't practised that particular language for many years. It came back in the end, though. A very interesting story he told me. If it's true, it may well explain a few things we've experienced."

"Bullshit! How could you possibly speak their bloody language?" accused Travis

"By studying it, of course," answered Arlon, without pause or rancour.

"You just happen to have studied their nonsense language?"

"Hardly nonsense. Yes, theirs and many others. As I've said already, I had lots of free time as I grew up. I didn't want to waste all that time being bored, so I studied as much as I could about...well, everything."

"How many languages do you speak, Arlon?" asked Clarice.

"I've never counted them all. I found learning languages easy once I learned the first hundred or so."

"Hundred?"

"Well, if you include all the dialects, yes. Easily."

"So what did he tell you?" asked Bill.

"It was a lot to take in, and I became confused between what was told as fact and what was supplied as supposition. I'm not even sure if I should relate it all to you at this time, especially for your sake, Clarice."

"Why?"

"You are...somewhat susceptible to imaginative stories. I wouldn't want to add to your unease tonight," Arlon suggested.

"I don't think I could get much more scared than I am, Arlon. Besides, it would bug me all night not knowing what the old man said."

"Yeah, and we have a right to know what the old bastard said, too," added Travis.

"I think you've used up any rights or privileges you had quite a while ago, Mr Henderson. If I do relate the story, it will not be for your benefit, I assure you. You are perhaps my strongest case against revealing what I was told," admitted Arlon.

"Yeah? Why's that?"

"Because you are the least likely to believe a word of it."

A sliver of pale moon had ascended in the night sky, amid a brilliantly speckled backdrop of stars as only the outback can provide. A few entomological sounds had begun to colour the silence with their nocturnal entreaties. A whisper of leathern wings above heralded the flight of bats or flying foxes on their nightly quest for nourishment.

Arlon settled himself into a leaning repose on top of his lightweight swag. He had never experienced camping as a child or as an adult, not for the sake of enjoyment, at any rate. His parents had taken him on several holidays, where he learned a great many things but never camping. They always stayed at motels or in cabins, mostly at beachside destinations after moving to Brisbane. Arlon did not enjoy the sea, because he could not enjoy anything. It was simply being in another environment: interesting, to be sure, but never enjoyable.

He debated telling them the story he'd been told, leaning toward the negative, if only to avoid the derision from Mr Henderson. Whenever Arlon spoke, he did so in a deadpan manner that did not captivate or entertain an audience. He mostly bored people to the point of slumber if he was forced to indulge in a recital of any description. His teachers and classmates had made that point abundantly clear whenever he was called upon to read from a book out loud to the class. So much so, that his teacher had fallen into a deep sleep during one of those periods, snores and all.

Arlon had no cause to believe the old man had invented the story. He felt sure that it was based on solid history, even though much of the legend surrounding the tale may have been helped along with a healthy amount of imagination. It was the way of most tales handed down from generation to generation like Chinese whispers, always a little creative interpretation and embellishments along the way. The important thing was to separate the wheat from the chaff; attempt to establish how much trust to place on which part of the story to arrive at a likely truth, or, at least, the semblance of truth.

SIX

Inside the hotel in the main street of Mundubbera in 1935, sharing a laugh with some of his workmates at the hardwood bar, stood Big Tom. The nickname was not simply an affectation attesting to a stature that was the opposite, like Little John of Robin Hood fame. Big Tom was quite large by most standards, standing a shade under seven feet in the old scale, with shoulders as wide as an outdoor dunny.

He was neither overly liked nor avoided by his fellow workers at the sawmill in Allies Creek. Most found his company to be acceptable and sometimes downright funny. Big Tom had a way of telling a story that most people ended up enjoying immensely and often attempted to repeat in the same manner, only to fail.

The Friday night session at the pub had just about reached full swing by the time Big Tom had gathered an audience for a story he was about to regale them with, when...

"Ah, Tommy, me lad, I think ye had better take a gander at the front door," said Bob, in his thick Scottish brogue.

"Oh, and whoy would that be, Scotty-Bob? Oi was gonna tell yiz about me bleedin' ole man and his fish."

"If I'm not mistaken, me lad, that be your Black-Mary standing there at door."

"Why would ye be calling her 'moy' Black-Mary?" asked Big Tom, in a menacing tone that bespoke of his foul temper.

"Och, no need to be gettin' all riled noo, laddie. I only meant to say she was your house black, noothin' else," sputtered Bob.

Big Tom looked from Scotty-Bob to the front door, where he saw Mary Bone, his housekeeper, standing in the doorway, wringing the hem of her thin, dirty cotton dress worryingly as she searched the crowded bar for the person she was after. A few others had seen her standing in the doorway and stopped their conversations mid-sentence. The barman and proprietor gave Big Tom a filthy look and was about to say something when the big man gave him a signal that he would sort it out. Tom gulped the last of the jug of beer he held in his ham-sized fist and slammed the empty container on the bar.

He muscled his way through the crowd of boisterous men, beginning to quieten when they saw a black woman desecrating their sanctum sanctorum. Nobody, but nobody, interfered with a man's drinking on Friday night after a long week of work in the mill; not a bloody female at any rate, and especially not a black one!

Australia languished in that shameful state of unbridled, undisguised misogyny and bigotry for many decades. The scum of England and surrounds had been sent to the penal colonies to serve out their lengthy sentences. Learning the worst way to treat other genders and races, the convicts had continued the tradition in the new land down under for many years, before it was finally outlawed, well past its due.

It was illegal for a woman or a black to be seen in a bar with men. Blacks were served at the back door, where their money was accepted for booze and fags, while white women were allowed to be in the public lounges only, ostensibly to save them from the foul language and behaviour of men in the act of inebriation. Obviously, the lawmakers of the time had not visited the homes of any working men after they arrived back from a night of drinking with their mates, pissed to the gills and spoiling for a fight, and, more often than not, finding a ready target for their ire in their spouses.

Commonly referred to as colonisation, the invasion of Australia by the English was to blame for the shameful manner in which the indigenous persons of Australia were treated for many years afterwards. They were hunted like animals, with some tribes, especially the Tasmanian Aboriginals, savagely murdered to near extinction. This appalling treatment was carried down through the government agencies to everyday men in their dealings with the Australian natives.

So Big Tom made his way deftly through the gawking

'gentlemen' in the bar toward the invader, with the authoritative air of someone well within his rights, as provided by the government of Australia under the auspices of mother England and His Royal Majesty, King George V, to deal with the troublesome blacks as he saw fit. It also rankled Big Tom considerably, that Black-Mary Bone had been so indelicately described as being *his* Black-Mary.

"Come on, out of it. You should know better than ta stick ya nose in 'ere," said Tom, as he bundled her roughly out of the door and onto the footpath outside.

Inside, the bar erupted once more into the banal and inane talk of drunken brutes all vying for the attention they believed they so richly deserved, once the object of their derision had been shown her place outside. Bloody savages should know better, most of them thought, and some even stated. Digger Chester, the barman, sighed, as the potential for a Friday night brawl had been resolved peacefully: or so he hoped.

"Whatcha doin' coomin' inta da bar like that, ya silly black bitch?" roared Big Tom, after he'd dragged Mary Bone half a block until they were out of earshot of any nosy parkers.

"Mary gotta talk ta boss," murmured Mary coquettishly.

"Ta me?"

"Yeah, boss."

"What about? You done somethin' wrong in me house I'll..." Big Tom started, with one huge hand rising inexorably to strike.

"Mary done nothin' ta house, boss," she blurted out, wide-eyed and fearfully.

"Then what the fook you doin' here interruptin' me Froidy session, ya doomb, black coont?"

"Mary been doctor, boss."

"So fookin' what? What do oi care if you've been to see the bloody quack?"

"Late, boss."

"Late? Fook, Mary, make some sense, would ya? Ye didn't hafta coom ta work today at all. Ye only do Moondy troo Wednesdy for me. Today is bloody Froidy. Don't you foockin' boongs know how to tell what day-o-week it is?"

"Not late for work, boss. Mary late for blood-moon."

"If ya don't start ta make some bloody sense soon, I'm gonna have ta teach ya a lesson or two about interruptin' me Froidy sess. Now spit it out, ya fookin' hairy, smelly, black bitch!"

"Miss thum periods, boss. Blood moon? Yiz gonna be a dad, boss. Make-em baby wit Mary, eh?"

Big Tom stood stock-still for long moments, trying to comprehend what the darky was saying. Although one part of his brain registered the message, another part fought to deny he had heard or understood a word. Inside, whether it was acknowledged or not, his gut was turning somersaults. The gallons of beer he had consumed that evening all rose to the surface in one almighty, gushing waterfall that flowed into the gutter for an age as the big man let loose. Once he had successfully evacuated his stomach of all acid-inducing fluids, Big Tom finally straightened himself.

He peered about him carefully at the empty streets, ensuring they were completely alone, before he grabbed Mary Bone by the hair, dragging her behind him while she squalled and flailed uselessly at him. He dragged her the length of the block to his horse, waiting patiently at the hitching rail. He climbed onto his horse as quick as lightning, throwing Mary across the rump behind him, arms akimbo on one side of the horse, legs dangling and kicking on the other. He placed one massive hand on her back to pin her there while he kicked his mount into a canter.

It was in the early morning hours when they, at last, trotted to a halt outside his cottage at Allies Creek, his horse coughing up masses of foamy lather from the exhausting ride. Big Tom left his mount to find water on its own as he dragged the woman, who was still screaming obscenities at him, as she had all the way from Mundubbera, to his cottage. No man alive could swear and cuss better than a black woman believing she had been wronged. It was a well-known fact.

Big Tom shoved Mary inside his cottage and backhanded her savagely. She sprawled heavily on the bare wooden floor, hitting her head and burning her hand painfully on the edge of the pot-belly stove.

"Now then, ya lying coont. Ya better admit yiz was lying, or it'll go bad for ya."

"Not lyin', boss," said Mary defiantly.

Big Tom crossed the room in two quick strides, hauled Mary up into the air with his massive fist, and belted her squarely in the jaw with his other rock-hard fist, breaking bone and teeth.

"Ya better not've said noothin', ya doomb black bitch."

"Tol' him doc and Mary's family," she managed to say with great difficulty.

Tom was incensed, outraged beyond recognition. He paced about the small lounge like a caged tiger. He had committed a cardinal sin. He had used a black woman for sex. Of itself, it wasn't so bad; many white men used the local gins for sex. It was just never admitted openly or spoken about. No respectable white man would dare tell anyone that he'd befouled his body by having sex with a black. But as long as it was only sex which no one knew about, everyone held their peace.

Having a baby with one! Impossible! He would be run out of town quicker-n-he could fly out of a cannon. Nobody would ever want to know him, hire him, allow him to enter their bar or...marry him, if it became known. The big man was slowly working himself into a conniption, while Mary Bone watched in grave fear from the floor. Suddenly, he stopped, whirled about.

"Get rid-uv-it," he ordered with glee. "Find one-o-them what does it, ya know? How much, ya reckon?"

"N-n-n-no, boss."

"Don't ya fookin say no ta me. Ya gotta find one-o-them baduns that doos away with bastards," he muttered murderously.

"Hum-Jesus pella say no kill, boss. Baby and Mary go ta hell if Mary kill baby."

"What the fook ya think I'm gonna do if yiz don't?"

"Mary scared, boss. Hum-Jesus pella got big magic."

"Him-fuckin'-Jesus got nothing on me, ya doomb coont. I swear I'll break every fookin' bone in that useless fookin', stinkin', rotten, dorty black body if ya don't do what I tells ya. I'm gonna give ya fifty quid, and yiz'll pay back every fookin' shillin'-uv-it if it takes ya ten fookin' lifetimes at the rate yiz get paid. Yiz gonna take that fookin' money and find a quack what'll get rid-o-the filthy black demon in ya, ya hear me, Mary Bone?"

Mary remained silent, watching him with a mixture of hatred and fear. She took it all in. She knew where she stood in the eyes of the white man. It had been ingrained in her since childhood. While they might act compliant, and bow and scrape to the white man's ways and laws, the Aborigines seethed inside and passed down the tales of their subjugation from one generation to the next, until nothing but contempt and hatred existed in their hearts. Their utter loathing was rooted deep within the Aboriginal psyche since the invasion of their land.

Mary Bone was a direct descendant of a distinguished tribal elder, veritable royalty among the Aborigines, and she had been taught the hatred from birth, learned and experienced the despicable treatment of her people from the time she could understand words. This brute of a man made her cower, took her forcibly night after night whenever he felt the urge and was too ugly and ruthless to find himself a white woman, but she knew there was nothing she could do to stand up against him or any other white man. She also knew that she could not, under any circumstances, kill her baby.

No respectable black man would ever have her after she had been the white man's whore. She already knew that her people, her family did not want or accept her with a white man's baby. But she had been brought up as a Christian in a mission after she was removed from her parents as part of the stolen generation, and had the Bible preached at her more often than the ways of the tribe. She knew she and her baby would be condemned to the fiery realms of eternal hell and damnation if she killed the baby. There was almost anything that the whites could ask or demand of her except that. She would never be forced to kill her baby. She would rather die first, and with that realisation...

"Puck you, puckin' white pella," she screamed at him defiantly.

"What? What did ya say ta me?" Tom asked in a deathly whisper.

SEVEN

When Mary Bone regained consciousness, she sorely wished she hadn't. She wished she weren't alive at all because of the indescribable pain she felt. The midday sun beat down through the dense scrub around her battered and broken body, left for dead on a mound of rubbish somewhere near Allies Creek. She found it difficult to breathe, could not open her bruised and bleeding eyes and was unable to hear anything through her swollen, cauliflower ears.

The moment she attempted to move, the true extent of her horrific injuries became clear to her. Somehow, by some cruel miracle, some evil twist of fate, she had been spared death at the hands of the demon, Big Tom, whose bastard she carried...or not. She had no way of knowing if the beating he delivered had killed the unborn infant inside of her. In all likelihood, it was dead, as she soon would be. She had no illusions about her chances in her dire situation.

No one knew where she was even if anyone cared anymore. The moment she became the chattel of the white man at the age of fifteen, she was disowned by her tribe, shunned by her mother and father. She had mistakenly felt special, privileged, when the big white man chose her for his bed, despite all the ingrained bitterness against the whities, spoon-fed to her since birth. Like any hot-blooded teenager, she longed to be held and loved by a man; longed to be rid of that stigma of virginity; to be seen as a worldly woman by her peers and elders; to be a woman grown at long last.

Fifteen and pregnant to a white man, barely alive, to die alone on a rubbish heap in mortal agony, would be Mary's reward for her impatience. Tears would not come when she summoned them. She was too dehydrated to expend tears of self-pity. By late afternoon, with her dark skin blistering in the waning sunlight, Mary breathed on stubbornly, clinging to the last vestiges of life with pugnacious tenacity.

Early evening, when she awoke after falling unconscious once more, she sensed a barometric change. She could not hear, see or smell this alteration in the weather, but sensed it instinctively. Her broken, swollen nose would never again allow her olfactory sensations. Her damaged ears ensured she was incapable of auditory detection for a long while. She felt the change upon her pores and in her mind; a slight difference in pressure, a coolness penetrating the formidable heat. Possibly the only thing in all the cosmos that may have made a difference to Mary's condition, the one thing above all else that could have swung the pendulum in her favour, was that simple, crucial element without which nothing in all of creation can survive; water!

Rain.

The night Mary was left for dead upon a rancid heap of rubbish in the middle of the Australian bush in February of 1935, it rained for the first time in many months of drought. It wasn't just a light sprinkling that lasted a second or two with nary a drop fallen. It wasn't a gentle shower to do nothing more than settle the rising dust whenever a breeze stirred. On that night, a solid sheet of water descended from the heavens to soak the land thoroughly with its life-giving, life-saving goodness.

Mary opened her broken mouth with her shattered teeth, despite the intense pain it caused, to take great mouthfuls of blessed water straight from the sky. That simple and divine gift from nature did far more than slake the thirst of the parched land and the lost and forgotten female abandoned like last night's garbage. It did more than cool the blisters and burns from the scorching sun upon the exposed limbs and face of the suffering urchin left for dead. It even did more than wash away the layer of grime and dust coating the broken, bleeding body of the poor girl.

The purging downpour had the metaphorical benefit of cleansing that girl's soul of her imagined sins against humanity and her God. With every drop that fell on her, despite the agony the slightest touch produced, she felt her spirit nourished and nurtured until her determination and strength of will overcame any doubt that ever existed in her. With that wholesomeness that comes from lifting one's head to the sky during a thunderstorm with all the power and intensity nature has to offer, came the will to live for her and her baby, came the courage to fight for her survival, came the knowledge and the strength to persist against all odds as only a new mother knows how.

It would be days before she could move away from the rubbish heap, subsisting on the putrid scraps of food she found therein, and the water collected in the few cans and jars within her reach. Mostly, it was Mary Bone's indomitable spirit that saw her regaining enough strength to face the coming trials, to ultimately slither down the heap of garbage despite the exquisite pain, into a little hollow beneath a rocky overhang.

Intermittent rain over the following weeks and months, breaking the back of the drought and reviving the ravaged countryside, ensured Mary Bone was able to continue to improve, little by little, day by painful day. With what little knowledge she had gained from the mission priests and nuns, she managed to splint her broken legs with branches and stringy bark, plaited into a rope with her damaged, broken hands. The little she knew of bush lore, as taught by her grandfather, she employed to find protein-rich grubs and other insects, which she sucked dry. Her teeth were still far too painful to allow her to chew, and her jaw had failed to realign itself no matter how hard Mary tried to move it.

After a few months of desperate and daily challenges, Mary felt the first signs of movement within her womb, just the tiniest flutter to indicate a life within her, strengthening her resolve, her courage and her will to see her baby born. Every day saw a little more movement possible from her broken limbs. Splinted fingers became workable once more, able to pick up a few small objects instead of Mary having to lie down into whatever she wished to eat or drink.

Only one of her arms was broken, so she had some functionality of the other; however, with severely broken and deformed fingers, she found the going very tough.

Every small advance was a victory which came at a cost. Movement of hands or fingers, while welcomed as a great achievement, caused immense pain. Rehabilitation of atrophied limbs, once she felt confident enough to remove splints, became lessons in the various levels of pain the body could endure without falling unconscious. Month after agonising month she gained strength and mobility, while also blossoming with the vitality and colour of motherhood.

In her seventh month, while enormous around the girth, her weight was seriously depleted for one of her height and age. She desperately needed something more substantial to eat than grubs and wild yams. Rummaging around her abandoned rubbish heap on her bottom, careful not to cut herself on the broken glass, she came across an old bicycle inner tube, much patched and worn quite thin from overuse. Mary smiled inwardly as the germ of an idea began to form in her mind.

After finding the right-sized branch to suit her idea, she used rocks to smooth the wood and remove the bark until her hands and fingers ached intolerably. Then she tied the ends of the tube to each end of the upper Y. She scoured the area around her little shelter for suitably-sized rocks, which she stockpiled to one side. Every day she practised with her slingshot, hitting the target only once out of every thirty shots. Within a month, she was hitting the cans she lined up on a fallen log three times out of every five shots.

One day, in her final month of pregnancy, feeling as bloated as a dugong, she made her first kill. It was only a skinny goanna, lurking around the rubbish heap, but it tasted like prime rib to Mary, who managed to chew with difficulty. The momentous occasion, and the bliss of that first real meal provided solely by her, lasted only briefly, as the first spasm of pain gripped her around the midriff and groin.

Mary had no idea what had happened when the paralysing agony slowly evaporated as mysteriously as it had appeared. She felt a moistness beneath her bottom, almost as though she had wet herself. Mary had control of her bladder, as far as she was aware, so the presence of liquid between her thighs baffled her

Mary had been naked for months now as the thin cotton dress she wore the fateful night she informed the evil white man that he had become a father, was nothing more than tattered rags which no longer covered any of her body.

The dress had slowly torn away in strips as she dragged her body over the coarse earth. She was unable to see the area at her groin because of the enormous lump in her belly. She could only feel the moisture there as she probed the area with her fingers. She could not make out the reddish colour of the fluid when she brought her hand to her face. The moon was nowhere to be seen that evening. Then, as suddenly as the first, the second wave of excruciating agony overtook her, while, inside her womb, her baby squirmed.

An intense pressure asserted itself, urging Mary to bear down, to push with all her might. She didn't understand, so she resisted as the wave of pain cascaded over her and slowly decreased. It returned at regular, agonising intervals over the following twelve hours, while her depleted energy levels were drained even further. Her screams silenced the surrounding bush, where she would normally hear thousands and thousands of cicadas and crickets. With increasing intensity and at shorter intervals, the waves of nauseating, back-breaking pain enveloped the confused child in its throes.

In the early hours of the morning, when Mary was all but done in, when she firmly believed she would be joining her sacred ancestors in the Dreamtime, one final, all-pervasive, agonising wave took hold of her, This finally managed to get Mary to push with all her remaining strength, with every ounce of courage and will she could muster from her aching body, forcing from her nether regions a squirming red and black mass. As Mary did everything she could to prevent herself from sliding into unconsciousness, she finally understood that she had just given birth to her child.

She clutched blindly for the unmoving, slimy package between her legs. Instinctively, she unwrapped the umbilical from around the baby's neck, fearing it might be too late. Groping in the dark, her hands explored the wet lump for signs of life, only to discover gross deformities where there ought to have been limbs, a distorted head with a face that told the tale of abnormalities. Regardless of what Mary Bone, new mother, discovered as she ran her hands carefully over the mass, she clutched the bundle to her naked bosom just as protectively as if it were the most perfectly-formed child in the world.

In that instant, when bare, warm, wet flesh met Mary's chest for the first time, the bond was made with that intrinsic intensity, certainty and permanence known only by a mother. Her fears were swiftly cast aside when she felt the first faint movements, followed by a muted mewling, a whistling, strangely distorted, in Mary's opinion. The sound was not as she remembered a baby's cries when she visited her cousins and aunties with newborn children.

It didn't matter to Mary Bone. The precious life, that had been the sole reason for her survival against all odds, had arrived at long last. That wet bundle at her chest gave Mary more courage, hope and strength than she believed possible. She would show the white bastard, she would show them all, that nothing could stop Mary Bone now.

Nothing in all the world would stop her from bringing up her child; the child his father did not want; her father and mother did not want, but Mary wanted with all her aching heart. She would bestow a love on the child that would never be broken as her parents had broken theirs. She didn't need any of them, especially...him! Deep down in Mary's psyche, a seething, boiling, roiling, tempestuous alchemy had been forming, a burning hatred so strong no earthly source could ever extinguish it.

Her son, for she could feel it was a boy by the large appendage between his legs, would learn of her hatred. He would be taught to nurture that red hot rage she felt, take it on board as his own, to make good on Mary's solemn promise to get even with...him, with them all. All the cursed whities and her kind who abandoned her, left her to deal with that monster that so nearly ended her life, she would make them pay, dearly. She would exact her revenge through the boy, Birrani Nullah, roughly translated as boy and war club or hunting stick, wielded by Aboriginal warriors. Birrani Nullah Bone would become her weapon of revenge against...everyone.

The following days were a balancing act of patience, perseverance, instinct and survival, all teetering precariously on the scales of life and death, weighed down sharply to one side or the other alternately. Mary's milk came down as nature intended, but her malformed infant had difficulty latching onto the swollen nipples. In the brightness of full sunshine, Mary was able to take in the extent of the damage her life-threatening beating had taken upon the unborn child within the womb. The child was very lucky, or unlucky, depending on who was asked, that he survived at all.

While the presence of all toes and fingers and other bodily parts assured Mary that Birrani was complete, the shape of those appendages, and his head and jaw, had her gasping with fear. The feet were cruelly curled under from the toes as though bound in the fashion of the Japanese geisha for a life of servitude, no matter how much Mary attempted to massage and manipulate them back into a semblance of normal feet. The hands were perhaps the best part of the boy, strong, large and dextrously perfect, while the crooked arms they were attached to left Mary frowning with concern.

Worse by far was the mouth. While his upper jaw appeared relatively normal, the mandible remained askew and formed a wide gap rather than the rounded shape ending in a chin associated with nature's design. His windpipe and voice box also appeared damaged beyond any semblance of normalcy. The boy did not cry like a normal infant, though he must surely have the need, considering his extensive injuries. Instead, he almost whistled and squeaked like a dog's rubber toy, giving him a plaintive 'scree, scree' sound.

After much fuss and worry, Mary found a means to feed the infant through a mixture of harsh and ineffectual sucking and expressing milk from her breasts manually, squirting the life-sustaining fluid directly into the baby's mouth.

Mary found new strength and firm resolve in the days after the birth, killing a few birds in flight with her practised eye at the slingshot, ensuring she ate enough, though barely, to keep up her supply of milk. Mary forced herself to consume the protein-rich amniotic remains of birth. It was, perhaps, the only reason she survived those crucial first days after the traumatic delivery. Mary was unable to attend to the torn perineum and parts of the vulva, damaged during the tough birth. She bled sporadically, and the injuries caused untold pain and discomfort during urination and excretion of solid wastes thereafter.

The days grew into weeks and weeks into months as the pair learned from one another how best to cope with the deficiencies the monster had thrust upon them. Mary had to find a permanent source of water once the area surrounding her pile of refuse and her meagre shelter had dried up. Plaiting together more of the stringy bark, which she softened with her saliva and wickedly-broken teeth, she created a sling in which to carry her growing boy, increasing his weight alarmingly for Mary, who struggled with the burden.

She still required branches fashioned as crutches to perform the basic function of walking any distance on her weakened and grossly bowed legs, thanks to bones not knitting into normal alignment. It was an ordeal for her to cover even moderate distances each day, travelling deeper into the bush as far away from the accursed town of Allies Creek and its dreaded population of demon whities as possible.

Exhausted beyond comprehension, yet compelled to venture ever deeper into the area that would eventually become known as Allies Creek State Forest, Mary Bone and her son, Birrani, finally arrived at a picturesque billabong. It was surrounded on three sides by steep escarpments, sheltering and covering the oasis in shadow for most of the day, thereby minimising evaporation of its precious liquid sustenance. A plethora of wildlife attracted to its water's edges each day provided Mary with all the game she required to gain strength and vitality. Within the steep walls of the ancient and worn volcanic caldera, Mary discovered a deep cave capable of protecting her and Birrani from the elements.

Utilising her vast store of patience, Mary was able to make a fire from two sticks, as shown to the boys in her family by their aging grandfather and Elder of the tribe passing down his valuable knowledge. The painstaking process, employing her aching hands and fingers for nearly an hour, eventually produced the first glowing embers. These took root in the soft bark she placed at the sides of the impression within the bottom piece of wood, where she placed the upright, hardened stick.

Producing the fire under the cover of an overhang at the entrance to her cave meant she was able to keep the fire going at all times, negating the need to repeat the fire-making process. She would learn over time just how much due diligence that task required. However, having achieved the task once meant she had the confidence to repeat it at those times when she foolishly allowed the fire to die.

Collecting the amount of wood a fire requires to burn all day and night kept Mary Bone working until the sweat threatened to drown her and her tears of frustration and pain to break her spirit. She soldiered on, in all weather, against all opposition, to feed herself and her growing infant. Often, when the infant bawled for one reason or another, the screee, screee-sound reverberated out of the cave and became amplified by the natural walls to create quite a loud and bone-chilling effect.

Mary Bone and Birrani continued to survive, to grow and to learn as time marched on. Their life at the oasis passed idyllically and harmoniously until the arrival of noisy and dangerous interlopers, making their passage to the waters of the billabong each day at dawn or dusk. The sounder of feral hogs showed no signs of fear for any foe, as the massive boar that led them was effective and remorseless in the protection of his harem of sows and offspring. Mary and Birrani watched on in awe from their lofty platform as young boars ready to accept the mantle of the alpha male, keen to rob him of his plentiful females, challenged the old boar for the position as head of the family.

The old, cunning boar, with tusks the length of Mary's forearm and possibly of the same girth, made light of all and any challengers. He dispatched them effortlessly with nothing more than a shake of his massive head as they charged, slicing them open along their entire length. It was not enough for the old boar to disable or frighten the young contestants: the beast then turned on his foes to devour them in a cannibalistic orgy of feasting for all, after he had eaten his fill.

Mary and Birrani learned to avoid the fearsome beast. She instilled in her child, using the language of her people, the consequences of not heeding her when he came into the age of understanding, somewhere between his second and third year of life.

Often, Birrani Nullah would stand at the lip of the cave to view the sounder as they came to drink and cavort playfully around the billabong, and let loose with a powerful screech that had the hogs scattering in a wild panic. Even the old boar became confused and disoriented at the strange sound echoing all about them. He tore off in every direction in an attempt to locate the source of the sound so that he could kill its owner. This usually ended in Birrani's approximation of a laugh that came out as nothing more than a high-pitched squeak, invoking great mirth from his mother as well.

Mary Bone schooled the boy relentlessly in all things from bush lore and survival to tribal customs, traditions and language. Mostly, though, she taught him to hate anything associated with anyone other than their tight family unit of mother and son. She told him what had happened to her, and indirectly to him, at the hands of the white dog called Big Tom O'Hare, the descendant of an Irish convict brought to this country in chains by the hated English overlords who nearly succeeded in decimating the Aboriginal population. They took away the black children from their parents to 'give them a better chance in life', and performed unspeakable acts of atrocity upon their fathers and forefathers.

Mary Bone drilled into the boy the need for revenge, to make his father pay dearly for his gruesome sins against them and 'hum-Jesus-pella who lived up in the sky'. Birrani listened in rapt attention to every word spoken by his beloved mother; caught up in the rhetoric with fervour; spurred on to shiver with murderous zeal; to exact his revenge on the demon whitey, Big Tom, his father. He had yet to understand what the word 'father' meant. He had no concept of any humans besides his partially-crippled mother.

Birrani practised diligently with Mary's slingshot until he bested her for accuracy and distance because of his increasing strength and size. By the time the boy reached his fourth year, he had overtaken Mary in height and weight. Even standing bowed and bent, with his deformed feet causing him to hobble rather than walk fully upright, he towered over his diminutive mother. One other curious change took place in the boy as he grew older; an inordinate amount of coarse body hair, especially on his back.

Mary became concerned at some point around the fifth year of Birrani's life. At times, if she twisted her bent body in a certain manner, either while ambling along behind her son or during her troubled slumber, she found herself short of breath and coughing up small amounts of blood. As time progressed, her problem escalated, causing her nights of endless coughing and sharp, intense jolts of white-hot pain knifing through her.

She felt she understood what was happening to her and worried fearfully for their future. Feeling about her ribs delicately, she believed that one of her broken ribs from the beating had never healed correctly. She assumed the splintered bone had worked its way slowly into one of her lungs, causing the shortness of breath and the bleeding. Slowly, day by day over a year, Mary deteriorated and grew more and more solemn.

She explained her condition to Birrani as best she could by using the carcasses of dead wallabies to demonstrate what she meant. She warned him that her time approached to join her ancestors. She made her son promise to carry on the vendetta she had taught him, to deliver retribution for her against the evil man, his father. She made him take a blood oath to swear his allegiance to their united cause, swiping a gash across both their palms to share the blood in a handshake.

She instilled in the boy all she had learned to ensure his survival in the harsh environment. She hoped he could survive long enough to perform his duties.

While in the throes of a delirium one evening, thrashing about on her bed of fresh straw, gathered by her son the previous day, a sudden shadow cast by a passing figure caused Birrani to screech in alarm. The wild screams of torment and suffering by his mother had attracted the presence of a stranger to their cave.

Standing at the entrance, in the light of the fire, stood an old man dressed only in a colourful loincloth. The man struck the pose of the stereotypical Aboriginal, with one leg raised and resting on the inner thigh of the other while supporting himself with a long spear held in one hand by his side. Birrani rushed at the man to scare him off, to protect his mother, only to be brushed aside and pushed back into the cave by the strong, wiry old man, who was far more dextrous and immeasurably quicker than the deformed Birrani.

As the boy backed into the rear of the cave, hovering over his mother, he screeched his annoyance at the intruder. He rushed to retrieve his mother's slingshot from its position on a small natural ledge within the cave, but they had not thought to gather any stones for ammunition in the many days since his mother became weak and ill.

Showing no fear, nor presenting himself as a danger to the pair within the cave, the old man moved forward to sit cross-legged beside the boy's mother. In hushed tones, Birrani could hear the pair speaking in a language he did not know. He paced impatiently out of reach and earshot of the strange man and his mother. He felt helpless and angry, wanting desperately to help his mother and be rid of the nuisance making her weary with gibberish.

After many hours of this, Birrani watched in dreaded fascination as his beloved mother drew her last painful breath. Her chest rose one more time before expelling a mixture of air and blood that dribbled from her open mouth held in a rictus of torturous agony. Feeling her passing just as surely as if he had passed himself, Birrani screeched his unholy grief to the world in a display of sheer terror and sorrow.

The old man closed the eyes and said some strange sounds over the body, passing his hands and waving a smoking stick, which he withdrew from the fire, around and over her body and his own. Birrani could not be certain, but it appeared as if the old man had become sad as well, sharing in their tragic loss. He did not go forward, would not approach his mother while the man remained.

Then something very odd happened, which stunned Birrani to his core. The old man rose from his seated position, turned to face Birrani with a look of great suffering suffusing his features, and spoke to Birrani in the language taught to him by his mother.

"Ho, Birrani Nullah Bone," he said in a soft voice. "My heart is heavy and I grieve with you. I will return here to bring food, to help you whenever I can. I know your mother has told you never to trust another living person, and you must hate me for my part in her passing. She is in a better place, where she no longer suffers. I will not try to take you from this place you know as your home. I will respect your mother's wishes by leaving you to do your duty when you have reached the age. I will not stop you. I will not inform the mill workers or your father. See you soon," he said.

And with one last look at Mary, the old man was gone as though he had never been there at all. He simply melted back into the night from whence he came.

EIGHT

Arlon was still relating the tale the following morning, once the group had prepared and eaten a small breakfast and consumed coffee. Arlon had been surprised to see the group hanging onto his every word the previous evening, with no one nodding off. He had had to call a halt when he was too tired to continue. For Arlon, it was the longest amount of time he had ever spent speaking.

Clarice and Bill had groaned when Arlon ended his story without answering any of the million questions they had, though, admittedly, they were both dog-tired as well. It had been an exhausting day filled with tension, concern and doubt. While Clarice mistrusted her ability to get any sleep at all, she was pleasantly surprised to find she had fallen into a deep and dreamless slumber, waking only upon hearing Arlon stoking their campfire before sunrise.

"Tell me, Arlon, why did you end the story there?" asked Clarice, after the group had moved on again into the thickening bushland.

"The next part of the story, and it may well be just that, Clarice, a story, a tale to tell the grandkids, is mainly snippets, supposition and conjecture. The old man gave accounts of what he witnessed and experienced himself, and from what others had observed, and the rest he filled in with guesses and logical deductions," explained Arlon.

"Load of shit, if you ask me," grumbled Travis, from the rear of the group.

"Well, I don't recall anyone asking, actually, nor giving a shit what you think, for that matter," remarked Clarice.

"Is it the billabong, you think, Arlon? Is that where you think the tracks lead?" asked Bill.

"That depends, Bill. When I casted around the clearing where they had feasted, I saw tracks leading in every direction."

"So why choose this particular direction, then?"

"Although it was mostly covered, and I would say purposely, the tracks that I wanted to follow are the unusual prints that were almost inexplicable before last night. In light of the old man's story, the tracks begin to make some sense. It's those that I aim to follow."

"You can't possibly think they belong to the boy?"

"No, Bill, not the boy: the man. If it is Birrani Nullah Bone, he's over eighty by now and huge, by the look of the prints. The story of the toes curled under the feet gives the tracks I found a certain validity, making them possible and understandable. If the boy grew to his full potential, surviving out here, he's reached formidable proportions in any man's language. According to the old man, he is truly monstrous in size."

"So, who is *he*, then?" asked Clarice, being fairly confident she knew the answer.

"The old man from last night?"

"Yep, the creepy old geezer that just appeared from nowhere without a sound and spent nearly two hours talking with you in Aborigine, before disappearing back into the bush just as mysteriously," added Clarice.

"That man was Mary Bone's father, an elder of the Gureng Gureng tribe, the traditional owners of this land we're walking on."

"So, he was the one who found Mary dying in that cave?"

"No, Bill. That was Mary's grandfather, who taught her the traditional ways of his people when Mary was finally released from the orphanage. He saw to Mary's traditional education, while her parents were off to the city to fight the government in protest about the white man's treatment of the Aborigine. Jarrah Bone took Mary under his wing and showed her the old ways; where to find bush tucker, how to live off the land, even how to divine water. Jarrah Bone never forgave his son for abandoning Mary when he found out she was pregnant to the white man.

"When Jarrah found Mary dying beside the fire in that cave, he made a promise to look after the boy, and, when he could no longer do so personally, he commanded his son, Kami Bone, to pick up where he left off. That was the man we met last night. He related Mary's story as explained by her to Jarrah, then repeated what his father had seen and done for the boy himself, then what Kami knew."

"When you were telling the story last night, Arlon, it, I don't know, seemed like you were experiencing some of it as you spoke."

"I hoped that might be true, Clarice. Usually, I bore people to death whenever I have to relate anything of length. I tried to give some light and shade to the story I told, employed a certain amount of animation to make it more enjoyable to you all. I hoped so, at any rate."

"Worked for me, and I think you should try that more often in your normal speech, Arlon, not just when you're telling some story."

"Wouldn't it bother you that it would be pure acting on my part, that I didn't feel anything I was relating, that I was being false?"

"Hell, most everyone acts false in one way or another, Arlon. Some people tend to be pretty damn false all the time," explained Clarice.

"So, Jarrah was the paternal grandfather, and Kami was the father, you said, Arlon?" asked Bill.

"Yes. Jarrah had a deep love for his granddaughter. He also cherished his great-grandson, despite the horrific deformities and speech defects. Kami said that, when he took over in caring for Birrani, the boy had grown into an enormous man, horribly stooped and very hairy, with great strength.

"To hear Kami tell it, Birrani had the facial appearance of one of the hogs that milled around him at that point. His lower jaw was practically bifurcated, with the two pieces, tipped by teeth, protruding from his chin area giving the impression of tusks. He had never heard his father describe the boy as anything out of the ordinary, only that he had a deep, abiding love for him and his mother, and a tremendous sadness for everything that had occurred.

So when Kami finally saw his grandson for the first time, he was truly shocked. He also feared the boy, who stood at over two metres tall by then. Kami worried about revealing his paternal relationship to the boy at first, for fear he would be killed. Kami had been feeling a great shame for abandoning his daughter, augmented by the scolding from Jarrah after Mary had been found and related the truth to Kami."

"You believe we're on the trail of Birrani and his pigs?" asked Clarice.

"Yes, I do. I have no reason at this juncture to disbelieve anything I was told."

"Coming from a cynic like you, Arlon, I would have to take that as almost gospel."

"It may turn out to be something entirely different. I'm not beyond being duped, Clarice."

"But it all fits, doesn't it? What I can't work out is why Mrs Henderson was taken, if she was."

"I have a theory about that, but not one I'd like to share at the moment."

"Why not?"

"Ah, present company?" Arlon answered cryptically.

"If you're looking to spare my feelings, don't bother. I don't go for any of this bullshit. It's just a tall yarn."

"Then how do you explain what's happening, *Travis*?" asked Clarice, using Henderson's first name in a derogatory fashion.

"All I know is that my wife is missing and we're tracking a bunch of wild pigs for some arcane reason. Just because some old fart came and told us a ghost story around the campfire last night doesn't mean that I'm willing to be duped into believing a word of it, like you gullible lot."

"Then why are you following Arlon and the 'pigs' with us? Go conduct your own search...idiot!" she muttered the last word under her breath.

"Unfortunately, I am not as good as this fruitcake, Livingstone, at picking up the trail, otherwise I *would* be leading my own search."

"By yourself, because no one would be stupid enough to follow you," she spat.

Clarice smiled to see the man madly swatting away at a zillion flies while the rest were relatively comfortable in their fly nets. The ground over which they walked was rough most of the time, and the heat was building rapidly by mid-morning. Clarice was unable to make out the tracks that Arlon told them they were following. Although the hogs followed the leader, the owner of the strange tracks, in a deliberate attempt to obfuscate them, Arlon still managed to identify those tracks intermittently.

Bill Rogers had taken up a proprietary station directly behind Clarice, who followed on Arlon's heels. Henderson brought up the rear of the group, seething and mumbling away to himself most of the time. Clarice knew that Henderson would turn on Arlon the moment an opportunity presented itself. Arlon was unconcerned. Clarice considered that a mistake. In her opinion, Henderson should have been restrained again, and they all should have returned to Allies Creek and gone home from there, allowing the authorities to deal with Mrs Henderson's disappearance.

Arlon hoped that they would reach their destination before nightfall. If the story was true, Mary Bone could not have travelled very far from the township in the state she was in, however much she had healed after the terrible abuse she suffered. If she was on crutches and carrying a baby, the billabong had to be relatively close by. What they would do once they reached it was not something he could answer with any degree of certainty.

His main goal was to locate and free the Henderson woman. How he might achieve that he would not contemplate until he had more information. His theory at present led him to conclude that the Henderson woman was safe for the time being. He had tried to convey that confidence to Mr Henderson without success. The man was too riled to see anything that Arlon did or said as being helpful. Arlon recognised that the man was so confounded by the situation that he was unable to hear or see the truth even if it was obvious.

Arlon had taken control of the rifle which he had confiscated from Henderson. The man could not be trusted to use it properly or safely, especially around Arlon. Arlon knew that Henderson would wait for just the right moment to even the score. He could not dismiss the notion that he might be unbalanced enough to try to kill Arlon.

"Why did Mary's father decide to help us, Arlon?" asked Clarice suddenly, interrupting Arlon's thoughts.

"You misunderstand, Clarice. He didn't mean to help us, he meant to kill us," said Arlon simply.

"WHAT?"

"Well, as far as Kami was concerned, we were a search party formed to hunt down his grandson to bring him in to face justice or do him harm."

"He was going to kill us?" repeated Clarice.

"If he couldn't stop us, yes."

"Why didn't he do it, then?"

"Because I spoke to him in his language. Despite his intense hatred for the white man and his promise to care for his grandson at all costs, I gained his respect with the simple act of knowing his native language. I also managed to convey our fears for the safety of his possible captive."

"But, I mean, we do mean to harm his grandson, don't we? What then?"

"It's complex, Clarice."

"Complex, my arse! We find her and we shoot whoever or whatever has her, end of fucking story," stated Travis.

"If we find her and she's alive, then we have to do our best to see that she stays that way. If it is Birrani Nullah Bone that we're dealing with, he's organised a small army to help defend their position. If you want to go barging into that lot with one gun blazing, then be my guest; you do so on your own. Then you'll have his grandfather's tribe to deal with afterwards. And again, watch your language," warned Arlon.

"What is it with the pigs? How did they come to join Birrani?"

"Kami believed he knew how that came about. He told me and I'll tell you what he told me tonight. I have to concentrate on these tracks now, otherwise, I'll lose them," answered Arlon.

The heat grew fiercer as the day drew on. Arlon guessed the temperature to be somewhere around fifty degrees Celsius. At midday, he called a halt to their trek. He found a shady area to wait out the hottest part of the day while they ate and drank a little. Arlon advised them to ration their food and water sensibly. He walked over to Mr Henderson, who was sitting against the bloated bole of a bottle tree. He appeared to be bearing up poorly.

"Mr Henderson, did you bring anything at all along for yourself? Some food, a bit of water?" asked Arlon.

"Gonna say, 'I told you so'?"

"No. You don't understand my condition, do you? I don't develop or keep grudges. I can't give glib or smarmy comments because I'm not offended by anything anyone says to me. I don't feel anger towards you. I'm asking because I can see you're suffering from dehydration and the flies are just about driving you bonkers. Your shoes are about as useless out here as wearing bedroom slippers, and your feet are bleeding by the look of them," said Arlon gently.

Travis peered at him with eyes that were mere slits. Sweat caused runnels through the thick dust coating his face. He sighed helplessly.

"I fucking hate you, Livingstone. Trouble is, there's no point. Hating you doesn't affect you, does it? No, I didn't bring anything along because I truly believed we'd be back before now, and I was...trying to tough it out, to be a man, to be a bigger, stronger, more virile man than you or that other wanker, Rogers.

"Wait here, try to keep cool. I'll be back in a sec."

Arlon walked over to the rucksack he had removed. After making sure the other two were as comfortable as possible, he returned to Travis.

"First, wet this rag with some of this water from my spare canteen. Don't overdo it; you'll need to save that water as much as possible. Wipe your face and neck with the rag, gently, because I think you may have a sunburn. Then have one good swig of the water. Here's a cap and a fly net. Place the fly net over the cap. That way the peak will keep the net away from your face. Take off those shoes and I'll see what I can do with them."

"You sure you wanna do this for me?"

"Why wouldn't I?"

"Really?"

"Really. I have a spare shirt with sleeves that will probably fit you. As you can tell by all the scratches you have on your arms, the T-shirt isn't protecting you from the branches or the sun. Then I want you to have these sandwiches I made. Curried egg and lettuce, I'm afraid, nothing else."

"What about you?"

"I've eaten a full breakfast and I have my canteen. I don't expect to need much more. If we don't come across them tonight or early tomorrow, we'll have to return, anyway. We aren't prepared for an extended expedition. We weren't even well-prepared for a short one. The authorities will have to take over, I'm afraid."

Arlon sat next to Travis while he ate in silence and drank a little from the canteen. Travis' whole posture changed when his face was clean and fly-free, and he was wearing a fresh shirt and even a pair of sunglasses given to him by Arlon, having left his expensive Ray Bans behind. He attempted to smile at Arlon.

"Save the smile, Mr Henderson, it doesn't work on me," said Arlon dismissively.

"Had to go and undo everything you just did, huh? Just as well, I suppose. You are an easy person to loathe, Livingstone."

"I don't know what you hope to accomplish by trying to needle me with that name. 'Sticks and stones' has never had a more apt meaning than for someone like me. You can pretty much call me anything you like and it will never affect me, not in the slightest. I know I'm a target because of my condition; I always have been. I can't escape it and don't bother trying anymore. Waste of time and energy pondering circumstances over which I have no control. Feeling any better?"

"Sure," answered Travis penitently.

"I think we should stay here until around three, then begin moving again. Rest up and conserve that water. We'll need it for our return trip, especially if we have another person with us at that point."

"You don't think it's far then?"

"Can't you smell it?"

"What?"

"Water, Mr Henderson, or rather the droppings and other detritus of habitation around a waterhole. Every so often when the breeze blows from the west, I catch a whiff of it. I estimate that we are perhaps only an hour away from that billabong Kami described. See over there, those low hills? I think they are the time-worn sides of the extinct volcano's caldera. The billabong doesn't dry up because of the shade it gets and the fact that it's probably fed by an underground spring. The fantastic depth of that pool, if it is the ancient caldera, will ensure it stays that way for many years. A perfect, natural hideaway and a highly defensible position with only one easy way into the three-sided area."

"So, how do you propose to go in there?"

"I don't."

"Come again?"

"I have no intention of blundering into a trap."

"A trap?"

"Of course. We're being led there by whatever or whoever has taken your wife. Thanks to you, they now know we have only one weapon and very little else. We're being lured into a deliberate ambush so they can finish us all off, remove all signs of us, our tracks back from our starting point, everything, leaving the authorities no trail to follow."

"So, what do you plan to do?"

"Find the billabong first. Then observe closely from a vantage point whatever awaits us."

"What if they decide to kill my wife while you're...observing?" asked Travis guardedly.

"I think you know the answer to that question, Mr Henderson. Nothing will save your wife, nor could have, if the decision was made to end it before we're ready to activate a plan. I say again, you want to go straight in there with one gun blazing, you're on your own. I won't risk all our lives on a reckless and pointless strategy like that."

"I think you'd better fuck off now and leave me alone. You're starting to annoy the crap out of me again, Livingstone," stated Travis, with a hard glare.

Arlon wandered over to the other two, where he sat for a time, before closing his eyes for a mini-siesta. Bill Rogers and Clarice Manning succumbed to their weariness as well after a short time.

NINE

SCREEEEYAHHHH, SCREEEEEYAHHHH.

The hideous sound jolted everyone awake. All around them, a dust storm was building from the hooves of dozens and dozens of wild boar, cloaking the area, making it impossible to see anything. Arlon retrieved his neckerchief, which he tied around his face to keep from choking. He ordered the others to do the same as best he could over the deafening mêlée of pigs squealing and grunting, spurred into a frenzy by the leader's impossibly high screeching.

Standing in a daze, amid a confusing maelstrom of indescribable noises and swirling dust clouds, Arlon, Clarice and Bill huddled together protectively. Arlon assumed Travis would have found a safe location within the circle of frenzied action to wait it out.

Arlon believed it was an intimidation tactic being employed against them, though thinking was next to impossible during the fracas. It was disturbing to see wild animals, some of them immense, working in a coordinated manner to herd their meagre group into a position of helplessness.

SCREEEEEEEEEYAHHHH, SCREEEEEEEEEYAHHHHH.

With that piercing shriek, all circling action ceased and the individual noises diminished, with the animals bleeding off into the surrounding bushland under the cover of the billowing dust. Within moments an ominous, unnatural silence fell on the landscape. Clarice shook with fear, while Bill appeared to be stunned into immobility. Arlon waited for the dust to settle before he attempted to move.

When the air cleared sufficiently, the first thing they noticed was the absence of their fourth compatriot. There was no sign of him, and they did not want to call out his name. Their motivation to pursue any course of action regarding Travis' disappearance waned considerably the more they thought about the man. Arlon was in quite a quandary. Without Mr Henderson's constant insistence that he should mount a search for his wife, Arlon was reluctant to continue. He feared for the safety of the other members of the search party should they be foolish enough to follow a bunch of wild pigs, led by some unearthly...thing into a certain ambush.

"I'm worried about going on," he finally admitted.

"No argument from me. I'm scared shitless, mate," said Clarice.

"What about that lot, though? Will we be allowed to go back if that's what we decide? You said you didn't think so, earlier."

"The odds are against us any way we look at it. Going forward with two men, one woman and one weapon against that hoard of marauders doesn't appeal to me. Wild boar are extremely dangerous animals on their own, without being stirred into a frenzy by their leader. We're almost certainly being encouraged to move forward by them and to hurry it along, it would seem. They don't want us wasting time sitting around. If we decide to return, we have to make a mad dash for it or else we'll be overrun by them. Not sure any of us are up to a full run back to Allies Creek."

"I'll only slow you down if that's what you decide," agreed Bill.

"I won't be much better than Bill. I'm tired, hungry and bloody too scared to do much of anything, Arlon. Sorry."

"While I may be the fittest of us all, I seriously doubt that I could outrun those wild boar if they came after us. I couldn't keep up a trot for that long, let alone a full run. I reckon we have just two options. Either we find a place to hole up, a defensible position where we make a stand with our rifle, or we press on and hope for the best."

"What do you think we should do, Arlon?" asked Clarice.

"If it was purely up to me, I'd opt to go forward. Going back is impossible, as far as I can tell, and holing up somewhere will eventually see us picked off one by one. By my estimate, we have about fifty bullets for the rifle and, once they're gone, we have nothing but a club for defence."

"But, what do we hope to achieve? We can't possibly hope to rescue the Hendersons, so what's the point?"

"The point is we don't seem to have much choice, and I still think we have a chance if we employ our collective brains to nut out a plan once we arrive and have an idea of the layout. I wouldn't be too quick to count us as down and out just yet."

"Can't stay, can't go back and most likely buggered if we go forward, is not much of a choice, Arlon," she said

"I agree."

"Well, we may as well just get going, then."

"What about you, Bill?" asked Arlon.

"Don't see what else we can do. How far do you think it is, though? We don't have much left in the way of food and water. I'm down to a few drops and one last boiled egg, which I think is going off quickly in this heat," explained Bill.

"I'm counting on being able to refill our canteens, at the very least, if what Kami said was true about there being a spring-fed billabong. Who knows what we may find to eat growing by the side of it. Kami told me he'd planted some citrus trees there to help keep scurvy at bay for the boy."

"Citrus?" queried Clarice.

"An old sailor's trick to keep up the body's vitamin C requirements. Mundubbera is a well-known citrus growing area, so the trees may well have survived."

When the questions came to an end an awkward silence ensued, the group resigned themselves to moving on. Arlon no longer needed to follow any individual tracks. He was certain about the general direction they were headed to find their quarry's lair. He believed they would reach their destination before nightfall. Gradually, sounds of the bush returned as the threesome walked forward gamely.

The afternoon wore on and the heat became almost unbearable, the air redolent of eucalyptus from the forest of gum trees surrounding them. The sweat poured from their heads and armpits in uncomfortable rivulets. Arlon had previously taken the time to cut ventilation slits into all their clothing, which helped enormously to circulate the weak breeze, cooling their tiring bodies. Once, much to Clarice's great amusement, Arlon stopped suddenly to shinny up a tree.

"What the heck are you up to?" begged Clarice.

"Trying to ascertain the distance. I don't want us to simply bumble our way into the trap. If we know the entrance to the caldera is coming up, I need us to stop and reconnoitre."

"And is it?"

"Still some way in my estimation."

"Hang about! If we're that close we should be able to see a bloody great volcano, shouldn't we?"

"No, Clarice. This is an ancient and extinct volcano, worn down through the millennia, leaving only a surrounding wall of around two or three stories high, if my information is correct. High enough and close enough to protect the billabong at its centre, but not high enough to be seen as anything all that different to the surrounding bushland when seen from above. I imagine this waterhole is only about ten metres or so in diameter, for it to have remained undiscovered. Believe me, if a permanent source of water was discovered by white men, they would have found a way to exploit it or settle there."

"Why haven't the Aborigines settled there?"

"Ancestral taboos, I believe. Aboriginals are very superstitious and highly respectful of their ancestors' resting places or lands of sacred value. There may be ancient cave drawings there to indicate early occupation, not unknown in these parts. We'd better get going again."

"Arlon?" said Clarice, after they had walked a few paces.

"Yeah?"

"Can you tell us the rest of the story now that you said you don't have to concentrate on the tracks?"

TEN

Birrani Nullah Bone stood over the prone form of his dead mother for a long time, wailing, which came out as a high-pitched keening. Then he began pacing, panicking. He wasn't sure whether to trust the old man, who said he would return. He wasn't sure of anything anymore. He was hurting inside, as though everything had turned sour and rancid. He found it hard to breathe, as if an unbearable weight had descended upon him. He ached deep down in his person, somewhere he was unable to provide relief. His precious mother had gone to her Jesus-pella, as she had often foretold.

He did not understand much of what she had said about all that stuff, three-headed gods that lived in the sky and the bad one underneath, the debil-pella. He didn't care about all that. The one constant in his troubling life of hardship and enduring pains associated with his condition was his mother. The woman who loved him unreservedly, who had saved him from certain death at the hands of his evil father, the detestable white man who had caused so much heartache and physical trauma to them both.

His tears brought him confusion without the relief he sought. He knew physical pain, was able to deal with that problem daily. He was unaware of the emotional ache associated with grief. His inexperience sought to destroy him from within, to make him curl into a foetal ball and wither into inexistence, to join his mum, wherever she was.

The pain was too great, with no solution or reprieve presenting itself. He lay next to her decomposing body within the cave for days, inexplicably distraught and unwilling to continue with his life. He slept fitfully, tortured by dreams and memories of his time with his mother. At times he would wake in the middle of the night to keen in mourning and desolation.

Those keening sounds, amplified by the cave and the amphitheatre-like geography outside, caused unrest to the animals, often adding their voices to the piercing shrieks. At times it was as if the entire bushland had come alive and shared the boy's intense heartache.

Jarrah Bone, camped several kilometres away, also shared in the boy's grief, mourning for his beloved granddaughter and fearing the outcome for his unholy great-grandson. Though he visited the cave every day, carefully speaking softly in the old language, the boy remained inconsolable. Jarrah worried that Birrani might not survive, and yet secretly hoped for it. He could not understand how the boy had survived to date with the horrific deformities he displayed.

Though he was inordinately proud of his granddaughter for managing to survive her ordeals and her significant injuries, which she had admitted while relating the tale to him on her deathbed, he did not understand why she had not simply allowed the boy to strangle by his umbilical when she saw how grotesque he was. It would have been a favour to the boy, to save him from the anguish and severe suffering his body would inflict upon him.

Jarrah paled at the telling of it. He had listened, with growing horror and immense pride, to how his lovely Mary believed she heard him in that first raindrop to fall on her face as she lay broken, bloody and dying upon a trash heap. Mary said she had heard her poppy singing and saw him dancing in the deluge that followed. It gave her the strength, the will to ensure she lived, to give birth to her baby, no matter what.

Mary had struggled from one puddle to the next, to gain a precious sip of life-giving moisture for her parched lips. She had licked the putrid remains from an old can of baked beans, or spam, or whatever else had been thrown away by the white mill workers. She was always in agony from her broken bones, swollen limbs and unseeing eyes. Mary had eventually regained her sight when the swelling receded, though it remained somewhat impaired. A fuzziness had crept into the edges of her vision, causing her to turn her head in the direction she wished to look.

Jarrah could not imagine himself as resilient or as brave as his granddaughter if he had been in her situation. He could understand her reluctance to allow the baby to come to harm. Mary had been raised in a mission, taken away from her father and mother as a young girl, to be brought up in the white man's world. The priests and nuns at the mission were strict Catholics, instilling in their charges the doctrine of their faith zealously. Mary had come to love and cherish their God and that 'Jesus-pella' she spoke about on the rare occasions she had been allowed to visit her natural family.

Mary had not wanted to end up in that hell place where the debil-pella made a permanent bushfire for all the 'ebil' ones. Jarrah hadn't understood much of what she related, but he certainly didn't like the idea of an eternity of living in a bush fire. He'd seen first-hand the intensity of an Australian bush fire, even started a few of his own to cleanse the land around their camp.

While Jarrah lamented his granddaughter's passing with the boy, whom he heard clearly day after day, he felt an indentured obligation to him. He felt an ingrained compulsion to take Birrani under his wing as he had done with his Mary, teaching her the people's way, the old way, the real way: not the vision of the life she had learned at the mission, but her culture, her heritage, and he felt he must also pass that on to her boy.

He did not know how he could accomplish the task. If the boy continued to mourn his mother to the exclusion of all else, he would perish alongside her. Jarrah thought that would be a blessing, yet he could not convince himself to allow it to happen. The boy was growing weak by the third day and showing signs of dehydration and starvation. It would be a day or two at most before the boy succumbed to the laws of nature governing the human body. To survive, a body required energy derived from food and water, the most basic of necessities.

It was the morning of the fourth day after Mary had passed. He would have to return to the cave to attend to the 'sorry business' of her remains. He was forced to divorce himself of her name, substituting Kunmanara, to protect her spirit from venturing back into the land of the living. It would have been his family way to have her body within the camp on a raised platform, where her family members could gather to mourn respectfully, but Jarrah could see no way of removing her body from the cave without incurring the boy's wrath and mistrust.

He would have to find a way to explain how the boy's mother needed to be sent away properly to ensure her spirit joined their ancestors. Without that, her spirit was condemned: unsatisfactory and frightening to a traditional Aboriginal. It was imperative to impress upon the child the need for a ceremony of song and dance, to commemorate her passing while they either buried or cremated her remains.

Reluctantly, Jarrah forced his aging body to rise from his squatting position by the morning fire. Dressed in a dirty pair of stockman's jeans and a long-sleeved, faded red shirt, Jarrah sighed heavily as he contemplated the difficult task ahead. Pushing back the ragged Akubra from the front of his head, he mopped his brow, beginning to sweat already with the rising heat, with the back of his wrinkled, bony hand. As a jackaroo for many of his younger years, Jarrah had worked hard to maintain a firm and strong physique for one of his age. He knew he would require all of his considerable strength and guile for the day ahead.

As he neared the cave's entrance, facing the short, steep path up to the cave, Jarrah steeled himself. Inside he smelled the ghastly corpse of Kunmanara. His resolve galvanised into an unyielding force of determination to see the plan through. He squatted a little way behind the boy cradling his mother. He spoke softly in the old language, the only one the boy understood.

"Ho, Birrani Nullah Bone. I feel your great grief in my heart. I share the rot in my gut. I feel the agony eating me from the inside.

You are not alone in this. Your whole family feels this with you. It is why we need to share this burden. It is time for Kunmanara to be free of this world, to join her ancestors while we grieve her passing. It is time to set her spirit free."

Silence.

"I am Elder, grandfather of the Gureng Gureng tribe, Birrani Nullah Bone. My name is Jarrah Bone, your great grandfather. You will hear and obey me; it must be done. You will have to help me, or I will be forced to do it all without you, and you will not be able to set your mother's spirit free."

Jarrah rose. The instant he heard the movement, Birrani leapt from his position beside his mother to a crouching defensive pose, hissing with fear and objection to the old man's words and possible interference. Though immensely large for his age, Birrani was no threat to Jarrah, yet would still be able to inflict severe injury with that separated bottom jaw and jutting teeth that resembled a boar's tusks.

"Ho, Birrani Bone. It is wrong for you to fear me or challenge me. You know already that I am stronger and faster than you. It is for you and your mother that I do this. It is right and proper, the people's way, to set her spirit free. If you prefer, she has to go meet her 'Jesus-pella'."

Birrani balked slightly at the mention of that name he knew well after hearing his mother mention it so often. It still didn't mean he would allow the interloper to interfere with him or his precious mum. He might know the language they spoke, but he was not to be trusted, not to be allowed to sway his mind like all the evil ones that had hurt Mary, the detestable whities and the awful black ones who abandoned her. No one was to be trusted in Birrani's mind. His mother had taught him that well. His hate was all-consuming.

He launched himself at the old man with a speed and ferocity that stunned Jarrah. Almost too late, Jarrah was barely able to thrust aside the charge with a well-placed blow to the side of the boy's head, utilising the momentum of the charge to inflict the maximum effect. Birrani stumbled and fell against the rear wall of the cave, where he shook off the dull ache in his head.

Silently, stealthily, Birrani rose to his full height, filling his lungs with air.

SCREEEEYAH, SCREEEEEEYAH, SCREEEEYAH.

It was the first time the boy had found his mature voice, if that's what it could be called. The intense screeching was deafening within the cave, making Jarrah hold his ears and tremble with superstitious awe. He thought the previous wailing he had heard was loud and unnatural enough. What the boy let loose with then stunned him completely. He did not think anything in the world was capable of making such an unearthly sound. It was like nothing he had ever heard, somewhere between an eagle's mournful cry, echoing off the walls, and a wild pig's noise.

Somehow, in the boy's damaged larynx, which prevented any type of speech being formed, he found a screeching cry of overwhelming volume, which evolved from the plaintive keening Jarrah had first heard.

The bushland outside the cave suddenly erupted in a cacophony of sounds and movement. Hundreds of galahs and sulphur-crested cockatoos took to the wing as one, swirling and screeching in a holding pattern above the oasis. The wild boar, frequenting the waterhole each morning and evening, were sent into a panicked frenzy, causing mayhem and chaos among the other denizens of the bush, including lizards, frogs and insects. Everything joined the commotion to create one unholy concert of nerve-fraying and ear-splitting intensity.

As Jarrah watched, agape, even the boy seemed to be stunned by the development of his vocal range and the tumult it caused. The interval lasted only a moment, as once again Birrani focused his rage on the old man, emboldened by the ruckus he had triggered. He charged again, head down in a bull's rush on his ungainly feet at a fast hobble.

Jarrah once more swatted him aside effortlessly. What the boy possessed in courage and ferocity, he lost in lack of experience and wisdom. Birrani shook his head as he sat in the dust. The last blow stung. His weakened condition began to tell on his body. He was out of breath and feeling exhausted by the ridiculously small amount of movement. Though every muscle and tendon in his body quivered with the challenge he faced, he understood that he was unable to conquer the foe. The old man was incredibly fast and wiry, and his fists were like steel maces, which stunned him. His anger grew.

SCREEEEEEYAHHHHH, SCREEEEEEEEEYAHHHH.

Birrani screeched his indignity and defiance even more loudly. Once more, the world erupted outside the cave. It seemed to Jarrah, once he regained his senses, that Birrani had somehow tapped into the animal kingdom with that sound. He was able to commune with, and maybe even control the animals on multiple levels. Whether the animals identified with the sound or sympathised with it or Birrani simply intuited an ancient form of communication long-forgotten by human beings, Jarrah couldn't be sure. It scared the old man to the marrow. It was supernatural and unlike anything from his people's memories or folklore.

Jarrah braced himself for another charge. The boy was not about to relent in his attacks, no matter how he fared. Jarrah could see the determination set in the boy's ugly features. The cold, hard stare penetrated Jarrah's defences, boring through to his spirit. It was time for a different tack. It was time for Jarrah to utilise the brain and the good instincts he was born with that made him a natural leader of his tribe. He prepared himself for possible injury on the next assault.

When it came, it was considerably slower than the previous efforts. The boy was running low on energy after days without food or water. It was a pathetic display of pure courage alone, as the weakened boy ran squarely into his great-grandfather's enveloping, steely embrace. The old man turned and twisted him easily so the boy couldn't bring his fearsome mandible to bear. Jarrah held the boy's hairy back to his chest with all his might, trapping the head and arms.

Jarrah whispered to him softly about the great love and respect he had for the boy and his mother, while Birrani struggled gamely and noisily within the man's grasp. He thrashed and kicked with all his waning strength while hurling a continuous stream of unintelligible protests and screeching. Jarrah held on. He held on for an eternity while he soothed the savage beast with words of love and undying affection, with high words of praise and pride for his great-grandson and his granddaughter.

Gradually, the noise abated and the struggles lessened as the boy grew weary. Outside, the world seemed to settle in tune with the boy. Jarrah continued in his calm, mesmerising tone.

"Ho, Birrani Nullah Bone, you are loved by me and your people. Kunmanara was wronged by her father and mother. You were wronged by us all, especially your white father, but we love and cherish you now. Know of the great healing spirit and strength of the tribe, of the people. Feel that in your heart, Birrani. Feel the love we have for you. You are strong and young, though you have suffered more than you deserve. Let us help you now on your journey to manhood. Take strength and wisdom from us, from me, your great-grandfather, Jarrah Bone."

Finally, unable to resist any longer, Birrani wept bitter tears of frustration, grief and the inability to break free. He wept for all the injustices he and his mother had faced. He wept for the pain he felt in his heart, for the loss he was unable to comprehend. His great-grandfather spoke to him so softly, and he strained to take in the words spoken with such devotion and sincerity. He wept for the longing of familial love and nurturing provided by his mother. He longed desperately for a father who cared, who wanted him for who he was. He longed and wept for another human to need him. He wept long and hard, clutching desperately at the old man for comfort, and Jarrah wept with him.

They clung together in that familial embrace until Birrani had expended the last tear from his great store of misery. Jarrah never once let up with the stream of heartfelt condolences and passionate pleas for the boy to understand and accept his love, all delivered in a soft, endearing yet commanding tone. Jarrah honestly felt what he said. He had thought bad things about the boy, wishing for an end to his suffering, without realising those thoughts caused much of the pain. The boy instinctively read Jarrah's mind, knew his thoughts and intentions. He did not communicate on a human level; he understood the depth of a human intuitively.

Jarrah was deeply ashamed that he had added to the boy's pain. He felt great remorse that he had allowed his great-grandson to know that Jarrah had wished him dead, regardless of the intentions. The boy had no speech, no other way to communicate, and therefore picked up on these extraneous gestures and movements, the facial tics and expressions, the eyes, that told the whole story, which words could never adequately convey. Birrani was one of those rare individuals that could see through to the essence of a person, read his soul as easily as Jarrah read the tracks of his prey in the dirt.

It was a lesson well-learned for Jarrah. He would never again underestimate the boy, attempt to be clever or false. He would need to be very certain of his inner thoughts while dealing with him. The slightest doubts or uncertainties would be picked up immediately. Any falseness he showed might be seen as a ruse. If he hoped to gain Birrani's trust, Jarrah would have to purge his mind of all impurities and prejudices against the deformities or shortcomings he saw in the boy.

For the moment, feeling the back of his great-grandson pressed firmly against his chest; feeling the talon-like grip of the boy's hands on his arms; feeling the heaving sobs slowly diminishing, Jarrah was at peace with the world, smiling and confident that he would succeed in teaching the boy as he had the mother. Though the rest of his tribe would probably never be able to accept Birrani as one of their own, he was sure that he had conquered his initial revulsion. With some luck and guidance, he might bring Kami, his son, around as well.

Jarrah was still very angry with his son for the shameful way he had treated his only daughter. It was right, though, that Kami should have a chance to make amends for that transgression with his grandson. All Jarrah needed to do was to convince his stubborn son.

Jarrah understood that his son had very little to do with his daughter being taken away by the whites, but he could not condone the banishment he forced upon her for becoming pregnant to the evil white man, Big Tom. Kami's daughter was only a young girl at the time, still inexperienced in the ways of men and women. Impatience was always a villain when it came to dealing with teenagers, especially females, who matured so much more quickly than males of the same age.

Jarrah released the boy when he felt assured that he would no longer be the target of his aggression, and Birrani displayed the first signs of being uncomfortable. He waited while the boy steadied himself emotionally, before turning to face him with his curious, intelligent brown eyes that looked right through him.

"Ho, Birrani Nullah Bone, you are family, you are needed and wanted by your relations. We, the tribe, hold this place sacred. See those drawings on the rock walls? They were put there by our ancestors many generations ago. It shows the rich history of our people, hunting the strange animals that were here at the beginning of time, the fires they used and their way of life. We don't come here out of respect for them and to leave their spirits in peace. Your mother, Kunmanara, must join them now. I must prepare the path for her.

"I see you do not understand why I call her a different name. It is no longer right for us to use her given name. If she hears her earthly name used, her spirit might be tempted to stay among us, causing upset and mischief. We call the dead by a general name to make sure they know there is no longer a place for them here with the living.

"Birrani, I must see to the 'sorry business', the preparations. I will not bring our people here to this sacred ground, and I will not try to take you to them. We will do this thing together, here, you and me. I will need your help to take Kunmanara down to the billabong, where we will build a fire around her. Normally, we would bury her after days of customary singing and dancing, while the tribe mourns the passing of a loved one. We have waited too long for a burial. Kunmanara smells bad, Birrani. This is not the way to treat a beautiful person. One day, I hope you can understand this and appreciate it. One day, this ceremony will be performed for you as a revered and respected member of our race and our family."

Without waiting for acknowledgement or acceptance, Jarrah turned around to see to the task of transporting the body down the narrow, steep path to the billabong. He knew he took a great risk in turning his back on the dangerous child, but he firmly believed that trust had to be shown before it could be reciprocated. He walked purposefully to where his granddaughter lay. He stood at her head, poised to bear her weight, waiting patiently.

It was an age before Jarrah heard the slightest movement from the boy. With his awkward gait, he made his way to his mother's feet. Jarrah nodded his head in approval. He bent to the task of lifting her under the arms and around her chest. The moment she was disturbed, and the gases escaped her body, the stench became almost overpowering in the cloying atmosphere of the cave. The boy lifted his mother by the legs and followed the old man out of the cave and down the treacherously steep path.

The sole reason the marauding pigs had left them alone in the cave was the hazardous incline of the path, which deterred even the most curious from ascending it. Slowly and carefully, Jarrah led the way while Birrani hobbled behind. They had to pause several times to adjust their grip on the precious cargo, ensuring they carried her respectfully, without dropping her along the way.

Jarrah found a small clearing a suitable distance from the surrounding trees, enough to ensure they would not set the bush alight. They lowered their burden gently to the ground.

"Birrani, we need to build a nest of dry wood and leaves for Kunmanara to rest on; then we will find more wood to place around her. The fire in the cave is almost out and I have no matches. Will you take some wood up to the cave, rekindle the fire, and bring down a burning branch to light the funeral pyre?"

Birrani peered at Jarrah thoughtfully, weighing the options, calculating the odds of betrayal or misadventure on the old man's part. He did not want to leave his mother alone for even a moment, but understood that fire was needed if they were to accomplish this... 'sorry business'. Birrani looked down at his mother's pathetic body, so horribly pale in death compared to the rich shiny blackness when she was alive. He pitied her, he pitied himself.

Everything would change for him, he knew that and feared it most of all. The happy time he had spent with his mother was over, and he faced a hard and lonely life without her loving guidance. The old man had told him that Birrani belonged to a family of some sort, that he was loved, honoured and respected as a member of the tribe. It didn't seem possible to the boy after being abandoned by them, according to his mother, and every word spoken by her was the only truth he had ever known.

Jarrah watched closely as the conflicting thoughts waged a battle within the boy. His need to be close to his mother, to protect her, outweighed almost every other consideration. This would be a telling moment in their association, Jarrah felt. If he was unable to gain the boy's trust enough for him to believe that he was able to leave his mother's side, he might never achieve it. The eyes darted back and forth between his mother and Jarrah. The boy moved closer, cautiously, to stand a mere arm's length from him.

It was disconcerting in the extreme for Jarrah to face the boy's fierce scrutiny, his soulful eyes boring directly into Jarrah's essence, almost causing him to recoil in horror and fear. Jarrah stood his ground, despite every nerve ending compelling him to retreat, to look away. He forced himself to open his heart, to remain stock still and not to blink at any cost. He was being tested as he had never been tested before. One false movement or aversion of his eyes would see the destruction of the temporary truce he had gained. The sun beat down upon the pair in all its fierce glory, causing sweat to run down their faces.

The entire area seemed to be subdued into submission by the intensity of the standoff, caught in the silent pall of the building tension. The only sound to be heard was the squeaky breathing of Birrani as he studied the old man for signs of falseness. He did not want to entrust the body of his mother to anyone else. The old man had fought and bested him, but he knew he could bide his time, attacking the man if he could catch him off guard. Something deep inside him advised against it, however. The air, the soil and bushland spoke to his inner mind, where no one else could hear or communicate.

Jarrah sighed inwardly when Birrani shrugged his hunched shoulders before wandering off in the direction of the path they had descended moments ago. That sign of acceptance encouraged Jarrah to believe everything would turn out all right for the boy and himself. He sensed an opportunity in that small but certain gesture of compromise shown by the boy. It was not capitulation by a long shot, but rather a show of temporary trust which he dared Jarrah to betray.

An hour later, with both faces and naked bodies adorned in the traditional patterns of their tribe, as taught by their elders, Jarrah and Birrani stood by in reverent silence as the body burned. Their body markings, adhering strictly to their origins within Jarrah's family, signified a connection to their spiritual ancestry, communing with them to introduce a newcomer to their community.

The singing and dancing had fascinated the boy, who felt compelled at one point to join in, despite having no idea what to do or what it meant. He simply became enamoured of the ritual, wishing to participate in some fashion, becoming one with the land, the funeral pyre and the passionate old man.

The boy remained mostly untouchable, however, and Jarrah observed his limitations with respect. He did not attempt to do anything without first explaining himself. The body painting had been a trial, a great effort to explain the significance and an even greater effort to proceed. Jarrah always carried a pouch of the material he needed to create the markings of his people. It required only the addition of water to produce the ghostly white paint, which consisted, predominately, of powdered clay and animal fat.

When the fire burned down to nothing but ashes, and the bushland resumed its natural sounds with the onset of evening, Jarrah bade the boy farewell, with a promise to return. He informed the boy of his wish to continue his education in the ways of the people, to teach him to hunt successfully, to make tools and weapons from the natural resources around them.

"I will teach you to create, decorate and use the turndun, the bullroarer, to make the sound of the Rainbow Serpent whenever you need me. If you call me from the cave, I will hear you, Birrani, and come to you, night or day. What I show you is secret men's business only, which is why Kunmanara could not show you. I will teach you the histories of our people and the customs we follow, the ceremonies and the dancing. You do not have the voice for the singing, great-grandson, but I think you will like dancing.

"You will learn the bush lore of the hunter, how to approach in perfect silence and disappear the same way. I will show you how to cover your tracks so none may follow or discover your whereabouts. I will teach you where to find food when there is none to see. Kunmanara did not wish you to learn the tongue of the white man; I will honour that wish. I will also honour your wish to be left alone at any time. If you do not wish to learn one day when I come, you will show me your fist to warn me. We will teach each other hand signals for you to communicate with me...and your grandfather."

Birrani hissed in revulsion, understanding too well whom Jarrah meant. His mother's father was to be hated as much as the white man, his mother had said, for he had abandoned her.

"Ho, Birrani, sooner or later I will join Kunmanara in the afterlife, for I am an ancient man now. See my grey-white hair? It shows how old I get. When the grey-white hair falls to the groin, leaving a snow-white bush down there, you and I will know it is time to plan for an end. I will live until I have taught you as I did Kunmanara, not longer. Then will be the time your grandfather must watch over you. You are right to be angry, Birrani, as I was when I found out he rejected your mother. You must learn to accept him when it is time for him to take over from me.

"You must accept this because it is the only way of keeping in touch with the most important aspects of life, family, custom and history passed down through the generations. Your story, too, will one day enter into our sacred history, to be told by the young ones who take over as elders. I will see you in two days from now, before the sun rises, to begin your lessons. For now, I want you to eat and drink and grow strong again. For the memory of Kunmanara to continue, you must recover, Birrani."

Before Birrani became aware of it, the old man had slipped out of sight into the gathering darkness like a magical wraith, leaving him truly alone for the first time in his short existence.

ELEVEN

Birrani slept fitfully that night, with recurring visions and memories of his mother and the old man coming together to speak to him. He made sure to have the fire well-stocked before he went to sleep, waking every so often to replenish the flames with a log. He did not need the fire for warmth or cooking, requiring instead its calming goodness and promise of hope.

He had listened carefully to the words spoken by the old man, words of kinship and belonging, inclusion and respect. Birrani secretly looked forward to learning any tricks the old man might have for acquiring food, and how to make weapons for the hunt. His mother's old slingshot had snapped and been retied so often that it was getting too short to be of practical use. Birrani could barely manage to launch a stone with it as far as he could throw the same projectile by hand.

He had taken the advice offered to him to eat and drink, despite not feeling hungry or thirsty. He was unsure about his future and felt afraid to be on his own. He longed desperately for the comforting sound of his mother's voice and her gentle, reassuring touch. He knew he could never feel another's love for him like hers, and neither could he love another as he did her. He did not know if he could ever again have feelings like those he had shared with his mother.

A great and terrible sadness threatened to destroy him. He fought the temptation to give in to it, to accept that his life was over. While he did not believe everything the old man said about family, he hoped some of it might be true, and that helped him to push away the melancholia attempting to control him. Loneliness weighed heavily in his young heart.

When Birrani woke, he squinted at the bright beam of sunlight penetrating the smoky gloom of the cave. He had opted to sleep closer to the cave's entrance, to feel and breathe the fresh air as it wafted in from the billabong below. The boy felt an instinctual urge to be close to nature, to allow the spirit of the earth to invest him with its goodness. It was a tangible essence that he was able to identify and immediately grasp; something even his mother could not explain or appreciate when she saw him suddenly relax and wanted to know why.

They had never communicated in auditory terms: only emotionally could he convey his feelings to her. It was always frustrating for Birrani not to be able to voice his concerns or ask a multitude of questions. The old man had told him they would find a way of communicating with hand signals. Birrani looked at his slightly twisted and gnarled fingers and wondered how they might be used to say everything he needed to say.

The knuckles on his hands were becoming hard and calloused from his way of movement, changing dramatically as he grew. With his stooped and hunched back making it difficult for him to walk on two legs for any length of time, he had taken to using his arms as a second pair of legs. As he ambled along, he used his hands to relieve his crippled feet from taking all the pressure.

Birrani knew he was different in the way he moved. He saw how his mother walked, albeit painfully and with restrictions. He saw how the old man walked. He longed to walk that way also. When he looked at his feet, he saw why he needed to walk the way he did. His mother and the old man had feet that touched the earth with relatively flat surfaces, while his toes were curled under his soles.

His mother had tried to correct the deformity by manipulation and massage while he was young and more flexible. She told him she had tried splinting his feet while he still only crawled. Unfortunately, without help from the whites' hospitals, she could not succeed, and she would die before venturing back to ask the whities for help.

Birrani had learned to cope with his afflictions as he grew, not knowing anything else. A large dent in his cranium, from where his skull was damaged within the womb, ached intolerably at times, driving him close to insanity on his worst nights. If he remained upright, it did not happen; only when he laid his head down to sleep. Some nights, he would nap in a slumped sitting position with his back against the rear of the cave, where the faded drawings of men with weapons hunted strange animals.

The handprints fascinated Birrani most as he grew to understand how they came about. His mother had demonstrated the process to him once. Holding his odd little hand against the cave wall, she had blown a clay compound, coloured with ochre, from her mouth over it, leaving an outline of his hand when removed.

The old man said the drawings came from their people, who lived here at the beginning of time. He also said that, eventually, Birrani would join the people and his family, and also the ancients, when his time came. With his handprint on the wall with the others, he knew he had already entered that coveted place of honour, at least, to his young mind. There was so much he had yet to learn that he didn't think he could ever know it all.

He stretched to the extent he was able as he gradually worked the sleep from his eyes. His first day on his own marked a significant entry into his mental library of knowledge and memories. While he had been grieving, lying next to his mother, it had not felt as though he were alone. Without her physical presence, alive or not, he felt truly alone, anxious and troubled.

Below, around the billabong, he heard the cavorting pigs making their usual noisy progress as they drank, bathed and wallowed, and the piglets squealed and played. Always, the enormous boar watched over them with a menacing air, defying anything or anyone to interfere. Birrani knew to keep well clear of the waterhole at those times. He had witnessed first-hand the strength, agility and ferocity of the boar, fearing nothing...except when Birrani had fun with the pigs.

SCREEEEEEYAHHHHH, SCREEEEEEYAHHHHH.

The sounder ran in every direction, panicking, squealing,

together with every other animal and bird within earshot of the resounding screech. Birrani watched from his perch, rolling on his back in snorting mirth at the antics his call produced. It was one of the few things that had made his mother smile and even giggle. They had been his favourite moments with her. When she had smiled, and he had seen those jagged stumps of white teeth in her black face, it was like watching the sunrise for him, warming his heart and soothing the savage beast within.

When he knew the area below was clear of danger, he ambled down the steep path for a drink and a wash, something his mother had forced him to do as often as possible. She said it would cleanse his body of harmful germs that attacked the open sores and other abrasions he gained during a normal day. Birrani did not know what these 'germs' were, or how they might harm him if they were too small to see, but he respected his mother's instructions to keep himself clean.

As he grew older, he was fascinated by the amount of hair growth over most of his body, especially his back. The only part that remained completely hairless was his groin. He had seen the old man naked and marvelled at the prodigious growth of dark hair he displayed in that region, along with the enormous appendage protruding from that nest. The sack beneath that thing almost reached the old man's knees.

When Birrani looked at his puny worm extending from the bare patch of skin, he was saddened by his inadequacy for some reason. He felt envious. He knew only that it was used for peeing, and that he could do that while standing, while his mother had to squat. He was sad for his mother at those times, for it was obvious that she had lost her thing, maybe when she was hurt. She also had a thick black bush between her legs, but only a hole where her thing had once been. She explained that Birrani had come into the world from that hole. He wondered if she had lost her worm naturally to allow this great thing to happen, and that maybe he was wrong to assume it was damaged during the beating. He didn't know and couldn't ask;

just one of the many unknowns he faced.

At the water's edge, he steeled himself for the cold plunge, shocking at any time of day. The water in the billabong remained very cold because of the constant shade and the fact that it was fed by a natural spring. He immersed himself quickly to get it over with. Once he had smeared himself with the mixture of sand and mud from the bottom of the pool, he became warmer as he worked it vigorously into his flesh.

He winced as yet another small cut had magically appeared amongst the bruises and abrasions he had garnered from attacking the old man. His ego was more bruised than his body. He vowed to learn to fight like the old man, to be as lightning-quick as he. He looked forward to that particular lesson and might even show the old man a thing or two if he managed to learn quickly enough.

Birrani made sure to wash everywhere he could reach, including his backside and his worm. Mother had told him to be meticulous about that area. The trouble was, in the icy water it shrank so much he had difficulty locating it at times; it became almost inverted. He wondered if he might be losing it like his mother. Sometimes, if he washed it long enough, it grew hard. It often stayed hard for a time, which amused the boy.

Once Birrani had dried himself in the warm sun, he set about finding some food. He knew he had to find something more substantial than witjuti grubs, even though there was good protein in those. He yearned for some roasted meat, like a goanna or wallaby. His mother had often refrained from catching or eating game she was unable to chew properly, an affliction Birrani shared with her. He decided it would be good to hunt for some decent-sized game that morning.

With a selection of various-sized rocks in his dillybag and the old slingshot, Birrani stalked off into the bush. He knew of a favourite resting place the wallaby mob used to wait out the heat of the day. By mid-morning, the wallabies were beginning to tire from their night of feeding and would have to allow the grasses to digest properly in their gut. It was also a time for the joeys to gambol about in mock battle and play while the parents lazed around in the shade of a big gum tree.

As the single large gum was in a clearing, it gave the mob a good vantage point to detect any danger approaching. Birrani would have to move slowly and silently to get close enough for a killing shot. He would use a dead tree with a large trunk, on the edge of the clearing, to mask his approach. He believed he could wait there until the opportunity arose to bag a straggler.

The parched earth did not offer a profusion of edible grasses for the mob, so when Birrani spied a likely patch of semi-green stalks protruding from the barren ground a few metres from the old tree, he thought he might get lucky. With a clear view through the old trunk where it had been split open by a lightning strike years earlier, Birrani waited and watched with the infinite patience he had been taught and often intuited.

The mob of thirty or so grey wallabies lounged around under the enormous gum, which shaded them from the worst of the brutal sunlight, scorching by ten o'clock. Birrani enjoyed watching the young joeys at play, bouncing around awkwardly while they found their way around their long feet, often stumbling over themselves to end up in an undignified sprawl. Birrani imagined he saw the mothers shaking their heads in dismay at the clumsiness shown by their offspring.

After an hour, a few of the mob had begun a lazy search for grass at the verges of the shade, nibbling on stubs barely worth their effort. One, in particular, sparked Birrani's attention when it wandered in his direction, eventually standing tall to survey the area. It appeared to be making its way to the tufts of grass Birrani had spied earlier. Selecting a good-sized rock from his arsenal, Birrani prepared himself for a shot. He tested the strength of the rubber in the slingshot, hoping that it would not break at a crucial moment, like last time. He stretched it to its limits several times before being satisfied.

The wallaby, a mature buck, swatted away and growled at a youngster that ventured too close to him for comfort. Slowly, painstakingly so, the buck made its way inexorably toward the tempting bit of grass surrounded by bare dirt, baking hard in the unforgiving heat. Within an hour, it would be impossible for Birrani to remain in his position, as the sun would burn him and his thirst would be too strong.

In the blink of an eye, he whipped around the trunk of the dead tree and drew back with all his strength, releasing the projectile to strike the head of the wallaby a stunning blow. In seconds, the other members of the mob gathered their joeys and scattered in all directions, unsure from where the danger would present itself, knowing only to flee as fast as possible. The wallaby struck by Birrani lay quivering on the earth as he approached. Using a broken tree branch, he clobbered the wallaby with a killing blow to the head.

He returned to the cave with the dead wallaby over his back, making the climb with the confidence of experience. He threw the animal onto the smoking coals, exactly as his mother had taught him; all the fur burned off instantly. In a short while, he would turn the animal over, ensuring that it cooked all the way through.

He would then use the sharp rocks he and his mother had formed by hitting the shale against harder rocks to shape them for use as knives, to cut the meat up into sizeable chunks for eating. He would store the rest in a hanging bag his mother had made by plaiting strands of water reeds she removed from the billabong. In the shade provided by the cave, the cooked meat would last a day or two before it began to turn. Tying the bag at the top, making sure the ever-present flies were unable to lay their eggs onto the meat for the hatching maggots to feast upon.

Birrani took a sip of water from one of the cans his mother had brought from the rubbish tip with her. It had been his duty to keep the cans filled with fresh water when he grew old enough. His stomach growled when he caught a whiff of the roasting meat, causing him to salivate in anticipation.

When the meal was ready, or about as long as Birrani could wait, he sat down to devour as much as he could in one sitting. His gluttony did not come from a need for excess nor even from his decision to take the old man's advice, but rather from a practical standpoint. He needed to eat as much as he could as quickly as possible before the meat spoiled. His mother had instilled that discipline in him from the moment he could comprehend her words.

There was precious little to eat in the Australian outback, proving even more difficult to attain when it was available. So it was imperative not to waste a single morsel. Thinking of his mother's lessons brought on another pang of heartbreak and yearning in the boy. He was only five, going on six, even though he stood nearly as tall as a grown man when he extended himself. He needed his mother desperately at that young age.

Feeling exhausted after his successful hunt and consequent meal, he felt his eyelids drooping as the afternoon wore on. Before the sun had set he fell into a deep and satisfying slumber, leaving his fire to burn down to ashes.

TWELVE

"Ho, Birrani Nullah Bone!" accused Jarrah. "Have you learned nothing? You sleep like a baby while the fire goes out. How do we eat breakfast, make tools and weapons without a fire? Did Kunmanara not bring up her child to be vigilant always, and to keep the fire burning through the night?"

Feeling chastened and growing angrier, Birrani listened to the tirade of annoying questions with a sense of shame. He did not think it right that the old man should be acting like his mother. He didn't need another mother. There was no replacing his precious Mary in his mind. Besides, it was pointless to ask him silly questions. He was unable to answer them.

"Go, get wood, lazy child," Jarrah barked at him. "We must be out early to find a meal."

Birrani rose to the bag he had stored the previous evening, throwing it at the old man's feet with contempt. Jarrah bent to pick up the plaited reed bag, surprised at the weight it contained. When he untied the neck to look inside, he beamed at Birrani.

"So you think this means I am wrong to call you lazy? It is good that you hunted yesterday and ate as I instructed, but you must be alert every day and keep the fire burning. Why didn't you bring wood up yesterday while your meal was on the coals so you could feed the fire once it was cooked? The people do not rest until the work is done...all of it. Go, get wood. We need a fire to make weapons for hunting like our ancestors. See the spears, Birrani, in the paintings? We will make them and the spear thrower, the woomera, to make the spears go far and true.

"Once we have eaten and made the weapons, we will go walkabout, boy, into the old country where the red dust blows into the sky like a storm from the earth. We will be gone for a long time and I will teach you the old ways. When we return here, you will no longer be a boy, Birrani Nullah Bone, but a man, a man of our tribe, the Gureng Gureng. When I am gone and I have joined Kunmanara and the ancestors, your grandfather will be elder of our people, then you, when *he* is gone. You must be ready with the knowledge and the experience to accept the title and the honour when it comes to you. You must earn your place in the tribe by learning the ways of our people. The first thing you must learn is an ancient custom. Make a fist and raise your thumb like this? Good boy. That means, 'yes'. Okay, it's not from our people, but it means that, anyway, and pointing the thumb down, means, 'no'. Understand?"

Birrani raised his hand uncertainly, made a fist and raised his thumb. His mother had already taught him to nod and shake his head for the same reasons, so he did not know why he had to now talk with his fist. Birrani was not to know that Jarrah would teach him a host of other signals to indicate different meanings and moods. He also did not know why the foolish old man was making strange sounds like his mother giggling, only much stronger and deeper. He was afraid of the sound even though it looked like the old man was enjoying himself, smiling.

"Ho, Birrani, you do not understand joking or laughing. That is sad. Have you not had fun with Kunmanara, did she not make you laugh?"

Thumb down.

"Life is not meant to be serious all the time. Part of life is to relax and have fun, laugh. It clears the heart, makes us stronger and healthier, Birrani. You must learn to have fun as you grow as well as all the other stuff, otherwise, it is all for nothing. Go and get wood for the fire. We will talk more about fun later," said Jarrah, still smiling.

Jarrah was not laughing at his attempted joke. He was relieved that his first real attempt at communication had succeeded so well. He was overjoyed that he had taken his first step on the road to establishing a bond with his great-grandson. He had made progress on his promise to Kunmanara, to care for the boy and teach him, help him to become a man. It was her dying wish that he does this for her and Birrani.

Jarrah reflected on Yindi, his woman, after the boy left the cave to collect firewood. He had told her, his sun, moon and stars, that he would be leaving her and might not return. She cried all night long, wailing like she was in mourning. He had explained carefully how important it was to make good all the wrongs done to the boy and his mother, to make up for the love they had been denied by their kind.

"Yindi, I must do this," he said, "but I am old now, and I don't know how long I have. The boy must become a man, and I am the only one to show him the way. Your job will be to make sure that son of ours does right when the time comes. Tell them, Yindi, if I cannot make it back. Shhhhh, don't cry. We've had a good life together. We've done everything together since we were only a boy and girl, sneaking off behind your father's back."

"Jarrah, my husband, why you?"

"Who else, if not me? I have to make it right. He's our family, Yindi. No good you cryin', woman. You do what I say. You tell that Kami to do his duty, you hear?"

Jarrah spoke harshly to her, even though he didn't mean to. He trusted it would not be the last thing she heard him say. He hoped he could survive until he returned with the man. Jarrah was nearly ninety and felt every one of those years in his old bones that almost creaked when he woke each morning. His arms were as thin as kindling and his legs were not much better. He had stripped down to a mere loincloth for his walkabout and was a little surprised at how thin he'd become when he peered at his reflection in the billabong.

As Jarrah watched the boy hauling a pile of wood that would make an adult stagger under its massive weight, he noted the ease with which he navigated the steep path. He stood back to observe Birrani stack the pile of wood near the rear of the cave, then watched as he went about starting a new fire by rubbing sticks together as his mother had taught him. Jarrah admired the dexterity shown by the lad in the swift rotation of the wood through his gnarled hands and along his forearm. It was evident he was both skilled and knowledgeable in the art, so Jarrah intervened.

"Ho, Birrani Nullah Bone. It is good that you know the way of making fire as your forefathers have done since the beginning of time. Now I will show you the magic of the white man," explained Jarrah, as he reached into his dillybag for a match.

Birrani nearly toppled backwards in panic when he saw the flame appear at the end of the small stick when the old man rubbed it on a flat rock. He watched with awe as Jarrah set alight the fine bark and leaves he had placed in the middle of the fire circle. On these, he placed some twigs and then larger kindling. Within moments they had a roaring fire.

"It is a wise man that understands his enemies and makes use of their talents. Our people have been hunted and killed in great numbers by the whites, so we watch and learn. We use the matches he gives us to save time in making fire. While we teach our youngsters that time will go at a pace that we can do nothing about, and has no meaning to our people other than recognising the passing seasons, it is not always to our advantage to ignore progress. By making a flicking signal with your thumb, you can imitate the lighting of the match. That will be your signal for fire. Do you understand?"

Raised thumb.

"Show me 'fire'" commanded Jarrah in a gentle tone. "Very good. Fire is at the heart of everything we do. It does not just cook our meals. We gather by the fire to tell our stories, to keep warm, to give us light in the night, to round up our prey, to harden the points of our wooden spears and to replenish the forest. Some of our trees will release their seeds only with fire. Our people must help nature at times when the lightning does not provide the spark. While this fire is burning bright, we must go and find the wood for our spears and woomeras. Come. Crooking the forefinger like this, backwards and forwards, means 'come' or 'follow'," described Jarrah as they left the cave.

They searched the entire area around the billabong before they found several lengths of straight hardwood that Jarrah decided might make good weapons. At his waist, from a sheath of crocodile hide, Jarrah withdrew a modern hunting knife with a keen edge. He observed the wry look on Birrani's face at his use of the modern tool.

"I am an old man, Birrani Nullah Bone, I do not have a lifetime to educate you using only the old ways. As I told you, it is wise to use any advantage if it aids us in our task. Only when we rush for no reason is it deemed a waste. I will teach you everything I know, and I have only a few years to do it.

"There are certain codes our people understand and follow without question, and others we may bend a little to suit our purposes. One of those rigid codes we may never bend, I will explain to you now. I see many dead birds here, the noisy ones, cockatoos the white men call them. They are fresh, so I know they are recently killed. Did you kill these birds, Birrani?"

Birrani raised his thumb with glee.

"It is not good to be proud of unnecessary death, Birrani," said Jarrah, shaking his head in admonition. "I understand that they can be very noisy and bothersome, but only the white man kills for fun or sport. Listen very closely to what I tell you. It is the most important rule we have. You eat what you kill. Never harm another living thing unless you intend to eat it, never! Disregard this rule and you will not enter the lands of our ancestors: your spirit will be trapped between worlds forever and you will never be with Kunmanarra.

"If you want me to teach you our ways, if you want to be part of our race and our culture, you must never disobey this rule. You may kill anything the land provides as long as you eat it. No exceptions! If you want to practise, use anything you can find other than living things. You may practise when you hunt. If you miss a hundred times, then you go hungry a hundred times. You will be amazed how quickly you improve if your life depends on it. Do you understand and agree, Birrani Nullah Bone?"

Jarrah waited patiently for the boy to answer his question. While it was certainly a way of their people, it was by no means the hard and fast rule he made it out to be. Jarrah had a very specific purpose in mind when he related the command. It was not to save the life of a few noisy white birds. Though it was wise not to kill indiscriminately, it was to give the boy pause in carrying out the sworn pact made with his mother, to avenge her. If he instilled his embellishment of this code of common sense in the boy, he hoped it would dissuade Birrani from carrying out the pledge. Surely the boy would balk at eating his father?

He would do everything in his power to indoctrinate the boy with that one directive, to save his life and prevent a war with the dreaded white man: a war the black man could not win. Their wooden weapons were capable of killing a single white man who was taken by surprise. However, they could never hope to withstand attacks by the white soldiers armed with rifles that delivered death to his cousins and friends from a great distance. Unless the black men were armed with those weapons, they would be slaughtered...again.

Birrani must not be allowed to carry out the debt he owed his mother; it would guarantee the end of his people. The white men would not rest if one of their own were murdered by a black. It was the ultimate crime in their eyes and many blacks would pay the price, not just the culprit. The only alternative was to take the boy under his wing, teach him of love and respect, to shower him with wisdom and affection to guide him on another path.

Only as a very last resort would he commit the unthinkable on a family member in the event he was unsuccessful. It would break his heart to do so, and bring unending shame upon him but he would not hesitate to do so if all else failed. It was for the good of all his people that Birrani must be made to understand and follow his rules. In this, he would not bend. He stared long and hard at the boy, penetrating his depths to see the truth in his eyes.

Birrani tasted the words of the old man, delicately manipulating them around in his misshapen mouth, testing the texture and the flavour, mixing them and tonguing them to find out if they were palatable. He sensed a challenge within the instructions that he did not quite grasp. He pondered the principle and found it wise to a certain degree.

It was a waste to kill for no reason, he could see that in the carcasses of the dead white birds littering the ground. It served no purpose other than gratification and practice to have killed them. They were annoying when they descended in their thousands to drink from the billabong, making so much noise it was impossible to think. Yet, did they not have just as much right as he to live and drink and feed? Mary had taught him that every animal had a right to live on the land they shared, and to honour them even as they died and were consumed by them.

What the old man declared was no different from what his mother had said many times. Yet, there seemed to be something missing in his limited understanding. A thought continued to gnaw somewhere at the extreme edge of his mind. It would not make itself known to Birrani, no matter how hard he pressed. An elusive fragment of information hovered just out of reach, frustrating the boy because, without it, he felt he could not answer the old man truthfully.

If he had to agree to the rule, he had to be sure of it. It was not in his nature to lie. His mother had drilled him with that almost every day. That would lead to 'hum Jesus-pella' sending the boy to the other place, with the bushfires burning all the time. That thought frightened Birrani. He had accidentally burnt himself when he rolled into the fire one night during a troubling and painful sleep. The sting of that burn on his leg and back he had felt for many weeks as it gradually healed under Mary's careful ministrations.

He had been taught not to trust anyone, black or white. Yet he was only a youngster in an adult's body. He was too inexperienced to know what he must do. The old man had said many things that made sense, and Birrani seemed to be no match for him despite being much heavier and taller. He wanted to know more things like those he had already been shown. He desperately wanted to belong to something now that he found himself without a mother. It was confusing and upsetting to be so unsure. The old man waited for a commitment from him, a promise of sorts to abide by the law of his people.

Birrani had been told that he was half white, yet he could see no dividing colour line on his body. The old man was as black, maybe blacker than he, so it seemed safe to assume that he must, in some way, be related to the man? The man knew the language he spoke, that of his mother. His mother had also entrusted the man with her memories. She would not pass those on to just anyone. Lastly, she had smiled when she saw the old man, a broken-toothed smile she had reserved for Birrani alone up to that point.

Reluctantly, painstakingly, Birrani raised his fist, poised to angle the thumb in either direction, wavering, squinting at the old man with a mixture of doubt and respect. With his version of a sigh, that sounded more like an asthmatic wheeze, Birrani eventually raised his thumb. Jarrah simply nodded as though it meant nothing in the scheme of things, downplaying its immense significance.

Jarrah sighed inwardly as he led the boy back up to the cave, where he would start by showing the lad how to strip the bark off the straight shafts he found.

THIRTEEN

Allies Creek State Forest, Jarrah State Forest and Barakula State Forest were all one massive tract of eucalypt bushland before they were officially designated as state forests. Nestled in the curvature to the north, bordering this mighty forest, was an area of desert-scape. Rocky and desolate, it accommodated a city of termite mounds rising from the bare red earth. Made by the tiny insects from a mixture of wood pulp, mud and saliva, these termite mounds were homes to trillions of the insects and their larvae, rising to several metres in height and rock-hard.

Birrani learned of their solidity the hard way when he attempted to kick a smaller one down. He screeched in agony, hopping around awkwardly on one foot, cradling the other in his hands until, unbalanced, he toppled over. He became even more incensed when his antics attracted the mirth of his great-grandfather, rolling on the red earth in fits of laughter.

SCREEEEYAHHHHH, SCREEEEYAHHHHH.

When Jarrah finally mastered his compunction to bring more shame to the boy by continuing to laugh, he stepped over to the prone figure.

"Was it me that kicked the mound and made myself look silly? You are angry at me for laughing, so you seek to punish me with that demented sound. Why? If you cannot laugh at yourself and understand that sometimes we do stupid things and must pay the price, then you will always be miserable. I have no time for someone that is only misery. If I cannot enjoy my time with you then I may not be able to continue with my quest. I am a volunteer, Birrani. I do this for love, not only duty. If I had kicked the termite mound and hurt my foot, stumbled around, cursing like a madman, would you not have laughed? Tell me honestly."

Birrani nursed his swollen foot as he looked up at the old man, hearing his words of wisdom, wishing all the time that he could make the old bastard eat those words. Admittedly, he felt ridiculous. He knew he had done something quite stupid. Had he not examined the hard mounds himself for nearly two days as they wandered through them? Had the old man not explained how they were constructed from mud and saliva to make them impervious to weather...and foolish children?

He imagined how he would have reacted to the old man doing the same thing, and he smiled inwardly, knowing he would have found it very funny. Unfortunately, he was not able to produce the same sound as his mother and great-grandfather when they found something funny. Whenever Birrani was amused he snorted and grunted, spraying phlegm and spit around him, much to his mother's dismay. She had never berated him for covering her in fluids because she had understood his shortcomings and was only too happy to see him amused, but it was an unpleasant experience just the same.

Birrani scowled up at the old man, despite the reasonable statements he made. Birrani's pride had been hurt and his childish mind brooked no amount of logic at those times. His stubbornness had seen him in trouble often enough, yet he did not seem to be able to work through it himself. Birrani glared with contempt at the proffered hand. He batted it away rudely, retaining his uncomfortable position on the scorching earth.

Birrani was sick of the landscape, tired of the relentless sun beating down upon them without surcease. He did not understand why they had left the relative comfort of the forest to walk endlessly among the mountains made by insects. The old man prattled on incessantly, explaining everything to him, forcing him to indicate his understanding with the annoying raised-thumb gesture. It was annoying because a simple nod of the head as his mother had taught him would have sufficed.

"Ho, Birrani Nullah Bone thinks he is a man already and has no need of help when it is offered. Then stay down there all day if you want. I have to eat tonight and I will find something for myself. You will go hungry again because you want to stay down there and sulk like a child. Your rubber thing is broken and you have not yet mastered the spear. How will you eat tonight?"

Jarrah stalked off at a swift pace and had created quite a distance between them by the time the boy rose from his position. Birrani blinked. The old man had disappeared! He shook his head in disbelief. It was only a moment ago that the old man had walked off in a huff. He could not have gone far in that time. Yet, he was nowhere to be seen, unless he was hiding behind one of the massive mounds.

As Birrani advanced he peered behind all the mounds he came across, which were many. By the time the sun began its ponderous descent, he was feeling the first vestiges of panic. He did not think he could find his way back home if the old man had left him for good. He turned every which way to find some trace of the man. It all looked identical to him. There were no differences to be found in the desolate landscape, no way to gain a bearing or a direction to travel. He was hopelessly lost.

As he picked up the pace in his panic to find the old man, his thirst and hunger stabbed at him. His panic grew exponentially with every passing hour, building until he could barely think. He ran blindly into the mounds and stumbled over mere pebbles. As darkness encroached upon the land, Birrani wanted to scream out for all he was worth. Only his stubbornness kept him silent. His pride would not allow him to cry out for help, no matter how desperate he became.

The night descended with rapidity once the sun had sunk in the west. The cool night winds wafted over Birrani as he crouched among the mounds wondering what to do or if he would make it out alive. He felt a great sadness for the possibility that he would never see his home again. He also felt a seething, irrational hatred brewing inside, bubbling and belching its noxious gases until Birrani was ill from it. He could do nothing to quell the upset he felt in his stomach and had no target for his rage.

About to give in to the tiredness in his weary bones and sagging eyelids, he lifted his head to the sky. The breeze carried a scent he had not noticed until that moment, a familiar scent that made his mouth moist with drool. Hovering just above the recognisable smell of wood smoke was the unmistakable aroma of roasting meat.

When Birrani stood as tall as his hunched body allowed, he was unable to see any glow, yet sensed a direction from being downwind of the fire and the meat cooking upon it. After twisting and turning around the multitude of termite mounds in his path, Birrani finally glimpsed a distant glow in the solid darkness of the moonless night.

It seemed to take an extraordinarily long time to finally come within eyesight of the flames leaping high into the sky, throwing sparks and embers upon the breeze. The old man sat to one side of the fire, munching on something with great relish. Only, when Birrani had walked around yet another termite mound to enter the area of light cast by the roaring fire, the old man was nowhere to be seen. More importantly, there was no sign of the food he had been eating.

Frustrated beyond measure, Birrani collapsed by the fire in a desultory heap. He sat alone for around an hour, loneliness and hunger clawing at his insides. He was sad and confused. Deep melancholia threatened to sweep him up in its tide of misery. He felt the first traitorous tears welling in his eyes. He felt ashamed for the way he was feeling, yet could not help himself. He allowed his tears to flow regardless.

"My great-grandson gives up too easily. He does not see that everything I do is for him alone, to teach him the ways, to make him proficient and independent. He wants to make anger with me instead of finding great comfort in my lessons. He wants to encourage the rage within him, the hatred. Ho, Birrani Nullah Bone. Hatred leads only to more hatred. Hatred has no brothers or sisters; it will never be sated nor conquered by anything but its opposite. If you fill your heart with hatred and anger, you will die inside. It will twist your guts and make you do things that you will regret. Your hatred may have consequences for others if you allow it to take control of you," whispered Jarrah, as he suddenly came into view a mere metre away from where Birrani sat.

Birrani's surprise soon turned to misery once more when he deduced that the old man was not about to give him any of the food he had been cooking. In the fire, not a morsel remained.

"Ho, Birrani Nullah Bone, have you learned nothing at all from me in the days we have been together? I saw you running around all day looking for me. Looking everywhere but where you should have been looking. Look at your feet, Birrani. See the track? What could have made that track? It is a straight line leading from outside this clearing right up to the fire. It is not the serpent leaving that straight line. You have seen the tracks of the serpent. I showed them to you and explained how they were made by the twisting curve of the serpent.

"Neither is it the tail of the goanna, because there are no feet tracks at alternating intervals either side of the line, like the one we saw. So what could have made those tracks?" asked Jarrah, as he stood in his typical manner, one foot raised and resting on the thigh of the other, hand holding his spear by his side, planted firmly on the ground.

Birrani peered at the track by his feet, entering the circle of light from the same direction as he not so long ago. Birrani racked his brain to think of the animal that could have made that track. Nothing he conjured up in his memories or imagination could have been responsible for the single track. He looked about in bewilderment until his eyes came to rest on the old man again. He inspected the man's open features, imploring Birrani to arrive at the answer. Birrani scratched his head and concentrated all the harder. Then he turned his head to the side and spat in disgust.

Jarrah watched as the boy came to terms with the knowledge, nodding his head sagely. "Now you see? You see the mark I made with my spear that a blind man could follow? Everything I taught you about tracking you lost with that anger inside you, blinding you and taking control. If you had looked down as I taught you when I left you earlier, you would have found me easily, watched me make the kill and shared in my supper. Now, you must pay for your errors by going hungry...again. Even now, you could so easily provide for yourself if you followed my lessons. Your dinner is at hand if you have the mind to listen."

Birrani looked away in disgust.

"You do not believe me?"

Thumb down.

Jarrah shook his head sadly. The old man's posture suddenly straightened and his head cocked to one side. The surrounding darkness shed only the echoing sound of the crackling fire. Jarrah stood stock still, without breathing. Suddenly, his stick-thin arm shot straight up into the air above his head. When it came back down, Birrani was flabbergasted to see a struggling, flapping flying fox in the old man's hand.

Jarrah broke the bat's neck before placing the body on the fire.

"Bush got plenty tucker, boy. You shame me and your people if you don't want to learn, if you keep anger in your heart with no room for anything else. I don't want to hurt you, boy. I love you. You're my kin. You don't need to be frightened of me or think I'm going to abandon you. I left a track for you to follow, but you didn't see it because you are so angry with everyone and the world. You gotta learn to love, Birrani: love for the people, for this beautiful country, for the stars and trees and everything else. Love will teach you more in one day than a lifetime of hate. Hate only teaches us to hate, nothing more.

Birrani tried vainly to listen to every word the old man was saying. The moment he believed he could eat the flying fox, he hastily removed it from the fire, tearing off the wings before ripping off strips of meat.

"Leave a bite for me, Birrani. I gotta eat what I kill, too."

The boy looked at the old man in surprise. He had wondered whether the same rules applied to everyone, especially the old man.

He was a cynic at heart, taught to be cautious in everything, so it came as a shock to learn that he was not to be alone in following the rules. He had berated himself severely for missing the obvious trail left by the man. The old man was right about one thing; Birrani's anger had made him miss the signs altogether. He had failed a task as simple as following an easy trail.

While he ate ravenously of the spare, stringy flesh from the bat, he commiserated with himself. He had only a young mind with which to formulate ideas and opinions, with a vast education awaiting him if he accepted it. He had some 'land-smarts' already, passed down to him by his mother, but he was severely lacking in even those basic concepts. He had been shown up in only a few days as a bumbling, mediocre child.

He began to appreciate that he could learn a great deal from the old fool staring at him with a look of such pity that it grated. Behind that stare, though, if Birrani took the time to see with honest eyes, he would find love and respect as well. Lessons of the emotional variety came slowly to youth. In Birrani, they became advances on a glacial level. It was unnatural for him to rely on anyone but his mother. Trusting a stranger was anathema to him, regardless of the man's claims of kinship.

However, Birrani had slowly come to accept that his previous life was truly over. He had realised with great sadness that he had lost his anchor, his touchstone with life and everything in it. Change was imminent, no matter how much he resented it. Faced with the prospect of surviving alone, something he might or might not manage, it gradually descended into his consciousness that he had few other options.

He grunted with pleasure at the feast he had been given, awed by how it had been attained. The old man's arm had flown into the air so quickly that Birrani had barely noticed the movement; then he had lowered it with a captured meal flapping about manically. Birrani had not even sensed the presence of the bat, not heard a solitary sound outside the fire and the roiling rage he felt inside, deafening him to all else. He understood with absolute clarity the truth of Jarrah's words at that moment.

It was a mini-breakthrough for the boy to use the man's name for the first time in his thoughts. It brought with it a sense of gratitude, acceptance and inclusion that warmed him more than the fire. That warming sensation alerted him to the fact that he must find a way to trust his great-grandfather, to learn, to live, to survive, to grow, to become a part of a family, a race and an ancient culture. Birrani had taken the first steps on his road to maturity and manhood, although that recognition would not materialise for a long time.

When he woke the following morning at the break of day, there was no sign of Jarrah. The fire had burned down to coals with a goanna roasting on them. If Birrani had been able to smile, he would have beamed. He understood. The game was afoot and it was a simple one. He must learn to track down Jarrah each day to receive a meal or other lessons. If he failed, he would be hungry, cold and alone.

He cast wide and near to locate a set of tracks to follow. While he knew instinctively they would not be as simple to follow as the previous day, he was baffled when he could find nothing. Two hours later, with the heat beginning to build, he saw what might conceivably be a sign. Animal tracks led to a small area of confusing activity, at the edge of which was his first evidence of the man, Jarrah.

Birrani skirted the entire area, attempting to make sense of the weird assortment of...signs? He was not quite sure what he was seeing. He sat down after a minute or two, almost ready to give in. He lacked confidence and experience. The previous day he lacked maturity and clarity of mind to see a track that anyone could have followed. Today, he ground to a halt because he didn't think he could do what was being asked of him, finding the challenge beyond his young years.

When at last he made up his mind to return to what was left of the night's cooking fire, he realised at once what he had been missing. He was sitting at the edge of the area where the kill had been made. The goanna tracks led to this place, where Jarrah waited patiently until it came within spear-throwing distance. Jarrah had set his foot down in a softer area of dirt to show him clearly what had transpired.

The wounded goanna turned, twisted and thrashed in its death throes, wiping away and making nonsense of the spoor. Naturally, Jarrah had then carried the goanna back to the camp, where he had waited until early morning to throw it onto the coals. Then he walked off quietly in a different direction, back along the single spear trail he had left the day before.

That was what Birrani had missed. He thought the footprints near the old trail were the ones from the previous day. The wily old man was walking backwards in his previous footprints along the same easy trail he had laid down for Birrani to follow like a rube, which is exactly what he was. When he finally realised his error, he was disgusted.

Assured that he had it right, once he had scanned the prints again with a clear mind, Birrani set off to follow. He made sure to keep a small portion of the goanna to share with Jarrah, to keep true to the credo set down by him. Without understanding it, Birrani had accepted the proclamation to 'eat what you kill' without fuss. He had unwittingly decided to accept and follow the unwritten code, taking it into his heart and head as a mantra he would often repeat to himself over the coming months.

With newfound confidence, Birrani quickened his pace, glowing with pride that he had accepted the challenge and had not been found wanting yet again. The trail led back to the site of Birrani's embarrassment, the termite mound that stood proud despite the boy's best effort to destroy it with his foot, which still ached.

A campfire had been constructed a little distance from it. There was no sign of Jarrah or food. Birrani sat near the fire to wait. The hours passed and the boy grew hungry and thirsty. The night crept in and the breeze turned cooler. The boy wondered what the game was. He had worked out the trail, as devious as it was, to arrive at the fireside he knew Jarrah had made for them. By rights, there should be some form of reward for his achievement, at least, according to his understanding of the rules.

"Ho, Birrani Nullah Bone, why are you not eating?" asked the voice from the bush.

Birrani was startled, though not afraid any longer.

"I lead you to food and you do not eat?"

With the odd question came confusion, for the boy could see no sign of food, a kill, nor his great-grandfather. The voice seemed to come from everywhere and nowhere at once. It was impossible to discern a direction. Though Birrani raised himself to search the area for many metres around the fire, he saw nothing edible, raw or otherwise. He snorted in disgust as he returned to the fire.

"If I led you back here, does that not tell you something? This is the place that shamed you, boy. You mistakenly assumed that, because that mound was so much smaller than the others, it would be easy to knock it over. It is always the way of people, to confuse an inferior size with an inability to defend itself. Yet, there is always a manner to defeat your opponent if you think about it using logic and good sense. Go ahead, kick the mound, Birrani Nullah Bone," commanded the voice.

Birrani shook his head miserably, jabbing his thumb down vigorously.

"I did not ask you a question. I ordered you to kick the mound again. You did so yesterday; do so again, with as much strength as you can muster. Or not. If you do not wish to follow my instructions, then I will leave and you can go hungry."

Birrani grizzled angrily at the instruction. He had no wish to repeat his mistake, causing him more pain and embarrassment. He did not understand why the old man wanted him to kick a silly mound again. It would accomplish nothing. Surely the fool did not expect him to deliberately hurt himself? Birrani shook his head with a stubborn refusal to obey blindly. He heard nothing more from the silent bush, only the sloughing of the breeze and the crackling of the fire. He sat alone in confusion and anger. It was unfair of the old man to ask Birrani to hurt himself. He could easily injure himself badly. His feet were not that good to begin with.

SCREEEEEYAHHHHH, SCREEEEEYAHHHHH, he screeched into the night, causing great unrest in the surrounding scrubland. A flock of nesting cockatoos erupted with a furious squawking, turning the night into a blinding profusion of white movement and ear-splitting sound.

Birrani stood with great reluctance, breathing in heavily with resignation. Despite the obvious reasons for him to ignore the command, grimacing in readiness for the agony he would unleash, he flew at the mound as fast as his deformed legs and feet would allow. With one mighty backward preparation, his leg was thrust forward in a kick any AFL player would have been proud of, hitting the mound with his full force.

His foot cleaved easily through the top half of the mound, with a soft slapping sound. Where there had been near rock the previous day was now a saturated mud heap, from which poured a colony of white ants, each bearing pupae to carry to a new and safer home.

Within the blink of an eye, Jarrah appeared by the side of the mound, greedily raiding the escaping hordes, scooping the protein-rich abundance into his mouth with glee. Birrani, still perplexed by the events, reluctantly followed suit after a few moments. Birrani was bewildered by many things that night, not the least of which was how Jarrah had managed to find enough water to soak the mound into a clay-like consistency and how he had applied the water to the mound.

After they had both fed on the meagre repast, Jarrah withdrew to the night once more, returning with a small wallaby. Birrani reached into his dilly bag to withdraw the small portion of goanna he had saved for Jarrah.

"Ah, my heart is happy, great-grandson. You remembered to

save me a piece. Very good. I am proud of you. You found my trail. I did not make it easy for you. You are still very young and yet you found a trail that most adults would not have found. I watched as you sat near the killing ground. I removed the blood so that it would not be easy for you to recognise the signs. Then I moved fast so that I could return here.

"I saw you looking confused about the mound. I think you are wondering where I found water to soak the mound?"

Thumb up.

"There is always water if you know where to dig. An old creek bed runs through here; that is why there are more trees, looking healthier and less stunted than the rest. A tree grows well only where there is water. I dug a hole with a digging tool I made. I then drank all the water I needed to quench my thirst, before transporting the water, mouthful by mouthful, to the mound.

"One thing, though. I knew it was safe for you to kick the mound only because I had probed into it with a twig. Sometimes, there is the trunk of a small tree inside a termite mound, one that has not yet been fully consumed by the white ants. Never kick a mound unless you are certain of that! It would have been far worse than the previous day, and maybe not so funny, eh?"

Jarrah placed an arm over the boy's broad, hairy shoulder. They watched in comforting silence as the wallaby cooked on the fire, the fur being singed away easily.

FOURTEEN

Birrani took in everything around him in an instant; the wind direction and speed; the angles of trajectory for the impending throw; the line of return and the receiver. He looked across at Jarrah, who stood quietly in the shade of an acacia, poised to throw his boomerang.

Birrani raised his eyes a fraction before lowering them again, squinting at him, then pointed his thumb down.

Jarrah, appearing to be disgusted with Birrani's negativity, let loose with a well-aimed throw for a man looking as feeble as he did. His hair was now a ghostly white, and his long beard matched. The years they had been together had not been kind to the old man, who hobbled lately, Birrani noticed. It seemed as if the old man was imploding slowly, collapsing in on himself. At over one hundred years old, it was no surprise.

The student watched as the boomerang sailed through the air as it was designed to do, arcing out at a forty-five-degree angle from the thrower to find its zenith, before completing the arc to arrive back at the point of origin. But three-quarters of the way to its zenith, the slight breeze picked it up and gently altered its path, which, by Birrani's estimate, meant it would sail well above his great-grandfather's head when it returned, as he had foreseen.

Birrani waited for the inevitable. The solid hardwood boomerang behaved exactly as it should by completing its journey to the end of its trajectory before making its path back to the owner. Jarrah could see that he had misjudged the wind and worried about where his boomerang might end up. He needn't have been too concerned, for the implement flew unerringly back in his direction. It was only when it was on the final approach that Jarrah realised it would fly too high for him to reach it.

He accepted the inevitable with dignity, knowing full well that it was impossible to be perfect all the time. When the boomerang flew above his head to strike the branches, he nodded to indicate to the boy that he had been right. What Jarrah did not know, when he had calculated all the factors for his throw, was the presence of a large paper wasps' nest in the branches above him. When the boomerang struck the fragile nest it exploded into a million pieces, all raining down upon the old man's long, springy white hair.

Even then, Jarrah thought that his errant boomerang had merely dislodged some dead leaves and accumulated dust that he brushed away from his naked black shoulders. Then he felt the first sting, then a hundred others, all stinging him, again and again, venting their wrath at him for interfering with their home. Before long, Jarrah was lost in a swirling mass of angry wasps, swatting this way and that in a mad panic to be away from the maddening insects.

Birrani had collapsed to the earth, rolling about in fits of mirth, snorting, grunting and spitting up a storm. Jarrah decided that he had better make a run for it. He ran as far and as fast as his spindly old legs could take him. Birrani was unable to follow, for the fit of laughter had him in paroxysms of gut-aching joy. His enormous, hairy frame rocked to and fro in uncontrollable snorts.

Jarrah kept running until he felt the last sting on his back. Though he had run without a destination in mind, he found himself coming out of the scrub right up to the lip of a manmade dam. Without hesitation, Jarrah plunged headfirst into the cooling, soothing waters of the dam, sighing with relief as he broke the surface.

"What the fook are ya doing, you bluddy black shite?" asked Jack O'Leary from the bank of the dam, covered in water from the splash caused by Jarrah.

Jarrah was startled after not hearing another voice in almost ten years. When he saw the owner of that voice he slowly shook his head in dismay. When he saw the fellow's friend stand up beside him, also wet from having been splashed, Jarrah knew he was in trouble.

"Sorry boss, sorry. I was..." Jarrah remembered too late that he was not speaking English.

"Don't ye be talkin' that gibberish to oos, ya black heathen. Whatcha reckon then, Big Tom, shall we teach the dumb black bastard a lesson in manners when he be addressin' us good folk?"

"Too roight," said the big man, smashing one fist into the palm of his other hand with a resounding smack.

With one mighty paw stretching out over the water as far as he could reach, he yanked the tiny form of Jarrah Bone out of the water and into the air as easily as lifting a one-day-old kitten. No amount of entreaties in English or otherwise could soothe the enraged mill workers. Jarrah held his hands up in a clear sign of supplication, total surrender in the face of Big Tom, whom he knew by reputation and sight. Knowing what the man was capable of and how he felt about Aboriginals, Jarrah showed only signs of submission.

Birrani watched from the tree line in abject horror as the two white men threw the frail man from one to the other as though having a game. Birrani knew that his great-grandfather was not feeling well of late, weak and short of breath at times. Jarrah had told him they were on their journey home, that Birrani was no longer a boy. Jarrah had gone through the ceremonies initiating Birrani into the Gureng Gureng tribe as a respected member and an elder once Kami, his grandfather, passed.

Jarrah had taught the boy everything he knew and then some. The boy had listened, grown and developed into an enormous man, albeit shortened by his gross deformities, which caused him to amble along on all fours most of the time. Jarrah knew he was slipping away. He meant to return to Yindi's side one more time before he joined his ancestors. Over the previous year, he had slowly been making their way back to their camp near Allies Creek.

His heart had soared at the thought of sleeping next to his sun, moon and stars again, nestled behind her sleeping form, spooning like young lovers. That thought had kept him going for months longer than his body deemed possible, eating less and less and sleeping fitfully for fewer hours each night. Birrani had to hold the old man in his arms many nights when Jarrah cried out in pain and desperation for his Yindi. The wheel had turned for the pair over the previous five years. More often, it was up to Birrani to provide for them, as Jarrah's aim with a spear became more of a joke with each throw. His feeble arms were unable to carry the spear for any distance. Only with the boomerang did he manage to out-throw Birrani consistently; a fiercely fought competition between them.

Big Tom had had enough of just tossing the annoying black bugger around like a rag doll. With a sickening thud, he launched a haymaker at the old man. The crushing blow from the ham-like fist of the towering Irishman flattened Jarrah; he dropped to the ground in an undignified heap of flesh and bones.

SCREEEYAHHHHHH, SCREEEEEEYAHHHHHH.

The bush erupted with the raucous sound of thousands of parrots and cockatoos taking to the air in a mad panic. Wallabies darted and bounded about in confusion and haste, while the pair of bewildered Irishmen stood stunned. When they caught a glimpse of the enormous boar heading their way, squealing like a banshee, they took off faster than they ever believed possible, especially for one as big as Tom.

They made it to one of the dormant milling sheds before they chanced a glance behind them. Whatever it was that had been chasing them could not be seen. They were thankful that it was not a normal workday, so the mill wasn't full of workers to see them shamed by running away in fear like that. It was only once Big Tom had caught his breath that he realised with a shock that the old man was no longer lying where they'd left him.

Big Tom and his mate guessed that the old man had recovered and was on his way to his next drink, assuming he had been pissed to the gills to end up in the dam while they were fishing. They chuckled nervously as they made their way back to Tom's cottage, the nearest one up the road. Jack gave an involuntary shudder at the eerie quiet that had settled about them after the madness of a few moments ago. He didn't think he would be going back to the dam to retrieve his bamboo fishing pole any time soon.

Birrani did not pursue the men, who could outdistance him quickly. He pulled up immediately after his initial burst from the scrubland surrounding the township. He went straight to where Jarrah lay, limp, broken and lifeless.

Screeee, screeee...

His big shoulders shook with the agony in his heart. Jarrah's death caused him such grief that he became immobile for a time. It was only with an extreme effort of will that he broke the spell to pick up the fragile, near-weightless body of his dear teacher, mentor and best friend in all the world. Gently he carried the old man in his outstretched arms as easily as carrying a child's doll, back the way they came, back to the only place he ever knew as home.

His grief knew no bounds as the afternoon gave way to evening. The surrounding landscape was devoid of sound or movement, seemingly in deference to the unmitigated heartache the young man felt as he cried bitter tears for only the second person in all the world he had loved. Two people of impeccable kindness and undying love had been taken from him prematurely by the same detestable white man, his father, Big Tom O'Hare, foreman of the Allies Creek sawmilling operation. Though he had never before seen his father, he recognised him easily from his mother's exact descriptions.

His hatred had all but disappeared over the years spent with his great-grandfather, replaced with purpose and loving goodness. His education on all things natural and ancestral, his feelings of being needed, loved and respected, had washed away all of the negativity that had consumed him. Those same emotions, steeped in the hatred and need for revenge, came cascading back into him like a tidal wave as he trudged back to his cave, where he would remain for the rest of his life, plotting the demise of his enemies.

Utter despondency and desolation smashed into him with every fond recollection that entered his mind. His years spent with the old man had been among the happiest of his short life. Once he had learned to throw away any resentment he felt at being dragged away from his home, where the spirit of his mother remained, he had opened his mind to the grand experiences on offer from a wise and gentle soul. Though irritating at times, he was always patient and kind as he tested and challenged Birrani to become a man, a leader, a worthy member of his race.

Everything good that had occurred over that decade together had been undone with one punch delivered by the big, ugly brute of a man from whence he came. Birrani understood how he had grown to be such a large person. He had inherited the genes from the thing that took advantage of and beat his mother, ensuring she did not survive her wounds.

The overwhelming emotions roiled within Birrani until there was nothing recognisable of the personality he had developed under Jarrah's careful tutelage. In the blink of an eye, the enraged boy had returned to the bulk of the man now occupying the body, with the penultimate hunting, killing and camouflaging skills taught to him by a master.

The seething maelstrom that occupied his mind controlled his future path. His destiny had been decided in that fateful moment when a white man created a monster to carry out the instructions given to him by his precious mother. What he had lost in ten years of absolute bliss had been rediscovered and honed to a razor's edge in mere moments. Gone was everything of a decent nature instilled in him. Gone was the good sense and any hope of living harmoniously with the world around him.

Only one mandate remained with him, one he would follow with unerring accuracy. He reminded himself of the one defining rule he must obey to the letter. He would make him, make them both, pay for his mother, himself and his great-grandfather; pay for all the wrongdoings of the white man in general; pay for every injustice suffered by the Australian natives at the hands of the insensitive and brutal whites.

Through the night, never pausing to rest nor deviate from the path he must follow, Birrani found his way to his cave with the lifeless form of Jarrah draped over his outstretched arms. He navigated the steep, overgrown path and reverently placed the old man at the rear of the cave. There he would mourn and plan. His duty would be to respect his great-grandfather's wishes, to see to the 'sorry business', to honour his life by making it possible for his spirit to join the ancestors.

FIFTEEN

Big Tom and Jack were downing a pint of the finest black gold in his cottage on Friday evening, six days after the incident with the crazy old drunk. Both fully in their cups by the time evening came around, they had elected to stay in Allies Creek when the rest of the crew opted to continue their drinking in Kingaroy for the night.

"Boi Jaysus, Big Tom, this shack-o-yourn is a doomp," Jack commented. "How coom ya don't get anoother black, then, eh?"

"Wotcha bleedin' tongue, gobshite. Don't need no more hired help runnin' orf now. What's wrong with it?"

"Stinks, don't it, mate?"

"Where you goin' then?"

"Gotta get rid-o-some Guinness to make room for more," Jack slurred, as he stumbled out the front door.

"Jaysus, Jacko, you moight use the back yard. Got some standards, you know?" argued Big Tom.

Jack seemed to be gone a while by the time Tom gathered his wits enough to notice. The enormous man struggled up from the wooden rocker in which he'd been relaxing all afternoon since work finished and the mill closed for the weekend. When he reached the front door and peered into the gloom, he could see nothing of his friend. Thinking the man might have collapsed into one of his untended gardens, Tom turned on the outside light, thanks to the newly-installed electricity. Then the lights went out again...for him.

When Big Tom finally managed to open one eye against the brilliant glare of the sun pouring into the mouth of the cave, his head felt as though a dozen sledgehammers were pounding away at an anvil. Slumped against a central pillar of stone, his friend was trussed up like a Christmas turkey. Milling around somewhere, out of his line of sight, he heard shuffling and saw a huge moving shadow. When he tried to bring his hand to the place on his head where a large lump had developed, he realised that he, too, was bound at wrist and ankle.

What he saw next robbed him of breath. Moving to a position directly in front of him was the ghastliest horror he had ever set eyes on. He had no idea what it was, but it smelt like death itself. He wondered if maybe it was the thing his blessed mam warned him about before Sunday school. *"Begosh and begorrah, the Divil take ya if'n ya don't go to choorch, Tom O'Hare,"* she would say to him.

It was enormous, drooling with evil intent and staring right through him. Predominately black, with a prominent brow ridge, it was redolent of prehistoric man, in Tom's opinion. *Bloody Neanderthal,* he thought. Fighting the rising bile from a hangover, coupled with the blow he took to his head, Tom braced himself for whatsoever was in store. Though much could be said of Big Tom O'Hare, cowardice was not a common complaint.

Tom recoiled as a waft of air from outside the cave blew past the creature directly into Tom's face. It had the distinct aroma of rot and contamination, of disease and open pustules. Incredibly, the thing held out a can of some sort to Tom, containing what he thought might be water. It clutched the can in a hand, to be sure, but a deformed and calloused abomination of a hand. Unfortunately, Tom's throat was parched from his excessive drinking, so he nodded reluctantly.

Displaying more dexterity and intelligence than Tom thought possible, it lifted the can to Tom's mouth, gently tilting it to allow him to drink the refreshing water. The creature then lunged on all fours to the opening of the cave, where he disappeared. Tom gradually cleared his head of the fuzziness, but he remained baffled.

He and Jack had been drinking at his place in Allies Creek. He recalled Jack going out of the front door to relieve himself. Tom remembered that it was taking far too long, even for Jack, who tinkled at such a slow pace everyone thought he might have a prostate the size of a grapefruit. It was generally joked about, but Tom had decided that his time went way beyond the bounds of reasonability, even for Jack. So he had ventured outside to look for him, thinking he might have fallen over drunk and couldn't get up. He turned the...

It was the monster! For one minuscule second, he had seen the monster in the light after he'd turned it on, before being clubbed viciously on the head, knocking him unconscious. The evil thing then carried them, after tying them up, he supposed. He would have carried them both at once, though, in Tom's opinion, or it would have been seen by someone returning from town.

Tom weighed an impressive twenty-two stone in his birthday suit, most of that pure muscle, with Jack adding his puny eleven or so. That made this brute of a thing immensely powerful. Tom had no idea where they were, or how far from the town they were, but it was one heck of an effort all the same. Had he known the cave was around twenty kilometres away as the crow flies, he would not have believed it possible.

As his head cleared and his mate slowly came to, he wondered what the beast could want with them. He remembered the boar from the weekend prior. He had assumed it was wild, as he had sighted wild boar on many occasions. Tom believed he may have mistaken the boar for the unholy vision before him, eyeing him steadily, as though it had some intelligence and purpose behind those penetrating eyes; a purpose Tom had yet to fathom.

Something glistened, catching the sunlight when the beast moved slightly. Though grubby and mostly covered by the matted fur on the beast's chest, Tom made out the rough outline of a cross, dangling from a solid chain hanging about its neck. In the centre of the cross, a cabochon of smooth green sparked a distant memory for Tom, one he could not quite grasp. It startled him to see any sign of humanity, apart from the loincloth it wore, connected with the supernatural thing in front of him.

When Jack finally raised his aching head from the ground, he was instantly alert and fearful of the large animal between him and Tom.

"Boi ya side, Jacko. Can o' water to clear away the cobwebs and the boodgy shite," said Big Tom quietly.

Jack saw the can of water nearby. He brought it to his lips with his bound hands and drank while watching the ugly maw of the beast as it turned to face him. His revulsion was plain to see, though it did not seem to affect the animal in any way. Jack could not believe such a thing existed on earth; he thought they were dead and had arrived at the place his mother had often predicted he would end up.

"What the fook is it?" whispered Jack.

"It's partly human. Has some sort of basic intelligence. Gave oos that water in those cans. Went to fill them after it gave me a drink. Knew we would be torsty," ventured Tom.

"Does...it...know what we're sayin'?"

"Not loikly," offered Tom.

"What the fook does it want?"

"Wale how the fook would oi know?"

Birrani watched and listened to the interplay with avid interest. While he did not understand the words, he supposed they were arriving at certain conclusions regarding their captivity, and asking questions of each other about him. They were eyeing him with dread and fascination. That was good. He wanted them to fear him, but not too much. He needed to gain their trust and cooperation in a few things.

He required their atonement for sins committed against him, his great-grandfather and, above all, his mother. The method of that atonement necessitated a ritual of sorts to precede the eventual punishment. It had, after all, been drilled into him for over a decade. He would ensure it came to pass.

To guarantee his success, both of these detestable things must be tempted to hunger. Water would be provided diligently to ward off dehydration. It would mean that Birrani would have to traverse the steep track to and from the cave many times per day. He accepted this onerous task with equanimity. It was simply something that needed to be done. Jarrah had chided him often enough about what he deemed as laziness in the boy. Birrani had known that Jarrah mistook his reticence to rise early or complete a task as a sign of laziness, when, in fact, it was pain that had kept Birrani from accomplishing his great-grandfather's request or command.

Jarrah was not to know that Birrani often suffered horribly during the night, finding no surcease to the constant strain on his deformed back when he attempted to sleep. His feet felt the burden of traipsing many hours over rough terrain, bleeding and weeping from old sores each night. As he grew, so did the pressure his weight asserted on those extremities and his lower lumbar region. His hunched back and bowed legs could not hold his weight erect for long, so he had to shuffle behind the swift old man on all fours like an animal.

Moments ago, he noticed a brief period of consternation on the face of the man who was his father, concentrating on something he saw when he peered directly at Birrani. The boy was not sure what it was that sparked the man's interest. He didn't think he had made any connections yet and hoped that would not happen for a time. He had preparations to make for the coming days and did not want the men to suspect anything until the appropriate moment.

While every intuition screamed at him to tear apart the evil white sinners for what they had done, he employed newfound patience, almost revelling in the dire consequences to come. Birrani had forsaken most of his lessons since the death of the old man, whom he had come to love more than life itself.

Without Jarrah in his life, there was no longer a reason for him to abide by some of the unwritten codes, to be a noble and respected member of his race. Birrani felt he no longer belonged to a race: it had been taken from him. Everything he held dear was gone at the hands of the contemptible piece of rotten garbage he saw before him. For that transgression, there would be retribution. The man would finally pay for the sins inflicted upon him and his family.

Big Tom watched as the beast swayed back and forth in front of him with an ominous leer, an expectation. Tom knew fear for perhaps the first time in his life, a soul-destroying, gut-wrenching fear that threatened to unhinge him. Something about this situation stirred a whole bunch of misgivings deep down in his Catholic soul. He truly felt as though he were about to meet his maker and pay for all the indiscretions of his life in one fell swoop.

"Ya all roight?" asked Jack, with growing concern.

"Hmm? Roight as can be. Where d'ya s'pose it came on that thar cross?"

"Holy mother-o-Chroist, I seen that n-all. Coulda found it?"

"Coulda," agreed Tom, with a slight nod of the head. "Reckon I moighta seen it somewhere, is all."

"Where, Tom, where ya seen it?"

"Don't roightly recollect," he admitted with a frown.

"Got me toid up toighter-n-a pig on a spit. How we gonna get oota here?"

"Do you see me any looser-n-you? Fooked if oi know. Wait for an opportunity, I s'pose."

The pair did not talk much after that, while the day wore on and the heat became a physical presence within the confines of the cave. Birrani had been back and forth to the billabong several times to keep up the water to his captives. In the late afternoon, he stoked up the fire in the cave, making it ridiculously uncomfortable. Once the fire had burned down to glowing white coals, he placed a couple of large steaks upon them, the meat sizzling and filling the cave with its delicious aroma.

Tom and Jack eyed the meat ravenously. Neither had eaten a decent meal since the previous day at noon. By the time the afternoon bell sounded for knock-off time at the mill, they had both taken to drinking their Friday night meal. They watched with growing suspicion as the thing carefully seared the meat on both sides, leaving a rare, juicy, succulent steak within. Tom did not automatically reach for the proffered steak. He folded his arms over his chest in defiant stubbornness.

Jack, on the other hand, accepted the meat with relish, salivating at the heavenly aroma. He ate greedily with his bound hands in front of him. Tom looked on, regretting his decision, growing hungrier and hungrier. When it looked as though the other piece would go to Jack as well, Tom capitulated, stretching out his hands to accept the meat.

Neither man spoke as they happily digested their fine meal in peace. The beast had returned several times to place more meat on the hot coals, roasting the portions meticulously on the outside while leaving the centre almost raw, just the way the two men liked it. Although they were still quite bewildered about the reason for their captivity and their mysterious captor, they relaxed appreciably once they were sated. Without realising it, they both drifted off to sleep soon thereafter.

The following morning, they woke to more of the wonderful scent permeating the cavern. The roasting meat almost brought tears to their eyes as they contemplated more of the delicious repast from the previous evening. Cool water from the billabong accompanied their feasting. The beast looked on impassively as the two men ate gluttonously.

They did not think to question why the beast was not partaking of the meal. They knew only that their tastebuds were being adequately catered for, whilst they were being held against their will. It had done nothing so far to indicate maltreatment toward the pair other than the first occasion when they had both been clubbed on the head.

By the third day, the portions grew smaller and smaller from breakfast to lunch. By early evening they were extremely hungry again. They waited impatiently for their evening meal to arrive. While they remained captive, they had little else to occupy their minds other than food and drink. The enormous beast had come and gone with scant regard for the pair.

When it returned once more, Tom and Jack could not see what it was carrying. With its enormous, hairy back to them, it began to distribute something carefully on the ground just out of their view. Curiosity overtook their hunger while they were unable to see what it was doing. After a few moments, the beast stepped back to allow them to witness his creativity.

In an ungainly, haphazard pile, they saw fresh bones of varying size with rag-tag pieces of flesh remaining on them. The pile was, predictably, unrecognisable as the animal it once was. Tom and Jack assumed it was the carcass of a large wallaby, or even a wild pig, guessing correctly that the animal had been the sole ingredient of their banquet.

With solemn reverence and a gentility belying its huge frame and clumsy appearance, the beast then laid down another fragment of the carcass while his back was turned to the pair. When Birrani stepped back, the pair recoiled in horror. In front of the pile of bones was a head, a human head, identifiable as belonging to Jarrah Bone, the old man they had killed.

"Fook, Chroist, fook. Tell me we aint et 'im?" begged Jack.

"Ya fookin' evil demon. Whatcha make us do, then? Chroist'll have noothin' to do with us no more. Fook!"

Jack began heaving, his insides screaming to be free, while Tom just shook his head in horror. He was scared for his mortal soul. Cannibalism was a sin against everything he knew, everything he'd learned and everything he cared about. He, too, gave in to the pressures of his roiling guts, puking to the side.

Birrani stood before them with grim satisfaction. It did not please him to feed his blessed great-grandfather to the men. It pained him worse than he could ever admit. He stood over them, watching them vomit out everything, with fear and anguish contorting their faces. When he finally had their attention, as their heaves issued nothing more than froth, he pointed directly at Tom, then slapped his fist into his other palm with a resounding thwack! Then he pointed at what was left of Jarrah. Birrani then placed his fingers to his mouth to indicate eating.

Without thought or pause, Birrani retrieved Jarrah's knife from his dilly bag and turned to Jack. While Jack protested and screamed obscenities at him, Birrani cut away all of the man's clothing. Before either of them understood what was happening, Birrani had sliced a clean swathe of flesh from Jack's calf, which he threw onto the fire. While Jack screamed and writhed hysterically, Tom froze with his mouth agape, unable to utter a sound.

The smell of burning leg hairs and searing flesh filled the cavern with its unholy miasma. As the meat cooked on the coals, Birrani turned to Tom. He pointed to himself, smacked his fist into the other palm, pointed to Tom and Jack and then indicated the eating motion again. Tom thought he understood. He interpreted the action to mean that the thing was going to kill Tom and Jack, then eat them, just as they had killed the old man and been made to eat him.

"Whoy, for fook's sake? Whoy?"asked Tom desperately.

Birrani did not understand a word the man spoke, but he grasped the notion that the man needed a reason for his demise, judging by the desperately puzzled expression on his face: as if it required more reason than the unnecessary death of a hundred-year-old venerated person. Tom watched in growing fear as the big brute reached toward its chest, grasped the minuscule cross in its huge paws and showed it to Tom. He inspected the cross closely, with a glimmer of recognition that turned into full-scale terror when the glimmer escalated to a certainty. He gasped as he remembered clearly where he had seen the small silver cross before.

"It... can't be. Mary... Mary Bone's. Why do you... Fook! No, no, no... You're her bloody bastard sprog," he whispered. "She lived, she survoived? That were her'n. I knows it now. It were on her neck that noight. Thought about nickin' it, oi did. That... Oy, that means oim yer da. You know what a da be? Father. Oim yer father, boy," Tom announced with some measure of pride.

Tom received a resounding backhand that cracked his bottom jaw, dislocating it easily. Birrani retrieved the piece of flesh from the fire and began the distasteful act of eating it in segments, just as a presence filled the entrance to the cave.

SIXTEEN

Kami took in the horrible sight at a glance. He instantly recognised his father's head beside a pile of bones. He noted the extremely ugly boy he had been told about by his mother, Yindi. Big Tom, bound at ankle and wrists, he recognised as the boy's father and the man who had killed Kunmanara. He did not know the man howling in agony, attempting to clutch his badly injured leg, which spurted blood in every direction.

Kami peered gravely from the boy-mountain eating some undercooked meat to the man with the fresh injury. Cannibalism was not unheard of in their histories and the cultures of many different races, especially the natives of Papua New Guinea. The thought disgusted him. Dressed in dirty jeans, long-sleeved shirt and riding boots, his working gear as a jackaroo on a nearby cattle farm, Kami strode slowly into the cave, tilting his dusty Akubra to sit back on his woolly skull. He squatted before the remains of his father with intense sadness invading his bearing.

"Who killed him?" he asked the boy in the language of his people.

Birrani pointed directly at Big Tom. Kami turned to glare at the man poisonously.

"Oi didn't mean it, honest. He was... Oi was... Fook, he was just an old..." Tom did not finish, knowing he was about to commit further insult. "He made oos eat the fookin' man! He needs to be arrested. Look what he did to Jacko, there. He's eatin' 'im aloive, the dorty, rotten heathen," Tom spat with contempt at Kami's boots.

"They arrest you, white pella, for killin' a man?"

"It, it was an accident. I only tapped him to teach him a..."

"One hundred-year-old man! You punch a one-hundred-year-old man? You, big as a mountain and him, like a sapling? You kill my father?"

"You're...? Fook me!"

"You kill Kunmanara, then you kill my father?"

"Hold on, hold on. I never killed no one boi that name ye said, and I told ye it was an accident with ya father," explained Tom, confused.

"Killed the boy's mother. Killed my daughter, Kunmanara. My name is Kami Bone. I get justice for what you done in the white-pella court?" Kami spat at the feet of Big Tom to pay back the insult.

"You're Mary's..."

Kami and Birrani both hissed at the mention of her name, fearing her spirit would be disturbed.

"No say that name. No more that name. Call her Kunmanara now, leave her spirit in peace. You done bad things, gotta pay."

"Fook ya. The police will hunt you down loik the dorty dogs ye are, then ya will pay for what you doon."

Kami turned to his grandson, who was still gnawing at the flesh, dribbling bloody juices down his chin and neck. Kami could see that it was difficult for the boy to chew food properly with the split bottom jaw. How he managed it at all, Kami could not imagine. It didn't appear as though any alignment existed, making mincing food between the upper and lower molars almost impossible. Instead, it seemed that the boy had to tear away small enough sections that he could swallow whole.

"Birrani, you know who I am?"

Thumb down.

"I'm your grandfather, Kami Bone. I'm Kunmanara's father. This man killed my daughter and my father. It's good that he's punished, but what you do is an abomination, bad thing. Did my father teach you this thing?" asked Kami, pointing to the head.

Thumb up.

"Pah! He teach you this for animal, not human."

Thumb down.

"You bring shame and danger to our people, Birrani. White man hears of this and we pay. They hunt us and hang us by the neck, everyone. Who saw you take them?"

Thumb down.

"No one?"

Thumb up.

"Shut him up. Can't think with that."

Birrani swiped Jack a vicious blow across the head, silencing the man at last.

"Oh, you coonts, ya dorty rotten, black coonts," screamed Tom.

"You want the same?" Kami asked him softly.

"Take me back to stand trial for what oim accused of," demanded the big man.

"Hah! No justice for the people in white-pella court," argued Kami.

Kami rose to stand before Birrani, arriving at a decision.

"Birrani, I need to take my father back to his tribe so that we can honour him and set his spirit free. Will you allow this?"

Birrani peered at him intently with those eyes that saw through anyone. Slowly he raised his thumb.

"I do not approve of the way you bring justice to the white man. It is not our way. I will not try to stop you, though. You must do what is in your heart. I ask only that you kill them first. Make it painful if you like, but please do not eat them alive. It is forbidden, bad medicine. Will you do this for me and our people?"

Reluctantly, Birrani raised his thumb.

"Thank you, my grandson. I will look to the 'sorry business'. I will place his bones next to his wife, who passed a year after he left. I will return once a month, on my day off work, to visit with you. I know you have reason to hate me for the way I treated your mother. I now regret my actions. I failed you and her. For that, I am truly sorry, my boy. It brings great sadness to me to bear that shame. I hope one day you may forgive me.

"Birrani, understand this, if anyone finds out what has happened here, the white man will hunt us down like animals and kill us all.

There will be no peace between us. Make sure there is no sign afterwards, nothing. If I hear of talk or suspicion among the white men, I will tell you, and you must leave this place forever. Cover your passing so that no man can follow. He has taught you this?"

Thumb up.

Kami nodded his head sadly, then removed his shirt and packed the bones and head of his father into it. When he had finished, he turned to face Big Tom.

"You gonna pay for crimes against my people, against my family. No white-pella court for you. No one know you here. No one come rescue."

"Ah, ya fookin' gootless shites. Oon-toi me and oi'll show ya joostice the man's way."

"Birrani, he believes you are too cowardly to face him man to man in a fair fight. He challenges you. I would not do this. If he wins and leaves here, we will all be in grave danger. Make sure neither he nor the other man can ever leave here. I must go now; there is much to do before I return to work tomorrow morning."

Just as his father had done, Kami merged with the scenery outside the cave as though he had never existed. Tom glared at Birrani in open defiance, daring him to accept the challenge. Birrani ignored him, turning instead to inspect his other captive. His grandfather had made him promise to kill them first. He would honour that promise. He deftly gripped the puny, unconscious form of Jack O'Leary, lifting him with consummate ease before throwing him face down on the coals of the fire.

Tom screamed for his friend, who woke to excruciating pain from which he was unable to escape. Birrani kept a huge hand on top of Jack's back, making sure he could not escape or rise. Kami had said he could apply pain while administering his justice. He took him at his word. The agony being suffered by the puny white man would be like nothing he had ever experienced before, yet might do again when he met that 'debil-pella'.

Tom shook with rage and empathy for his dear friend suffering the torments of hell, being roasted alive. Eventually, Jack quietened as the pain caused him to black out. The mind, being unable to cope with the messages being received by the receptors, began to shut down in defence. The sickening stench of his body voiding itself on the coals made Tom retch pathetically.

Throughout the night and the following day, Tom sat in torment as he watched his friend slowly being consumed by the thing that was his son. Shame, disgust and anger filled him to overflowing. He cursed the bastard with all the invective his dull mind could muster, shouting and screaming the obscenities till he became hoarse.

He understood that it was all to no avail, that the stupid brute could not comprehend what he was saying, but it made no difference. It made him feel better, and while he had breath in his lungs he would keep up the barrage of insults. Tom had never imagined that he would have to answer for beating the young, black bitch he had made the mistake of bedding while drunk...a few times. With a shudder, he realised he would be next to die in some horrific manner devised by this insane...thing!

It didn't seem right, yet, in the back of his mind, he recalled how the Irish had been treated by the English and couldn't help but make a small comparison. The Aborigine was on the bottom of the totem pole list for any whites, regardless of the nationality. The Irish were only one rung above them on that pole in the eyes of the British. Small wonder they began discriminating against the blacks so heavily. It lifted their status in their eyes, to be off the bottom of the pile in the new land.

Descendants of convicts transported to the penal colony in the Antipodes, the Irish were quick to exert their superiority upon the hapless natives, along with everyone else. Laws prevented the blacks from entering respectable bars and taverns, being served their alcohol at the rear. Segregation was enforced by law and opinion, often brutally.

Tom supposed that Kami was right not to trust the white courts to deliver justice for the death of his daughter and father. It would cause an almighty backlash if Tom were convicted, setting an ugly precedent that the general public would not accept. In truth, it was why Tom demanded it, knowing he would not be convicted in an English court, even if he was just a lowly Irishman.

Before Big Tom could finish his musings, the brute had picked him up and cast him over his hunched shoulder as easily as toting a woman's handbag. While he grunted with the movement of having his stomach compressed by his weight, Tom foresaw his inevitable demise now that his friend had been consumed. Knowing the pain Jacko had experienced before his passing, Tom was in no doubt that his punishment would be far worse if that were possible. He couldn't think of a much more painful end than being roasted alive on hot coals.

Tom gasped, with each movement causing him to expel air, as he was jostled about down the treacherous, twisting path. He watched in awe from his unique perspective the sure footing displayed by the creature as it wound its way down the steep decline. Tom did not recognise the setting. He glimpsed the area through periodic openings in the thick vegetation growing either side of the path. At the bottom of the path was a dark, smooth section he could barely make out in the gloom of the shade, after being blinded by the sunlight strobing through the trees they passed.

At the bottom, Tom understood what the smooth, black surface represented; a billabong. He was deposited roughly on his back in a small clearing, obviously used by animals as they gathered about the watering hole. Tom squirmed uncomfortably on the dirt, attempting to get to a sitting position.

SCREEEEEEEYAHHHHHHHHH, SCREEEEEEYAHHHH.

The big man winced as the piercing, deafening shriek emanated from the beast. He could barely imagine anything in the animal kingdom capable of making such a sound, let alone something of a semi-human nature. He'd read somewhere that the loudest animal on Earth was the howler monkey. He felt sure the howler monkey had nothing on the thing a few paces away.

Big Tom gaped in awe as the bushland erupted in a cacophonous commotion. The raucous cries of sulphur-crested cockatoos, the shrieks of galahs, and dozens of other bird varieties, all taking to the air at once, filled the natural amphitheatre with a resounding din. The creature screeched and the world about it seemed to react in empathy, spurred on by its call to add to the mêlée.

Suddenly, at Tom's feet, a knife magically appeared, speared into the ground. It had missed him by only a fraction. He looked up to see the brute standing a short distance away, indicating the knife and then pointing to Tom. Sensing a trick, Tom was reluctant to make a move for the knife. He slid backward on his backside, farther and farther as the beast approached the knife. It bent down, never once removing its defiant stare from Tom.

The knife was thrown once more, with unerring skill, at Tom's big feet, clad in his work boots that he had not taken off that Friday evening before the nightmare began. He had no idea how long it had been. It felt as though weeks had passed. The knife was thrown with incredible force and precision, quivering when it landed point-first in the hard ground. Once more the creature seemed to want Tom to use the knife to cut himself free.

It dawned on Big Tom that his challenge might have been conveyed by Kami Bone and the creature had accepted it. He did not understand a word of the Aboriginal language. It would have been far beneath him to learn even a few basics, even though Mary had been using it around him more often than not after lessons with her grandfather.

The more he viewed his situation, the more he became convinced that his...son was willing to accept the challenge. It wouldn't be the first time in history that a son was willing to challenge his father, having reached adulthood. Usually, such a challenge was premature; the challenger realising too late that he lacked the experience or maturity to succeed. Strength or size seldom became a factor.

Not so, in his present circumstances: Tom knew that strength and size deserved consideration in a contest between him and his offspring. He conceded the enormous strength inherent in the creature when it carried him over difficult terrain. That it carried both Jacko and himself for a considerable distance added to that realisation. Though Big Tom was larger and stronger than the average man, often towering over his fellow workers, he was less than confident about the outcome of the contest. Unfortunately, the number of options available to him were severely limited.

Fight or flight? The primordial instinct battled within him as Tom eyed the knife still sticking out of the ground within reach. He contemplated cutting himself loose, then making a run for it. He had observed one thing that gave him confidence in such a scenario. The creature suffered from horribly deformed feet, making it slower and clumsier than he had first thought. He didn't think he would have much difficulty outrunning it.

The bushland had settled into an eerie silence, as though everything was waiting with bated breath for him to decide his future. The creature had taken on a stance of almost amused contempt, as though it had figured all along that Big Tom would be unworthy of the challenge, a challenge he would not accept. Tom weighed up the probabilities, taking into consideration that he would be armed once he was free of his restraints, facing an unarmed opponent.

Two major obstacles prevented him from acceding to a plan of flight. The first of those was that he had no idea where he would go if he chose to run. The second, and more important, was that he was practically trapped within a natural pen on three sides. The only route out of the bowl with high sides was directly behind the brute. He would have to face the creature, regardless of his choice.

Reluctantly, he removed the knife from the ground with his two hands bound at the wrists. Watching the creature, he sawed away at his leg restraints, some sort of animal-hide strips, plaited and soaked with water to make them shrink into a formidable braid. With difficulty, he then managed to saw the bond holding his wrists together. It was a great relief finally to be free of the fetters, though he felt the sting of pins and needles as the blood coursed back into the starved extremities.

Big Tom rose unsteadily to his feet, staring at the creature with a seething, roiling anger causing the bile to rise in his stomach. He remembered every last sound and movement made by his friend as he died in the coals. Those tortured, anguished screams before his face melted would remain with him for eternity. Every bite of his friend the rotten creature placed in its mouth, Tom tucked away in his memory banks. He allowed the images to fester and boil in him till his rage pushed all the uncertainty and fears aside.

Before he could make his first charge, however, a loud commotion near the entrance to the bowl caused them both to turn that way. Tom was confused about the interruption; having steeled himself for the action, he was champing at the bit to be in the fray. He was a big man and had never had to fear an opponent. He always bested anyone he faced.

Almost too late, he recognised the cause of the disturbance. The family of wild pigs, headed by a boar bigger than anything he had ever seen before, was stampeding in their direction. Panicking, Tom twisted around to find any means of escape. He knew all too well what a wild pig was capable of, with razor-sharp tusks slashing from side to side as it charged. He had seen his prized Pitbull terrier ripped to shreds by one on a hunting trip only the previous year. The culprit of his dog's demise may well have been the monster bearing down upon them like a steam train.

Without waiting to witness the outcome of the creature's encounter with the marauding pigs, Tom sprinted to the nearest tree that would accommodate his large frame, shinnying up it faster than a lizard. The moment he was settled at a height that was out of the pigs' reach, he turned to watch the outcome of the contest.

Birrani wheeled about at the sound he dreaded more than anything in the world. He had finally been caught by the mean bunch of pigs he had been teasing and annoying with his screeches for years. Luckily for him, the pigs seemed to be intent on chasing the white man, who had clambered up a tree. Birrani did not know what had caused his good luck. Perhaps, with the amount of dust being kicked up by all the hooves, they did not see him clearly as they entered the clearing. Maybe his dark, hairy back camouflaged him slightly against the backdrop of bushes and trees.

Birrani did not know if pigs were intelligent enough to have memories or carry grudges against humans for transgressions. If the pigs were heading straight for the white man, perhaps they had a grudge to settle with him, making him a priority target. He was unsure about a strategy. He could run past the pack up his track to the cave, he thought. Or he could turn around and escape through the entrance to the bowl.

Something inside prevented him from choosing either option. He was tired of having to run scared of the pigs all the time, deferring to them so they had the run of the billabong whenever they chose. He was sick of having to wait hours for them to leave the vicinity before he could venture down to have a bath or a drink in the mornings and the evenings. He was fed up with being scared of them.

Birrani knew he was at a disadvantage, greatly outnumbered by the pigs, some of which were huge. The alpha male was the largest, most aggressive animal he knew. It was about the size of a small Brahman bull. He had seen the humped cattle grazing in the area from time to time, seen his grandfather mustering them with the other jackaroos, rounding up the new calves for branding. He and his mother watched them secretly, many times. What they never knew was that he and his mum stole calves over the years for food.

The pigs were milling about underneath the tree, where the white man waited above them with a look of concern, hoping the branch would hold his weight. The large boar, squealing its annoyance at being unable to reach the man, galloped around the tree in a maddened frenzy, urging the rest to follow suit.

Standing his ground at the edge of the clearing, Birrani let out his blood-curdling screech, instantly bringing a confused halt to the disturbance beneath the tree. Birrani was surprised by the reaction. Normally his screech from above them would have stirred them up to a fevered, frantic restlessness. Maybe the sound was less ominous coming from ground level, where the pigs could finally see the animal that was challenging them? Either way, he now had their full and undivided attention, especially that of the alpha male.

Birrani wished he had not thrown Jarrah's hunting knife to the white man. It would have come in handy for the fight. The boar had long, lethal tusks protruding from its jaws, while he had no similar defences. His pair of jaw pieces, jutting out either side of what would have been a chin on any other human, tipped by a couple of broken teeth, did not begin to compare with the weapons facing him as the boar began its murderous charge.

The enraged pig, defending his harem of sows and piglets, ploughed the ground as it dug in its pointed hooves to gain traction and speed. Grunting, snorting and squealing, it ran straight at Birrani like a runaway locomotive; inexorable, immutable, lethal. The rest of the sounder stood about uncertainly, witnessing the contest.

Birrani barely managed to sidestep the initial charge, the tusks tearing through the air only millimetres from his thigh as the giant beast crashed by him. Before it fully passed its target the boar let out a shriek as it felt the blow hit him from the rear, sending him sprawling in the dust.

Birrani had mustered every ounce of strength and speed he could muster to leap into the air after the decelerating boar, punching its rump with a sledgehammer blow that would have killed or maimed anything else. The boar rose from the earth, shaking itself vigorously to get rid of the stunning lethargy the blow had induced to his rear musculature. Working up its level of indignation and menace, the pig accelerated once more in Birrani's direction.

On the next pass, Birrani felt the first sting of the razor-sharp tusks ripping through one of his thigh muscles as he moved too slowly to cleanly miss contact with the rampaging pig. The pain was bearable. Birrani had suffered horrific agonies throughout his life from the burdens of his own body. The tear felt like nothing more than a scratch to him, despite the profuse amount of blood pouring out.

The remainder of the sounder grew restless with anticipation of the kill, with the scent of fresh blood in their nostrils. They knew the big boar was a consummate killer and provider; they sensed a victory looming, from which they would all share in the resultant feast. Nothing had bested their leader in known memory. They felt sure nothing would. They milled about the perimeter of the battleground.

Birrani tensed himself for the next onslaught. The magnificent, ugly beast announced the killing lust with a loud squeal that sent the others into a frenzied fervour. Birrani let loose with his deafening screech that caused the entire bushland to erupt. The boar ran straight for him, its head tossing those enormous tusks from side to side as though scything grass to make way for its charge. The second before contact was made, Birrani leapt high into the air above the brute, smashing his huge fist into the side of the boar's body, easily breaking several ribs.

The boar squealed with the pain and indignity of suffering a blow from the ineffectual thing he believed his opponent to be. It was frustrating and maddening that he was not able to simply pierce the stupid thing with his mighty tusks, providing a banquet for his family.

Birrani stood his ground, bleeding from the open gash on his thigh, surprised to see his manhood fully erect under his flimsy loincloth. It appeared that he enjoyed the life and death challenge, revelled in it, found it intoxicating and highly erotic. It was the first time in his life he had experienced the sensations in his groin. His masculinity had not presented itself in his previous years; only occasionally did he wake with an erection before his first urination of the day.

Big Tom man sat statue-still on the limb of a tree, observing the battle taking place with great interest. His fate would possibly be decided on the outcome of that battle. Birrani watched as the pig reversed his direction at the end of his third run, albeit with a slower and less agile movement. Still, it came on, relentlessly, mindlessly, a juggernaut with but one thing on its mind; ending the life of the challenger.

Birrani did not think he could fool the pig twice with the same methods he had employed on the first three runs. He detected a keen fighting intelligence in the mind of the boar. It learned and improvised, adapted on the spot during an altercation. The boar changed its tactic now to circle Birrani menacingly, darting in periodically to slash at him with the far-reaching tusks.

The circles became smaller and smaller, with the tusks only a hair's breadth away from delivering Birrani a mortal wound. Birrani's adrenal glands were no longer supplying sufficient quantities to keep his insensate energy alive, with the lactic acid build-up in his muscles slowing down his reactions. The rest of the sounder, intuitively sensing a victorious end to the contest, ceased their restless milling.

With the knowledge that the opponent was being worn down, the boar made ready for one last charge to gain victory. They came together in the centre of the clearing with a mighty thud of two leviathans meeting body to body in an age-old test of superiority. Birrani grasped the boar around the neck, twisting so it became unbalanced enough to fall to the earth.

The head of the boar was immensely difficult for Birrani to control. The beast's strength was formidable. With every movement, its tusks bit painfully into Birrani's arms and chest. They wrestled that way on the bare earth for many moments, neither party gaining the upper hand conclusively. It was all Birrani could do to keep hold of the massive boar's head. At a point where Birrani believed he had lost the battle, unable to keep the fierce tusks from delivering the fatal blow, he changed handholds before the boar could interpret his intentions.

Birrani grabbed onto both foot-long tusks. Drawing on every last vestige of his waning strength, he pulled the tusks in opposing directions, outward from the snout. The confused and enraged boar attempted to escape but found it impossible as Birrani wrapped his strong legs about the beast's belly and locked them together with his feet up on its back. Birrani reared back, straining every muscle, tendon and sinew in his upper body and arms until they were set to snap.

The boar squealed in panic when it realised what was happening, unable to counter the movement or escape. With a loud ripping sound, the boar's tusks were wrenched out of its jaws, snapping loudly as they were freed. Knowing that the pig had been defeated, denied the ability to inflict any more damage, Birrani might have elected to be merciful. It was not to be. Screeching with joyous victory, Birrani reared back with the tusks he had reversed in each hand, plunging them into the boar's eyes and through to the puny brain, embedding them full length within the boar's skull.

The rest of the pig family stood by apprehensively, wondering what had happened and why their leader was not moving. Birrani lay in the dust on his back, thoroughly exhausted and bleeding profusely from several deep gashes. He waited in silent resignation for his inevitable demise by the rest of the sows and smaller males, sure to be incensed by the death of their leader. He could not hope to continue to struggle against the rest of the family. He was doomed to die alone and his one regret was that he could not fulfil his promise to his dying mother.

When Birrani gathered the strength to lift his head he saw that Big Tom was no longer in the tree. He had used the battle to make good his escape.

SEVENTEEN

When his muscles finally stopped quivering and no longer felt like lead, Birrani rose to his feet. Expecting an attack at any moment from the remaining pigs, he steeled himself for the charge. When he opened his eyes, he became confused at the sight of the pigs seemingly going about their business of drinking from the waterhole, enjoying dust baths and generally cavorting in a relaxed manner, ignoring him completely.

Birrani knew he had to attend to his wounds to stanch the flow of blood. It would require stitching together the flaps of open skin as his mother and Jarrah had taught him. He had a supply of bone needles and roo gut with which to suture his wounds in his dilly bag within the cave. His mother had warned him about infections if he left his wounds open and unclean.

He hobbled over to the edge of the billabong, wary of the pigs as he sat in the water to wash his wounds. The pigs continued their activities without as much as a sideways glance. Birrani did not understand their behaviour. He had seen what could happen if the sounder converged on a target as one. Birrani stood no chance in that scenario, yet he was being ignored by the mature pigs. Only the piglets seemed to look his way every so often.

Once the wounds were clean and he felt sufficiently revived, Birrani made his way to the cave, watching the pigs warily. Hours later, the pigs were still at the waterhole when Birrani returned. He had delayed the pursuit of his father long enough. He had to track him down before darkness intervened. He could not afford to let the man reach the safety of Allies Creek, to inform the authorities. If that happened there would be no rest until he was found and captured, along with any other black man within cooee of the township.

He had to follow Kami's instructions in that regard, for all their sakes. He didn't think his father knew his way back to town, and certainly had no way of getting there before nightfall. He was confident in his abilities to track the man, having been taught by the best. That thought still created a pang of sadness in Birrani, who missed the old man greatly. Despite Kami's assurances of frequent visits, Birrani still felt the burden of loneliness crushing his heart in its vice-like grip.

The boy-man steered clear of the pigs as he made his way around the billabong, limping and suffering from the sting of his wounds. He did not think the boar had caused any major damage to him but knew he would have to be very vigilant about infections. Fortunately, Jarrah had shown him bush remedies and poultices that he could apply to the areas.

As he neared the narrow path leading from the bowl, a strange thing happened. Birrani heard a small sound behind him, turned, and saw the sounder of pigs lined up to follow him...or attack him, he couldn't be sure. Shaking his head at the impossibility of his situation, he turned back to face the track. Moving ahead, he heard the pigs following him at a steady pace. He was perplexed. The pigs were not making any overt moves to attack. They displayed no signs of aggression, fear or anything else.

Birrani almost gasped out loud when a couple of piglets scooted in front of him, snorting and grunting playfully. He was soon surrounded by the group, keeping pace with him, accepting him into their family. Although he could not be certain, Birrani concluded that his fight with the old boar was considered a legitimate leadership challenge to the family. If Birrani was not mistaken, he had become their new leader, their alpha male. *Did they take him to be a pig?*

It was a troubling development. He tried numerous times to shoo them away, discouraging their proximity, to no avail. The piglets, especially, saw it as a game, which they played with great exuberance. Each time they drew near, he turned to scare them off with a loud shriek. Off they would scamper, only to return within moments, ready for another round. The rest simply walked along, accompanying him wherever it was they were being led.

Birrani sped up to keep on the trail of his quarry, ignoring his entourage for the time being. The stupid, heavy white man left an easy trail to follow. Probably believing he was not being followed, possibly imagining that Birrani had perished during the contest, he made no effort to cover his retreat. Nor did the tracks suggest any effort to hurry; a slow, steady pace. Birrani ate up the distance readily, despite his ungainly method of movement.

The man had no water with him nor food, making his progress slow as the day drew on. Birrani saw by his tracks, veering off occasionally, that he was dehydrating in the formidable heat, wandering aimlessly. He assumed the man was lost and possibly delirious from thirst. It wouldn't surprise him to find the white man walking in circles before too long.

Birrani wondered how he might retain the element of surprise with his gathering of pigs all happily grunting and snorting as they ambled along. He need not have been concerned. Before the afternoon light began to fade, the sounder of pigs started to separate from him. The females and piglets veered off to stay behind him, and the younger males and large sows without progeny speared off to either side and in front of him.

As he came to a small clearing in the scrubland, he was fascinated to see the pigs surrounding the prone figure. As Birrani neared Big Tom, spreadeagled on the hard, baking earth, he thought he understood the strange behaviour evidenced by the footprints of the foolish white man. As Birrani leaned in to examine the exposed areas of his father, he came across the two fine puncture wounds on his forearm that he had been looking for.

Snakebite.

It explained why the tracks meandered so haphazardly after midday. The man had taken the time to rest, possibly beneath the shade of a gum tree. But a snake had had the same idea. Pissed off at the intrusion, it had struck him on the forearm. The man had not thought to bind the bite, bleed it, or apply a tourniquet; nothing. He was not yet dead, though. Birrani could see him watching every move he made.

Big Tom was unable to say anything through lips that seemed to be glued shut. His muscles did not want to work. The pain in his arm was an intense, burning agony that increased with each breath, marching up his arm and entering his chest. He had not seen the snake until after it had struck with lightning speed. The death adder was only a small snake, but it delivered a toxic brew that killed easily and swiftly when inflicted on lesser mortals.

Tom had disturbed the snake when he moved a broken tree limb to make room for himself beneath the tree. He had not seen the reptile until he almost laid his hand on top of it while bracing himself to sit. The only reason he was not already dead, hours later, was his great size and metabolism. Anyone smaller, older or quite young would have perished long ago. The neurotoxins had made their way through Tom's system, slowly paralysing him until he had faltered and fallen in the centre of a small clearing.

He did not know how long he had been wandering in agony and confusion. He had heard noises at different times but thought he might have been hallucinating. He stared at the ugly creature standing over him. He could not believe his loins had spawned such a horrible monster. It was a tragedy that the huge boar had not killed the abomination. Tom noticed the wounds adorning the creature's chest and arms with satisfaction, knowing that the boar had at least inflicted injury.

He watched through slitted lids as Birrani lowered his hand, offering him a hand up. He almost laughed at the useless gesture, but feebly raised his arm in acceptance. His eyes grew wide as the large hand enveloped his own and the creature's foot came to rest on his collar bone. Inconceivably, his arm was torn from the socket without any effort at all by the powerful thing that was his son.

Birrani wrenched the man's arm from his body with

consummate ease. He looked about the clearing, surrounded by his new family, all waiting patiently at the perimeter. Birrani tossed the bloody arm to them, whereupon they converged as one onto the morsel. He then turned back to the screaming, squirming mass beneath his hairy foot. Bending to catch the other arm, now flailing about in an attempt to avoid him, he tore it free as well. The legs followed, then the head.

Birrani snatched back the knife Jarrah had given him, sticking out from the belt of the man's trousers. He tore open the shirt on the torso at his feet and carved a chunk of flesh from the chest of his father. He chewed the meat raw and bleeding, then tossed the torso to his fellow pigs. The group engorged themselves on Big Tom O'Hare, father of Biranni Nullah Bone, while he watched with grim satisfaction, knowing his mother had finally had her revenge on the evil bastard.

He rested in the clearing while the pigs made short work of the man. The piglets frolicked about him gaily while their mothers gorged. Birrani was highly amused by the piglets' antics, picking one up now and then to hold. They were unafraid. He had been accepted as one of their own.

EIGHTEEN

"How could anyone possibly know that?" asked Clarice.

"I told you, many of the gaps in the story were filled by Kami with assumptions and rumour. He guessed some of it, heard bits and pieces from others. He pieced a lot of the story together from many sources, including personal observations," explained Arlon.

"So he looked that much like a pig that they accepted him?"

"If it's fair dinkum, and these tracks we're following lend credence to the story, then I doubt it had anything to do with his appearance. Birrani challenged the old boar and won. The others accepted that, supposedly."

"How much farther, do you think?"

"We're here."

"What?"

"That narrowing in the track in front of us? That's the entrance to the caldera. See how it rises sharply on either side?"

"I just thought we were coming to a hill."

"Yes, it's deceiving. From here that's exactly what it looks like. I reckon that's part of the reason it's stayed secret for so long. You can see up to the top and be satisfied that it's no different to down here, so why bother going up?"

"What are we going to do?"

"Go up, of course."

"Why?" asked Bill Rogers.

"Reconnaissance. We can't go blundering into a trap. We need to know the lay of the land and where the captives are being held. Then we need to come up with a plan that involves the least amount of danger possible. It's getting on to dusk. I'm betting on a fire being lit by Birrani, to watch over the prisoners. We need the night to mask our presence. Bill, I'd like you to stay here and watch Clarice if you don't mind..."

"No way, buster. I'm coming with you," declared Clarice, with a stamp of her booted foot.

"Shouldn't we consider going back to inform the authorities of the location? Allies Creek should be crawling with emergency services by now," recommended Bill reasonably.

"Have you heard any helicopters or seen any sign of flashing emergency lights at night? I haven't."

"What are you saying, Arlon?" asked Clarice growing worried.

"Look, I'm only guessing, okay? I don't think our Mr Gaze made it to Mundubbera. I don't think anyone has alerted the authorities or knows a damn thing about us and our situation here," explained Arlon.

"Why would you say that Gavin didn't make it? I don't understand," queried Bill, equally concerned.

"Do you both accept that we're all victims of Birrani Nullah Bone and his pigs?" asked Arlon, receiving reluctant nods. "Well, then we're dealing with certain intelligence, don't you think? I mean slashed tyres, kidnapping, leading us here?"

"Well, sure, but what are you getting at?" Clarice asked.

"If Birrani is still looking to prevent what he sees as a possible war between the whites and the blacks because he knows no better, and is unaware that the world has changed significantly since his youth, then he'll be doing everything he can to cover his tracks, so to speak. I don't think he would have allowed anyone to leave Allies Creek alive to inform the outside world. I think we can assume that Mr Gaze has become another victim. I'm convinced that the first grisly scene we came across is what remains of Mrs McAllen and possibly another. No one knows we're here, no one is aware of our plight. We're the only hope the Hendersons have of rescue at this stage."

"You paint a gloomy picture, Arlon. If those poor people have only us as a means of rescue, then they are doomed as well. What can we possibly do against an army of pigs led by an enormous human with unnatural powers?"

"Unnatural powers? What're these 'unnatural' powers you're alluding to? He has superior strength by being a large person who has lived all his life off the land. He has exceptional tracking and hunting skills, taught to him by Jarrah and Kami. We assume he has taken over as unchallenged leader of his pig family after he beat the old boar. Nothing unnatural about any of that."

"What about the sounds we heard, Arlon? Nothing natural about that?" questioned Clarice, with a shiver.

"That's just a mutation to his larynx caused by the injuries he suffered in the womb. He has trained and perfected that sound to great effect over the years, stirring the wildlife around him with it into a frantic panic. His inability to speak has made him concentrate on that sound as his only means of showing his emotions. Once again, nothing unnatural about it. Perfectly logical."

"Oh, Arlon, you make it sound as though it is the most normal thing in the world. Nothing about any of this is normal. People are dying here and you're dismissing it all as normal and natural," argued Clarice, feeling very frightened.

"You misunderstand me...again, Ms Manning. I don't dismiss anything and I haven't lost sight of the fact that we're dealing with anything other than normal. I'm simply saying that we shouldn't be ascribing anything supernatural to the situation or the man. Birrani has had a very hard life from birth onwards. He's had everyone that meant something to him taken away by the white man, his father. He has known nothing but hate and misery from anyone that was not his mother or great-grandfather. We can probably assume that his grandfather, Kami, does not engender as much love and devotion as his mother or Jarrah did.

"While he may derive some affection and loyalty from his gathering of wild pigs, it is obvious that they could not replace his beloved mother or great-grandfather. We're dealing with a very powerful human being here, one capable of atrocities in our eyes, to be certain, but a human being, nonetheless. We shouldn't underestimate him but we should not attribute anything beyond the natural to him. A worthy adversary and a clever one. It'll take some nous on our parts to effect a rescue. If anyone has second thoughts about that, you should speak up now. I only went along with this madness for the sake of Mrs Henderson. I'm still willing to proceed, as I believe I now have to do all I can, as we are not likely to receive assistance from any other quarter."

"All well and good, Arlon, but what can you hope to do?" asked Bill.

"Nothing at all..."

"NOTHING!" shouted Clarice and Bill.

"Why don't you both shout a little louder? I'm sure there were at least one or two bush creatures that didn't hear you?"

Receiving the appropriate amount of contrition for their outburst, he continued; "If you had allowed me to finish, I would have said that I can do nothing at all until I've done some research. As much as I don't have fear, I don't want to run blithely into a trap where we'll all be at the mercy of Birrani and company. I thought I'd made that clear?"

"Sorry, Arlon. You're right, that was uncalled for," admitted Clarice. "Let's say that you find what you expect. Can you give us an idea of what you have planned?"

Arlon sighed. He knew he had to toss them a glimmer of hope to gain their complete cooperation, yet he was reluctant to deliver false hope. He simply did not have enough information at hand to formulate a thorough plan. He explained in detail the need for proper surveillance of the area and conditions before arriving at conclusions. Though he had a hint of a plan in mind, he could not reveal it before his observations were complete.

He reminded the pair, standing before him with stress and fear etched on their features, that he would not risk further life and injury to anyone, himself included, unless he had assessed the risks and found the scales tipping in their favour. He would retreat to Allies Creek if he determined that the risk was too great. He did not believe they would make it back unscathed, but it was the lesser of two evils if they were faced with no alternatives.

The night air was sticky; heat and humidity making it uncomfortable, with a hot breeze wafting over them. Clarice and Bill were exhausted but determined to help their fellow humans if possible; admirable traits, no doubt, but most likely misplaced in their present circumstances. Arlon foresaw no happy ending for their group. He inspected his motley crew, wondering how in the world they had ended up in such a predicament.

He worried about his business if they made it back alive. Somehow, he didn't think his handling of the assignment would be seen by the solicitor as being in any way satisfactory. If word got out about the fiasco, he anticipated future contracts would be jeopardised.

There was much more at stake than simply reputations, however. Lives were hanging precariously in the balance and it was being left to him to protect those lives. He admired their spunk, especially his secretary. She had proven herself a force to be reckoned with, quite stubborn at times. He had found her to be resilient and dependable, though not always the most logical thinker.

If he were of a particular cast, he could do a lot worse than end up in a relationship with her. While her looks provoked no emotion in Arlon, he knew she possessed a rare wholesomeness and down-to-earth charm. He had seen much worse; quite recently. He prevented himself from thinking too much further. It was supposedly wrong to think ill of the dead...or endangered. However, he was not altogether convinced that Mrs Henderson was dead, nor even in mortal danger.

He had intentionally not revealed his opinion on that particular sunbect. It served no purpose. Speculation would only muddy the waters and he needed them all thinking along the same lines. If his suspicions were correct, their plight seemed doomed. Arlon fought to rid himself of negativity, to concentrate on the plan.

He had left Bill with his instructions and the signal to watch for, while he and Clarice walked off the track to approach the crater from another angle, a gentler ascension. While the walls of the caldera could be practically vertical on the inside, the outer walls were a moderate climb. Dusk crept in as they began their hike.

Once at the apex of their ascent, Arlon urged Clarice to lower her stance on the ridge, even though darkness obscured their profiles. From his rucksack, Arlon retrieved a pair of binoculars. He surveyed the area with a practised eye, taking in all the details he could by the glow of the fire within the cave, illuminating a little of the area below it. Inside the cave, he could easily make out the figures of Mr and Mrs Henderson huddled together, unbound, against the rear wall.

Below, near the edge of the billabong, Arlon witnessed Birrani, a giant hulk of a man sitting comfortably with the pigs as they settled for the evening. The idea he had originally entertained became his best, and possibly the only, option. He had banked on the notion that the captives would be kept apart from the pigs for their safety for the time being, while the leader waited below, ready to attack at the first sign of any activity at the head of the trail leading to the arena.

Arlon and Clarice now carefully moved around the ridge until they were directly above the cave's opening. Arlon checked once again with his binoculars to make sure that Birrani was still below, waiting for his pursuers to come barging in through the only entrance to the caldera. Arlon reached into his backpack once more and extracted a pair of coiled nylon climbing ropes complete with abseiling and repelling hardware, tying one end to a stout tree stump.

Clarice watched in amazement as Arlon formed slings with a complicated array of carabiners and other equipment any mountain climber would have been proud of, before explaining his plan in detail to her. Her eyes widened in wonder at the brilliance of his simple plan, yet frowned at the chances of its success. It required only one or two elements to go wrong for them all to suffer the consequences.

Arlon began to lower himself expertly down the steep slope

towards the opening of the cave. Once he was low enough, he would manoeuvre to the side of the opening to prevent any shadows from the fire alerting Birrani to their presence. He planned to keep well to the side of the cavern's entrance. The double sling around each leg was biting painfully into his flesh as he neared the glow emanating from the cave around a dozen metres below him.

Deftly, he lowered himself to a position above the opening, then moved a few paces sideways and lowered himself until his feet touched the earth. He crept quietly to the edge of the cave. He chanced a glance inwards, hoping that none of the pigs were present to keep guard, as strange as that thought seemed. From what he could tell by his cursory reconnaissance, there were only two people in the cave, sitting with their backs against a rear wall covered in ancient Aboriginal drawings.

Gloria and Travis stirred immediately when they heard a noise at the entrance. Arlon quickly held a finger to his lips to ensure their silence while he made his way around the cave walls until he was behind the small fire where he would not cast a shadow. He advised the pair to remain where they were.

He whispered: "They're all below, waiting for the rescue party to enter the caldera from the direction of the track. I have a sling set up outside the entrance, which I'll use to raise you one by one to the top of the ridge where Clarice is waiting. Once we're all safely up top, I've arranged for Bill to light a fire at the entrance that should prevent them from following us for a time. I'm hoping it will give us enough of a head start to make it out of here before they have a chance to follow. Are either of you hurt?"

Though they both shook their heads, Arlon was not certain about Mrs Henderson, who appeared quite dishevelled, with torn clothing and a vacant expression. Travis held onto his wife protectively. Arlon made them stand and hug the walls as he had done. At the entrance he made Travis stay behind while he ushered Gloria forward, placing her legs in each of the rope loops once they were outside. He then began to hoist on the trailing line, inching the bewildered woman slowly up the incline to the top. There Clarice would remove her, then tug on the line to inform Arlon to begin lowering the loops once more.

Arlon had raised Gloria no more than a few metres when her foot dislodged a small avalanche of pebbles that clattered noisily downward. Flattening himself against the hillside and warning Travis to do the same against the inner wall of the cave, they waited a few tension-filled moments in utter silence. When Arlon detected no movement from below, he continued to haul on the rope. Though he wore leather rappelling gloves, the rope bit into his hands painfully, making progress slow. Several times he felt Gloria attempting to leave the harness when he rested a moment. He was forced to continue quickly before she could attempt to remove herself and cause them all to be discovered.

Once she had been safely raised to the top of the ridge, Arlon received welcome relief to his straining muscles. He waited until he felt the signalling tug to retrieve the loops. Unfortunately, they dangled immediately in front of the cave opening, casting a dangerous, though slim shadow. To reach the slings by hand, Arlon would have to expose himself in front of the opening, backlit by the fire within. The shadow cast by the slings was enough of a concern without a human shape to add to the danger. He could not take the risk.

In the darkness to the side of the cave where the firelight did not reach, Arlon searched for a long branch. Unfortunately, any dead material around the cave had long ago been used as firewood. He needed a branch to swing the trailing slings across the opening of the cave. Without it, he would give away any advantage they retained by revealing themselves when exposed by the firelight. He cursed himself for setting up the equipment directly above the cave's entrance. Breaking a branch from a nearby tree seemed to be their only option, bringing its own drawback; noise.

Arlon slunk back from the cave's entrance cautiously and walked a short distance along the path until he came to a suitable tree with an appropriate branch. From his utility belt, he withdrew a Swiss army pocket knife with all the bells and whistles, including a small saw blade. Quietly, he went about sawing the branch through.

He succeeded in catching the swinging slings on his third attempt. He expanded the slings to accommodate the larger frame of Travis Henderson before taking up the strain to haul him upwards. He warned Travis that the going would be extremely slow because of his extra weight. Travis took that as an insult rather than a way of Arlon admitting that his strength was waning.

Resting every other moment, Arlon struggled gamely to hoist the man to the top as he had done with his wife. Twice, Arlon lost his grip with trembling hands, allowing Travis to sink precious metres before Arlon was able to stop the descent. His hands bled as the rope burned through the tough leather gloves. Arlon began to doubt his ability to endure the strain. Sweat beaded on his forehead and under his arms. The tension in his muscles caused them to quake and quiver.

Arduously, centimetre by centimetre, Arlon raised the man. Despite asking Travis to use his feet wherever possible to find safe purchase and push upwards, thereby relieving Arlon for a few precious seconds, the man did no such thing. Travis allowed Arlon to do all the lifting himself, figuring that he was helping not to cause any further rock falls. The debilitating haul left Arlon shaking by the time Travis finally reached the top.

Panting and wheezing as though he had just run a marathon, arms like jelly, hanging limply by his sides, Arlon fought to regain his regular breathing. He felt light-headed and almost delirious. When the empty slings arrived back at eye level, he contemplated finding another means of escape for himself. He groaned inwardly at the thought of raising himself to the ridge after his gargantuan effort. Raising himself using the rope brake and foot loop he added to the design would prove to be even more difficult and stressful.

By the time he reached the top, where Clarice and Travis assisted him to remove the harness, all he could do for the next ten minutes was remain collapsed and unable to move a single muscle.

Gradually, Arlon regained his composure, glad of the strict regime of martial arts training he had forced on himself from the age of ten. He recovered in due course to implement the second half of his plan. He shone a torchlight up through the treetops directly overhead. If Birrani saw the light from below, they would probably not succeed. It was Bill's cue to light a fire at the entrance to the caldera, blocking off all escape. If Birrani meant to follow them, he would have to do so by scaling the steep hillside above the cave. He would only be able to accomplish it on his own. The pigs could not follow on such a steep incline.

Moving as quickly as possible with the night firmly entrenched on the landscape, Arlon led his group downward, hoping to meet up with Bill at the bottom. Arriving out of breath from the short run, Bill burst into their group. Arlon quickly took a compass heading to get them pointed in the right direction for their return journey to Allies Creek.

Time was of the essence, to place as much distance as humanly possible between them and the enemy, trapped, hopefully, within the caldera for long enough to ensure their escape. There was no time for inspections of persons for signs of injury or explanations and questions about the Hendersons' ordeal. Arlon urged them to action the moment he had his bearings.

He pushed them at an onerous pace when it seemed the bushfire started by Bill had escalated alarmingly. The wind had increased considerably during the previous hour and changed direction. The conflagration behind them turned the night into an eerie muted orange hue. In the path of the fire, Arlon suspected that they would probably not be able to outrun it. The direction of the wind also meant that Birrani and company would not have been trapped for long.

It roared and hissed behind them like a living, breathing entity, as the tired group picked up their pace. It lit the way through the dense, dry scrubland beckoning to become fuel for the coming fire.

Arlon's main concern was not the fire catching up with them, although that almost seemed a certainty. His greatest fear was the fire leapfrogging ahead, trapping them between two or more fronts. An Australian bushfire, fanned by strong enough winds, becomes hot enough to create weather patterns, causing firebombs and burning embers to leap many kilometres ahead of its front, igniting the forest in many directions.

Arlon had misjudged the tinder-dry conditions of the scrub when he thought about creating a fire to trap Birrani. The drought conditions ensured a plethora of fuel for a fire to rage through the entire area. The heat began to encroach upon the hapless group, and the smoke caused visibility to decrease to near zero. They would not be able to breathe soon, overrun by smoke, heat, and then the flames coming horrendously close.

He pushed them harder and harder, urging them onward despite any chance they might have of surviving the blaze. Talking became a near impossibility as the fire crept closer and closer, dogging their heels. Almost at the end of their capacity to run, choking on the toxic smoke filling the air, the fire suddenly twisted all about them. Arlon and his group found themselves in a swirling vortex of flames, with the wind pushing outwards from the epicentre containing them.

Normally, a fire would consume every last vestige of oxygen available, causing anything organic to die for lack of it. By some quirk of fate, the fire continued to course all around the beleaguered group in a firestorm of swirling flames and lightning from clouds generated by the fire. In the eye of the raging maelstrom, the group huddled together in mortal fear, believing their end had come. It seemed to last an eternity for the forlorn members of the miserable clan as they waited within a small circle of scrub that miraculously remained untouched by the inferno.

In reality, the storm lasted only moments, as the kilometre-thick front passed their position to continue on its destructive path. In the area about them, many animals were also finding refuge from the searing heat. A few koalas, wallabies and even a wombat found themselves sheltering together. Rats, lizards, snakes and many insects were also sharing the small oasis.

Arlon had heard about strange phenomena occurring during Australian bushfires, had seen news reports showing whole towns reduced to cinders, while one house remained untouched amid the sea of black. He had always assumed the one remaining house had survived for some explanatory reason, such as reliable fireproofing by the owners: filling the gutters with water, having a sprinkler system on the roof; dousing the walls with water before evacuating, that sort of thing. If he hadn't experienced it himself, he would very much have doubted the veracity of a report outlining their survival due to inexplicable circumstances.

Arlon quickly set about providing water for the parched animals or smothering anything that smouldered. Clarice and Bill assisted, while the Henderson couple huddled together in fear and confusion. It was a surreal experience for the trio tending to the injured or to hold a canteen to a koala's mouth for it to drink. The animals would normally have nothing to do with humans and would naturally fight off any contact.

Wallabies allowed them to pour a little water over scorched areas on their bodies, goannas accepted droplets of thirst-quenching water in their mouths. Gradually, as the horrendous noise abated and the fierce heat subsided, the animals began to fade away into the encroaching darkness, leaving the baffled group alone and weary. Arlon considered their survival to be nothing short of phenomenal. He would not have wagered twenty cents for their chances. Only one upside to the fire presented itself to Arlon; that it had erased all sign of their passing. There would be no tracks for Birrani to follow if he were doing so.

The downside was that any direction they went now would leave glaring signs in the blackened earth, clearly indicating which way they were heading. With Birrani's minions scouring the general direction towards Allies Creek, it was almost certain that their tracks would be discovered eventually if they were being followed.

They were all exhausted, incapable of moving onward. Arlon suggested that they rest for a few hours until the surrounding bush cooled sufficiently and they had recuperated.

"Mrs Henderson, are you all right? What happened?" asked Clarice, with compassion etched on her features.

"I, I suppose, I'm okay, considering. Thank you for coming."

"They wouldn't have come at all if I hadn't made them, honey," argued Travis.

"Funny, they seemed to keep coming even after you were captured, husband," replied Gloria pointedly.

"What's that supposed to mean?"

"Figure it out," she answered.

Travis took the affront as a good excuse to create a little distance between them.

"She's right, Mr Henderson. We could easily have gone back once you were taken, but we didn't. And it wasn't on your insistence that we decided to come, either. You owe your lives to Arlon. It was his ideas alone that made your rescue possible. I'm fed up with you taking that high road and talking such bullshit, mate."

"I don't think any of this is necessary, Clarice. I don't care about receiving thanks or apologies..."

"Too bloody right, you shouldn't! Your actions nearly cost us all our lives. What the fuck were you thinking when you started a fire in this bush?"

"Now, Mr Henderson, it was a good ploy. It just didn't work out exactly as we planned, that's all," added Bill.

"Fat lot of good that did us, sitting here in the middle of a fucking fire!" came Travis' retort.

"Well, technically, we are no longer in the middle of it. It has somehow missed us and moved ahead at great speed. I admit that, in hindsight, it may not have been the best option. I couldn't see any other way of ensuring we weren't followed immediately if we managed to get you two out of that cave," explained Arlon.

"Do you have any idea what he wanted, Mrs Henderson?" asked

Clarice.

"He?" enquired Gloria, looking confused.

"Birrani."

"What the devil are you talking about?" she asked, looking even more bewildered.

"It's the name of your abductor, Mrs Henderson, or so we assume," said Arlon.

"It has a name?"

"We believe he is a malformed and wild, part-Aboriginal born alone with only his mother to raise him until he was about five," stated Arlon.

"Did he harm you?" asked Clarice again.

"N-no... Not really."

"But you're all scratched and bruised, and you look like you're limping a little," suggested Clarice.

"Well, so would you be if you were carried roughly through this infernal scrub on the back of that...thing," Travis spat.

"So, if he didn't hurt you, and he didn't eat you, what did he want?"

"Who can say?" said Gloria without conviction.

Arlon watched the interchange closely. He took special note of Gloria's reticence to answer the questions fully, holding back something and seemingly untouched by her experience. Gloria eyed him suspiciously as he nodded at her slightly, as though they were sharing a secret.

"Come on, Gloria, you have to know something about its intentions," urged Travis.

"Oh? Did you manage to ask him anything while you were there, Travis?"

"I was bloody unconscious most of the time and it didn't seem to be in a talkative mood when I came to," said Travis gruffly. The sheila has a point, though. You don't look too bad for someone who was kidnapped by a wild animal. Exactly what happened during the time you were alone with it?"

"I was kept in the cave the same way we both were after you showed up over his shoulder and were dumped at my feet. What do you think was happening, dancing?" she asked irritably.

"And just who are you calling 'sheila'?" Clarice demanded.

"Oh, don't you start with all that feminist crap."

"If you all keep this up we'll be discovered in no time flat," ventured Arlon. "I think you should get some rest before we have to get moving again. We've got a lot of kilometres between us and Allies Creek, and I don't plan on waiting around here too long. I'm going to sit down over there, have a bite to eat and a drink of water. I have a little jerky if anyone wants some?"

"Where the heck did you manage to get some jerky, Arlon? Don't tell me you had some with you as supplies for Allies Creek?"

"No, I didn't bring any with me, no."

"You took some from the cave. It was hanging there on drying racks near the fire. I remember," accused Gloria.

"What?" the others said at once.

"I managed to take a few pieces, so what?"

"After what we know? Arlon, no!"

"What are you talking about? Know what?" asked Gloria.

"Humans. He kills and eats bloody human beings. He's a bloody cannibal, and Arlon is thinking of eating it as well," said Clarice, feeling nauseous.

"I think you're all allowing your overactive imaginations to get the better of you. Anyone could see by the bones at the side of the fire that the meat was a wallaby."

"Well, some of us weren't in the cave, Arlon, so we didn't have the benefit of that observation," said Clarice.

"Which is why I can't understand your indignation, Ms Manning. I wouldn't be tempted to consume human flesh, nor would I offer it to others. If you don't trust my judgement on the source of the jerky, then go hungry, by all means. I, for one, intend to recharge my batteries for the long trek ahead," stated Arlon, as he went to sit a short distance from the rest.

"I'll have a little of that, Arlon, if you don't mind?"

"Not at all, Mr Rogers. It's very tasty, actually," said Arlon, as he handed Bill a few strips of the delicious meat.

Gradually, one by one, they each came to Arlon, sheepishly accepting a few pieces of jerky to satisfy their hunger. Gloria sauntered over last to sit by him. After accepting a piece of meat, which she chewed gratefully and hungrily, she became still.

"You, you... know... don't you?" she asked quietly.

Arlon nodded, unsure of his ability not to put his foot firmly into his mouth.

"How?"

Arlon weighed his words carefully. "I guessed. It seemed to be the only viable explanation."

"Will you tell anyone...?"

"Anyone?"

"My husband?"

"Not up to me."

"Would you? If you were me, I mean?" she asked, near to tears.

"You're asking the wrong person, Mrs Henderson. I can't begin to know how you're feeling or what your husband might feel if he knew. He may surprise you by working it out himself. How would you feel if that happened, knowing you could have told him beforehand?"

"Not, not good," she admitted after a short pause.

"What are you going to do?"

"I don't know."

"What if...?"

"That frightens the hell out of me, too. I don't know. Do you think it's possible?"

"Slim chance, I reckon, but always possible."

"I'd be so, so..." Gloria was unable to finish, feeling ashamed, confused and terrified. She began to tremble, crying softly. "Could you hold me for a moment?"

"I think you should ask your husband to do that, Mrs

Henderson. I am the very last person in the world someone should turn to for sympathy and comfort."

"Sometimes, it's not about having to say anything at all. Simply placing an arm around someone's shoulders can impart more comfort and kindness than all the useless platitudes we hear," said Gloria sadly.

Arlon nodded his understanding. Awkwardly, he placed an arm around her heaving shoulders, as she tucked her head against his chest. It was the first time in Arlon's life he had ever ventured such a strange action, that meant nothing at all to him. It was a pointless gesture on his part, yet Gloria seemed comforted by it. She allowed her tears to flow quietly while Arlon held her. Only Clarice appeared to notice the interaction, with a look of warm approval.

NINETEEN

"Don't think I don't know what's going on here," Travis whispered to Arlon as they resumed their trek over the charred, desolate landscape.

"You mean you know we're headed back to Allies Creek? That's very astute of you, Mr Henderson. Was someone trying to conceal that fact from you?" Arlon asked mordantly.

"I saw you with my wife back there, smartarse. Pretty dumb, trying to take advantage of a vulnerable person right in front of her husband."

"It never ceases to amaze me the heights of stupidity able to be reached by humans," said Arlon, shaking his head.

"Don't try to deny it, arsehole; I saw ya."

"You saw me offering comfort to a woman who has been through a tragic ordeal and the only explanation you can conjure up is an attempt by me to take sexual advantage of her? How many times do I have to explain to you lot that I have no bloody emotions? None! That means I do not have affections, I do not feel anything for another human. Just like the contempt I should be feeling for you right now is absent. It would do me no good at all to try to curry favour from a female. I am, to all intents and purposes, impotent because of my condition, Mr Henderson. Can I possibly be any clearer than that?"

"So you say," replied Travis gruffly.

"How many men do you know that would lie about something like that? Would you? I very much doubt it. You're judging me based on your immoral compass. That's a grave error."

"Is that a threat? You may still have hold of that rifle..."

"Would you like me to lay it aside so that we can have another round?"

"You know them fancy karate moves and think you're some kinda Bruce Lee, huh? Well, you'd better watch your back, mate.

You can't always be on guard."

"So, not man enough to face me? You'd rather attack me while my back is turned? I'm sure that will impress the missus."

"My wife and I are very happy, thank you very much."

"I hope you remember that in the days to come if by some miracle we survive this ordeal."

"Why?"

"Because you two will need every little bit of love and understanding you have together if you hope to stay that way."

"What the fuck are you on about, Livingston?" asked Travis, growing impatient and more than a little riled. "Did my wife say something to you? Something I should know?"

"Technically, no. Your wife revealed nothing at all. If you want to know what's on her mind, you'll have to ask her."

"You're not some priest, Livingston. It's not like you're held by some rules of the confessional or anything."

"Doesn't mean I'll go around discussing what people say to me."

"She's my bloody wife, Livingston!" argued Travis heatedly.

"And around we go again. Correct, she is your wife, not your chattel, and, again, you should ask her about our conversation, not me. If your relationship is all you say it is, then she'll tell you what you want to know. Now, I'm bored with this unending interrogation and your aggression. Either make your move, if you have the balls or leave me the fuck alone. We have a long way to go yet and we aren't safe out here. If you keep nattering on like a jealous fool in my ear, I won't be alert for any danger creeping up on us. It'll be light in a few hours; we need to be well away from here by then."

SCREEEEEYAHHHHH, SCREEEEYAHHHHH.

The loud screeching was all that could be heard over the deathly silence of the ruined forest about them. Arlon judged the sound to come from a great distance, but could not be certain of that. Night air carried sound a greater distance than normal, yet the surrounding landscape, devastated by the inferno, could have an altering effect on acoustics. Arlon called a halt to their advance and made sure everyone knew to remain as quiet as possible.

"Has he found us?" whispered Clarice.

"Hard to be certain. If I had to guess, I would say it was a call to arms; alerting the animal kingdom to be on the lookout for a bunch of humans in their midst."

"What do we do?"

"I think we have enough of a lead to beat them to Allies Creek if we motor on. Unfortunately, I don't think we have enough juice left in the tank. You look about done in and so does Mrs Henderson. Bill and I aren't that far behind you. Travis, how are you holding up, fitness-wise?"

"Why?" he asked, with more than a hint of suspicion.

"This is going to sound nuts, and might be extremely dangerous for you if you agree to the plan."

"Treading on thin ice with me already, Livingston," Travis warned.

"Travis, would you just for once shut up and listen to the man who is responsible for saving our lives?" objected Gloria impatiently.

"Gloria!"

"Well, it's true. I admit that Arlon Grey is possibly the hardest man on earth to like, but so far he's been calling the shots and managed to rescue us despite all the odds. I would think he has earned our deepest respect and appreciation for that, wouldn't you? Or would you rather we were still being held captive by that thing? I'm sick of your constant negativity and ill manners.

"Becoming rich is perhaps the worst thing that could have happened to us. We seem to have lost all our old values and common sense along the way. This decent, kind man and his associates have gone out of their way, far and above any sense of duty, to traipse all over this hostile terrain searching for me. I, for one, will be giving them all that they ask of me in return for that, whatever the cost. I expect you to do the same, or you can find yourself another wife if we ever get out of here alive."

"That's not fair, Gloria..."

"Don't you give me that, Travis John Henderson! I know all about your little trysts with Molly and the previous two secretaries. Why do you think I was looking afield myself? I adored you once, thought the sun shone out of your arse. Until you started screwing anything with a skirt once the money started rolling in. Thought you were God's gift to the female race, didn't you? Well, this young lady had me pegged right from the moment she set eyes on me, and I can see now what I was reduced to by your antics.

"I became a snob and a slut. I did try to get it on with Arlon when I arrived in Allies Creek. I tried my best, because of that 'business meeting' you were attending in Brisbane. My arse! You were screwing your bimbo before you deigned to join me in that shithole of a town. He rejected me, though, even told me I was not all that good looking. And he's right. I look like a freak after all the bloody surgeries. All that pain and suffering I went through just to get you to notice me, to make me number one again in your eyes.

"And what did it get me? Another freak wanting me. That's what I was talking to Arlon about. He knew. But my dear and loving husband didn't have a clue. I was raped by that thing, Travis. Thrown on the ground, stripped naked and brutally raped! I can only imagine how you will take that news. I can see it in your eyes already. The horror, the disgust, the..."

Gloria couldn't continue. As she wept, Clarice went to her and wrapped Gloria in her arms. Travis merely gaped, appalled. Bill gave the man a baleful glare, while Arlon stood by uncertainly, wondering how he should be acting, not having a clue.

Through the silence of the night, and the pregnant pause in the conversation came a whispered sound upon the air: a kind of irregular whooshing sound that went over their heads like the lopsided wings of a large bat flapping. Too late, Arlon thought he knew what it might be. With a resounding thud, it struck Travis squarely in the back of the head. The sickening sound made them all believe his neck had been broken, if not partially severed when they saw the blood. They watched in amazement as the heavy boomerang clattered noisily to the stony ground several metres away, with Travis collapsing from the near fatal blow.

Arlon warned them all not to move or make a sound. He knew their lives all hung precariously in the balance, depending on their reactions. From the darkness surrounding them came the indistinct sounds of animal hooves clip-clopping lightly over the rocky ground: a surreal and sepulchral movement outside the reach of their pathetic torch beam, a seemingly macabre death march by their pursuers.

"Ho, Birrani Nullah Bone," announced Arlon, using the greeting most often used by Birrani's great-grandfather, according to Kami.

The enormous shape emerging from the periphery of the torch beam stopped suddenly upon hearing the people's language, and the familiar greeting from the detestable white man's lips. Arlon peered at the hairy hulk with an openness of expression that left no doubt in anyone's mind that he was unafraid.

Birrani made a mock charge with a spear raised in one of his mighty paws directly at Arlon, who stood his ground firmly. The tip of the spear made from a sharpened shovel head, stopped short of Arlon's left eye by a mere centimetre. Unblinking, Arlon stared at the massive face with its grotesque abnormalities making it a fearsome beast in any circumstances, recoiling inside from the foul, fetid breath emanating from the cavernous mouth. Arlon watched as doubt crept into the eyes of his would-be assailant/murderer.

Birrani backed off a step, indecision playing on his mind, staying his hand. Arlon could almost see the play of questions and assumptions crossing the brute's mind as he weighed up the pros and cons of simply killing him and the others outright. Arlon correctly assumed the only reason he had not become a victim immediately was his use of the greeting. It was time to play his next card in the deadly game.

"You have been wronged by the white man from before you

were born, Birrani Nullah Bone, and you have no reason to trust me. Your grandfather, Kami, has told me of your struggles and the injustices perpetrated by your father and others on first, your mother, then you and your great-grandfather, whom we must now call Kumanjayi. I am very sorry for all that has occurred to you and your people.

"The government has also apologised for the way its predecessors treated your people, Birrani. It is no longer the same as it was. Although it is not perfect, it is better. Thanks to Eddie Mabo, the people now have rights and ownership of sacred sites around Australia. There is a large movement out there to secure better conditions, compensation and rights for your race. You do not know this, of course, because no news reaches your ears, and Kami will not tell you of anything good from the white man. He has been poisoned with hatred for them as you have been.

"Kami's daughter, your mother, was taken from him and his wife while she was still young and impressionable, raised in a strict Catholic mission by zealous priests and nuns, part of the stolen generation. He never forgave the white man for that transgression, even when the white man apologised. It is understandable but not necessarily beneficial.

"Hate is a powerful emotion leading only to more hatred. I do not hate. I do not love, I do not fear, I do not feel anything at all. In all honesty, I do not care about anyone or anything on an emotional level. I, too, have been deformed by nature as you were. I am seen and known as a freak by everyone who meets me. For that reason alone, you should not fear or mistrust me. I have nothing to gain by misleading you, and I have nothing to lose by standing my ground.

"You see the stick I carry? It is called a 'gun', a 'rifle', to use the white man's words. You have no name for this in your language. It shoots a projectile from the barrel that reaches a great distance. It can deliver death from afar. All the white men in authority have these, which they can use to shoot down criminals. Your primitive weapons are no match for the white man's modern weapons.

"The white man also has many means of transport to find criminals, including a machine that flies in the air, giving him a bird's eye view from high above. I say all this because, if you kill us, many white men will follow. They have sophisticated methods of tracking and locating their quarry. The death of many white persons by you will not go unnoticed and will incur the wrath of the police and the public when they come to understand what has happened here. They will carry the weapons I have spoken about and much, much more. They have glasses which will let them see in the night without these light makers I carry, called torches.

"They will not hunt all Aborigines for the transgressions of one or a few, though, as you have been led to believe. They will hunt only the culprits guilty of crimes, and they will most likely kill you without you ever having seen them. Taking the woman was a bad crime. You would be locked up in a very small room with no way out for the rest of your life if they catch you. She is not your woman, she is this man's woman, and you have also hurt him badly. Your crimes are many, Birrani, and the white man will never stop looking for you when they find out.

"I urge you to believe what I am saying and allow us to go back home in peace. If you do this, it will allow you to leave this area for good, to go far, far away, where nobody will ever find you. You can cover your tracks, you will have a good head start. You may succeed in eluding the authorities, whereas, if you kill us and stay here, you will die or be locked up.

"The pigs? They will all be slaughtered. Yes, I see you care about that. They are your family, you are their leader. You won that right to lead by conquering the old boar. They will all die if you persist with this agenda."

Birrani held his massive hand to his chest, then pointed at Gloria.

"No, Birrani, she is not yours, by claim or otherwise. She belongs to the man on the ground. They are husband and wife. Besides, she is no use to you."

Birrani screwed his face up in a question.

"What are you saying, Arlon? What's happening?" begged Gloria, having seen the beast pointing at her.

"I thought I warned you all to shut the fuck up," Arlon whispered urgently. Seeing Birrani reacting to his whispered instructions, he said aloud, "I told him you were too old to be of any use."

"How dare you say such a horrible thing?" Gloria exclaimed.

"Good grief, you really are quite dense, aren't you? Do you want this person to take you? To bear his children?" Arlon asked.

"What?"

"That's why he took you. He realises he will not live much longer and wants a son to continue the name of Bone. I was about to explain a woman's use-by-date, their...time of life, past the point of bearing children."

"Oh."

"Yes, 'oh'. You may well have eliminated the possibility of explaining that to him with your outburst. Birrani, this woman can no longer bear children, she is too old," continued Arlon in Aboriginal.

SCREEEEEYAHHHHH, SCREEEEYAHHHHH.

Birrani stormed and screeched around them in anger and frustration, not knowing whether to trust the white man's words, not wanting to make a mistake and ending up with a barren woman. He wanted a child of his own, one to love, nurture, train and raise, as a child should be. He wanted everything for his child that he missed, that he had in the beginning with his precious mother. He had decided long ago to capture a woman for that purpose.

The other one, the one that lived alone in the house in the empty town, had fought him tooth and nail, making it impossible for him to take her without damaging her to the point where she was unable to bear a child. He had to kill and eat her in the end. She was just too troublesome. If what the white man told him in the language of his people was true, then the new one would be unacceptable as a mate.

Birrani had learned the way of sex and babies from observing the pigs. Neither his great-grandfather nor grandfather had said anything on the matter, given him no instructions. He had never been with a female other than his mother.

He'd had no choice but to choose one of the detestable white persons. In truth, he was half white himself, so it wasn't quite as shameful as he had first thought. He didn't think it would start the war his great-grandfather spoke of. He had no idea the white man thought anything of their women, that they would miss them. His father gave him that notion when he abandoned his mother after beating her half to death.

He returned to the group, cowering together. Only the one who spoke showed no signs of any fear, which disturbed Birrani. He wasn't sure what to make of the queer-looking white man in the strange clothes and silly hat, carrying a stick he thought was capable of killing a man. Birrani had heard the bang-stick one time when the man on the ground used it. While he was very surprised that a stick could make such a loud noise, he thought nothing more of it, even though one of his family members rolled over for no apparent reason afterwards.

Birrani approached the group warily, inching closer. He then pointed toward Clarice after pointing to his chest in the same manner he had declared Gloria to be his woman.

"NO!" shouted Arlon, pointing to his chest. Then he realised he had spoken in English. "She is my woman," he repeated in the language Birrani would understand.

Birrani thumped his chest demonstratively, demanding to be obeyed. He would have the younger woman. He would not be swayed in his quest to father a child. They could keep the ugly old one if she was no good for him. He would take the nicer one and give her his seed. It didn't matter to him if she liked it or not. As Birrani was about to grab Clarice, Arlon fired into the air with the old carbine, startling him out of his intentions. Birrani then watched with amusement as the tiny white man laid aside the bang-stick and haversack.

"Birrani Nullah Bone, I challenge you for the right to take the woman," declared Arlon, placing his helmet, jacket and fly net with the weapon.

"Arlon! What are you doing? You can't possibly be thinking of fighting this moving mountain?" cried Clarice, not understanding the language but recognising the intent behind the words and actions.

"I told him you were my woman after he said he wanted to take you instead of Mrs Henderson. It's the only way of resolving this. A one-on-one, winner-take-all contest, as he did with the old boar."

Clarice wondered if she had heard right. She felt more than a little chuffed that the man of her dreams was about to wage battle on her behalf. What she wasn't too thrilled about was that her man was taking on a beast of mythical proportions and inordinate strength. While she did not for one moment entertain the idea of becoming a broodmare for the ugly monstrosity, she feared greatly for Arlon's life and did not wish him to come to harm on her account.

Arlon had carefully removed his jacket, shirt and boots, placing them on top of the growing pile by his side. He had handed his torch to Bill. It was a strange and surreal scene as the wild pigs stayed just out of range of the torch beams, yet were making their presence known by squealing and grunting. The two combatants could not have been more physically opposed as they circled one another warily.

Clarice marvelled at Arlon's rangy physique, his muscles bristling with kinetic energy, thrilling her to the marrow. He was a magnificent specimen of manhood. It was the first time she had seen him without a shirt on, the first time she had glimpsed the power and utter fearlessness in her boss. She surmised that it would be his ultimate undoing. Viewing the thing that was Birrani Nullah Bone left her shivering with fear and revulsion. No matter how hard his life supposedly had been, how much he had unjustly suffered, she could not bring herself to feel anything but revulsion.

The wild man, blending in with the background with his dark, hairy complexion, seemed to disappear at times, making Clarice imagine all sorts of supernatural elements occurring. She could not condone Arlon's actions, well-intended, heroic and selfless or not.

"Stop!" she shouted. "No," she said, placing herself between the combatants. "Enough of this. Enough bloodshed, enough hatred, enough, enough, enough!" She walked brazenly up to Birrani, stretching up on her tiptoes to slap him hard across the face. "Translate for me, Arlon," she insisted. "You should be ashamed of yourself, Birrani Nullah Bone! You think you were hard done by as a child and then a man? Big deal! No one has an easy life.

"Your mother would be ashamed of her son at the moment. Did she bring you up to do this, to make war against everyone, especially the white man? No. She wanted you to avenge her. She wanted to see justice done to the man who beat her and caused your injuries. That has been done. The rest, that is an abomination, do you hear me? It has to end, here and now. If you do not stop this bloodshed I will pick up that gun and shoot you full of holes myself.

"You simply cannot do as you please anymore. There will be grave repercussions for everything that has transpired here. You will not only lose your life, but the pigs and possibly your family could also die for aiding and abetting you over the years. This will undo a lot of years of struggle by your people to improve their standing in this country. Yes, we had a shameful past and your people were treated abominably by the white folk. That doesn't make what you have done right, nor will it help your people's cause.

"You cannot take a woman and attempt to impregnate her with your foul seed. The way you have acted, bringing great shame and danger to your people, means you do not deserve to be able to reproduce. We do not need more hatred in this country. We need love and understanding, cooperation and friendship.

"Take this opportunity to do the right thing for once in your life. Go, find yourself another home, away from all this hatred and hurt. Live out the rest of your life in peace and contemplation of your end.

If you meet your mother in the spirit world, you need to be sure you will be welcomed. At present, I would not want my son joining me if he behaved like you. What you are doing is wrong on many levels. Eating people is an abomination of the highest order, a crime against my people and yours, against the laws of heaven and earth."

Birrani reared back when he heard Arlon repeating that eating his enemy was against the laws of 'hum Jesus-pella'. He had often heard his mother speaking to him of the white man's god and the son that died for them all on a cross-stick. She had instilled in him the tenets of her white man's religion bestowed upon her by the missionaries who had taken her in as a young girl. That eating his enemy was a way for him to suffer the torments of hellfire for eternity came as a shock to him.

Didn't his great-grandfather tell him it was the unwritten code of his people to do so? If everything else he told him was true, then why had he lied about something as significant as eating what you kill, man or otherwise? Then there was the stuff about his mother not wanting him to join her if she knew what he had done.

That frightened him most of all. Every day he had thought about joining her at the end of his life. Often, he thought about making that end come sooner. Every hour of every day was a painful reminder that he lived and his mother had been taken from him before her time. The overwhelming sensation of shame and guilt, of religious condemnation, caused by the woman's words, retold by the strange little white man who spoke in the people's language, crushed Birrani with its intensity.

Confusion and remorse gripped him fiercely, causing his heart to palpate, attempting to rob him of breath and strength. He seemed to implode as the grief he felt over being unable to join his mother in the afterlife crippled him from the outside in. The loud, anguished cry which escaped his mouth had a more human quality than anything prior. It was a plaintive, pitiful sound full of torment and suffering.

Clarice could not believe her words had caused such utter

hopelessness in someone, especially the great lump before her, who crumpled to the ground in a heap. She began to feel a little uncertain about her involvement, as compassion and pity crept into her. Clarice had hoped to garner a speck of contrition within the beast but did not expect anything on the scale she witnessed. The mighty leviathan wailed in a heart-rending display of sheer despair at her feet.

Clarice supposed that there came a time in everyone's lives when they must take stock of themselves, a time to reflect on the deeds of the past and take responsibility for mistakes made. She tried to sort through all the information Arlon had given them to identify the source of Birrani's great lamentation. She could not quite convince herself that she alone had brought about such misery: a catalyst, perhaps, but not the sole cause.

A lifetime of stored beliefs and indoctrination had profound effects on a recipient. Birrani's advanced age meant that he had little to no interaction with any humans other than his older family members, which made him stubborn and recalcitrant, singularly focused. Interaction with peers and even opposing opinions often led to introspection, sorting through all the life lessons to arrive at conclusions based on many accounts, not just the biased few. She concluded that Birrani had never been told that he might be evil for doing as he was instructed, that he would end up in hell, according to his mother's beliefs.

As his racking sobs slowly subsided and he quieted, Clarice moved toward him, offering him a hand up. Her natural tendency to forgive and love all her fellow humans allowed her to ignore the gross abnormalities, to seek the truth of the person within. As was her custom, she could hold no grudge nor resentment for someone so hardly done by. Birrani's life had been one of extreme hardship, prejudice and hatred so intense it condemned all positive emotions to a dungeon deep within his mind.

Try as she might, she could not budge him from the ground when his huge paw was placed in her petite palm. Seeing her difficulty, the others quickly assisted, until Birrani was standing once more. Like a chastened dog with its tail between its legs, Birrani shuffled off into the darkness without looking back. He had been beaten neck and crop, shamed and vilified, accused of evil acts that would send him to the bushfire place. He was feeling every one of his eighty-odd years.

When everything had turned silent, and the circling pigs had merged into the night to follow their leader, a burst of raucous laughter from two adult kookaburras in the treetops heralded the first signs of the approaching dawn. As they waited for Travis to show signs of recovery, they watched as the morning sky lightened on the horizon, giving off a pinkish glow with the ascending sun.

All about them, the forest was a blackened wasteland, revealed by the encroaching daylight, with the smoking corpses of many animals adding to the pungent miasma. A distant rumble reminded them all of the healing powers of nature. One decent rainfall and the landscape would be magically transformed to a healthy green once more as new life took hold from the charred earth and nourishing ashes. The cycle of life would continue its constant mutability of death and regrowth, as it should when left to its own devices. Nothing healed nature quite as well as nature itself.

Fire is often viewed as an occasion of great fear and sadness when it should be seen as a necessity for the future welfare of the Australian bush. Of course, this philosophy does not hold water for civilised folk living in towns and cities that are easily destroyed by fire. A nomadic tribe like the Aborigines understand and appreciate the fire and use it to cleanse the earth, simply moving on to 'greener' pastures while their former settlement is rejuvenated. Their wandering trails will eventually lead them back to the same place, to begin the cycle once more.

Blackened, exhausted, emotionally and physically, the little group moved on once Travis had recuperated enough to walk, albeit with a very sore neck and a headache that seemed to overtake all his thoughts. After the emotional highs they had all experienced, and the adrenaline rush, they lapsed into an anticlimactic low, each one lost in his or her thoughts. The barren landscape added nothing to brighten the dreariness they felt.

Gloria had not spoken a word to her husband, knowing how he must feel about her. She was not altogether unhappy with the result. She had known for some time that their marriage was nothing but a sham. She had done everything in her power to accommodate his urges and preferences: bigger boobs; tighter...everything; make-up classes; exercising at the gym and her home equipment for endless dreary hours; reading everything on marital tricks and employing all manner of aids, toys, films. All to no avail; he still screwed everything with a skirt; all the mindless bimbos falling for his wallet in the hope of bilking her out of her share of the spoils.

She had descended to his level on more than a few occasions to elicit a jealous response, only to find he enjoyed the idea of her having an affair. He even suggested a threesome or foursome, believing his wife had accepted the status quo. Nothing could have been further from the truth. Gloria felt disgusted with herself and the men she bedded. She no longer had any ideas as to how she might dissuade her husband from his philandering.

What came as a surprise and a bit of a shock to her was the callousness he had developed. She knew that they had both become somewhat snobbish of late, parading their wealth around like a tool with which to bludgeon anyone less fortunate but she had not realised just how offensive he had become. He displayed complete indifference and even resentment toward her, not affording her a modicum of respect in their conversations or dealings. She had long ago accepted her banishment from all business dealings with him, whereas they used to share opinions and bounce ideas off one another.

Gloria could not remember the last time she had access to a bank where she could check on their balances or seek advice from a bank manager regarding a personal investment or business idea. He gave her a credit card with a fifteen-thousand-dollar limit, topping it up every month so she was never short of funds but that was the extent of it. She was no longer consulted on business ideas and ventures, such as his ridiculous plan for Allies Creek.

It was far too isolated from modern townships and infrastructure to entice the well-to-do crowd from the cities in her opinion. Unless it contained twenty-four-hour brothels and gambling, there was nothing at all attractive about the desolate little town. It might entice the odd nature-lover or seclusion-seeker hoping for a quiet sabbatical but that was it. As far as weddings or business conferences were concerned, she couldn't see it being successful.

Gloria had contemplated making a complete split from her husband a year or more ago. Her last-ditch effort to rekindle their relationship by agreeing to spend some time with him at Allies Creek had ended in a disaster beyond her imaginings. Feeling abandoned and isolated by him had left her bereft and seething. The last straw for her was the look of revulsion on his face when she admitted to being raped. She could not reconcile with him after that final act of abandonment and look of disgust.

She would have to find a decent lawyer the moment they returned to Brisbane. She could not trust the business lawyer they normally retained for all their dealings. If he was still on the payroll. She no longer knew or cared. She would have to find herself a top-rate lawyer and take the pig to the cleaners. She would cite every misdeed she was aware of, starting with infidelity. The list was long.

She knew he had several offshore bank accounts to avoid taxes wherever possible. If it came down to his denying their existence to escape paying her half, she would inform the Australian Tax Office of his nefarious activities. She might lose a lot as a result, perhaps all, she didn't care. As long as he didn't get to keep the lion's share. If he played fair, so would she. Otherwise, the gloves were off and she would prove the adage that there was nothing worse than a woman scorned. She blew out her chest in a stance of defiance and self-worth as she walked.

Travis had remained silent since recovering. His mind was a seething turmoil of emotions and embarrassment. He had been bested by the wimp, Livingston, and abducted and abused by the animal that had also raped his wife. He had been shown up and demoralised at every turn by the peasants around him, including his wife, who had made some worrying comments about their relationship. The last thing he and their various businesses needed right now was a messy divorce, revealing how cash-strapped they were.

In truth, Travis had been squandering away their amassed fortune on frivolous, high-risk ventures at a time when the markets were unfavourable. He had taken a huge hit by plunging a vast amount of his accumulated profits on the stock market, even going into debt to raise the amount he could invest. He was not to know that the tech company in which he invested had been under investigation for industrial espionage. Only the inner circle of company directors were aware of the investigations, hoping to have them sorted before the next AGM.

Travis had been convinced to make a takeover bid for the company by his business brokers and lawyers. The tech company's directors jumped at the chance to offload their shares and the company to avoid the ongoing investigation. They accepted the first offer, which should have had the alarm bells ringing loudly for Travis and his advisers. It didn't, and, consequently, the company went into receivership only months after the takeover, when investigators pronounced many of their patents to be questionable and suspended all trading until the matter was settled.

Travis had been left with a mad scramble to make reparations. Panicking, he latched onto the prospect of purchasing an entire town for a pittance compared to what he believed it to be worth. He immediately saw the potential in the town. The low purchase price, after it had initially hit the market for an exorbitant amount, induced Travis to speculate with borrowed funds. He fully intended to do nothing more with the town than gain the requisite permits from local councils, then offload the place for a sizeable profit once the approvals and a few basic renovations were achieved.

With Gloria potentially making waves for him in a divorce court, the extent of their ruined finances would become public knowledge. The sharks would then go into a feeding frenzy. His companies would go into liquidation and everything would be snapped up at cents on the dollar. Travis knew the shit would hit the fan well before any divorce talk, at any rate. Gloria's credit card was maxed out and Travis was unable to pay it down to zero again for the foreseeable future.

Travis had been living on a tightrope of emotions lately, knowing his house of cards could come tumbling down about his ears in the blink of an eye. His nerves had been stretched and frayed beyond endurance for the previous year. Once the news of Allies Creek became known, his plans would be undone. No one would want any part of the town after what had occurred. What no one knew was that he had already purchased the property, lock, stock and barrel. Walk-in-walk-out was the deal he had negotiated with the owner.

He had kept up the pretence of an inspection and all the other lies to keep Gloria busy enough to take away her curiosity about their finances, something she had brought up on several occasions over the past year. He had used another solicitor to oversee the deal as his usual lawyer had warned him off the purchase, threatening to inform Gloria of the risks involved.

When Gloria had been abducted, he had almost sighed with relief, knowing her death could alleviate much of the tension he felt. Unbeknownst to Gloria, Travis had acquired a five-million-dollar insurance policy on her. He then had to play the part of the aggrieved husband to maintain the illusion of a firm relationship between the two. Not that the peasants deserved anything or required proof. He did not count on that bloody fool, Livingston, being up to the task of leading them to find her. Once it became obvious that the meddlesome idiot might pull it off, he had to take measures to ensure their failure to locate his wife. All his inept attempts at sabotage, including taking a pot-shot into the dark, had failed miserably.

Nothing could dissuade this bunch of goody-two-shoes from abandoning their quest, no matter how unlikeable he made himself. When he regained consciousness to find her unharmed in that cave, it was all he could do not to strangle her there and then. Just when he thought it was what he might have to do, along came the idiot again to spoil his plans by rescuing them both. Travis could not remember ever hating a fellow more than when he saw Arlon sidling along the cave wall. If Travis hadn't been more afraid of what the animal would do to him, he might have been tempted to foul up the intended rescue.

He had been mulling over all the possible options in his mind when Gloria admonished him openly for the first time in their marriage, laying out their dirty laundry for all and sundry to view. Then her dreadful admission had left him stunned, incapable of normal thought. She guessed right that he was revolted, more disgusted and repulsed than he had could ever recall. Unfortunately, that display would cause his ultimate downfall very shortly. She would demand a divorce. Once the extent of their financial downfall was discovered, it would immediately be made public by the media. He ruminated on how he might bring about her 'accidental' death.

Arlon trudged over the crisp black landscape, still quite warm from the passing fires, marvelling at the perspicacity shown by his secretary in dealing with a very delicate situation. Had he the ability to feel anything, he assured himself that pride would be first and foremost among those feelings. Not only had she prevented a battle between them, a contest that he would undoubtedly have lost, but she had managed to turn the tables on Birrani completely. It was a feat that Arlon could never emulate because of the emotional sagacity it required.

His condition! It seemed that his whole life revolved around his condition, determining his future. Almost all of human interaction centred on emotions, without which it was near impossible to advance in either business or social status. Arlon had to struggle through life, battling everyone unable to understand or accept his freakish disposition.

Beginning with his parents, life for Arlon became a fight for his very existence from the age of four onwards. The diagnosis of his mild autism a few years later, though immensely relieving for the Greys, who had thought initially that they were doing something wrong, did little to alleviate the emotionally-charged battlegrounds he faced every day in the schoolyards. The other children just could not cope with nor understand his condition.

During his younger years, despite scrupulous instructions delivered by his parents, Arlon managed to say the wrong thing every time he was faced with the emotions of his peers or teachers. His lack of empathy, remorse, sympathy or any other human feeling left him tactless at best and habitually infuriating. Mostly, to avoid confrontation, Arlon became reclusive, throwing himself into such activities as his martial arts.

The training and discipline had a twofold benefit. He had something into which he could pour his energies while learning to defend himself in the inevitable conflicts. He mastered all disciplines with astonishing speed and agility and meditated for hours to seek a sense of peace within himself, one that he could not find in the life around him.

He changed schools often when it became apparent to his parents that fighting, for their son, was his only means of survival against cruel and harsh children. That he mostly won these conflicts only strengthened other parents' resolve to see him suspended for fighting. Arlon's patience would run thin, often making him strike before the first blow was delivered by an opponent, making him the bully in everyone's eyes.

The more he was ostracised the more he concentrated on his training, increasing his skills, strengthening his inner and outer core. He became a very powerful young man able to end any contest, against opponents far larger than he.

His parents also were a great disappointment to Arlon. They were fixated on love. They required that act of love from him as vindication, as a reward for their efforts as parents. They were unable to accept that their only son was incapable of love, preferring to believe he simply did not love *them*. Which, of course, was utterly ridiculous. Arlon was unable to love or even care for another living soul. He could not even communicate with his parents on the matter, as they were too heavily invested in the emotional aspects of child-rearing to truly understand his condition.

Though his parents never faltered in his educational requirements or his other essentials like clothes, good food and so on, they did not provide Arlon with unconditional support. It was not within them to give love when it was not reciprocated. Arlon, naturally, did not require their love on an emotional level, only where that love offered the support and understanding his condition required. Had they simply accepted him for who he was and what he could give, they might have found life with their son easier and perhaps even pleasant.

Instead, it was a constant source of pain for them to be ignored by their son when they offered a hug or a kiss. It became a sort of contest for them to finally crack the shell in which they firmly believed he was hiding. The reward for unlocking the emotional dam would be a final, all-encompassing outpouring of love from their son. They paid no attention to the medical fraternity, begging them to accept their son's condition as permanent and intractable.

Although Arlon felt nothing like loneliness or sadness at being shunned by society in general, it did reduce his ability to communicate effectively. Without a firm hand guiding him through the process of dealing with his condition, leaving it mostly up to him to persevere, it took many long years for him to develop coping mechanisms without the need for constant conflict. Generally, that meant fabrications; saying things that were not entirely true to keep the peace. Unfortunately, being emotionless made it extremely difficult for Arlon to lie effectively. Until he mastered that artificiality, he continued to attract the wrong kind of attention.

His tallish physique and strength enabled him to pass the physicals easily for his entrance to the police academy. His keen intelligence saw him sailing through the twenty-five-week initial course at Oxley in Brisbane, before being inducted into the first-year constable program, which took a further twelve months.

Arlon was required to continue as a constable for two more years before being encouraged to enter plain clothes training as a detective. It would take a further three years before he could request the detective title and the accompanying gold badge. While his solve rate was second to none, his inability to engage with the public caused great concern to his colleagues and superiors, eventually landing him in the shit when he inappropriately delivered the truth to the parents of a child in a particularly brutal rape case.

He could not recall the last time he had visited his parents, never knowing if he was welcome to do so. They had made it clear to him, at least in his mind, that his presence was tolerated at best. He never failed to bring out their anxieties and insecurities while he was there, as if it was all somehow his fault and his plan to be as obstreperous as possible.

Arlon supposed that others might have it worse, so he did not lose any sleep over it. His parents' shortcomings did not affect Arlon unduly. He couldn't be offended, something his mother and father also found difficult to process, as much of their efforts leaned toward that goal in their misguided attempts to bring about an emotional reaction from him. If it wasn't so pathetic, he might be amused, if he was of that inclination.

A sudden lightning strike broke the spell that bound them all in silence. Clarice and Gloria both shrieked in alarm, while the menfolk were startled but quiet. Seconds later the rolling thunder roared across the sky. While dark clouds obliterated the rising sun, they had not yet begun to unleash their burdens upon the parched lands.

Arlon guessed that they had perhaps another ten minutes or

more before the heavens opened up. That might result in a pleasant shower or a deluge, he could not be sure. He estimated that they had as much as five or more kilometres to go. Whether they would beat the rain, he could not venture an opinion.

TWENTY

The deluge expired as swiftly as it arrived, leaving the group drenched and cool. The clouds had not evaporated or moved on, but hung ponderously and pregnant in the air, ensuring the humans remained uncomfortably wet. Another inundation of monsoonal rain was imminent. Tired, hungry and exhausted, they stopped for a well-earned break.

"How much farther, Arlon?" asked Clarice, as she sat on a large boulder with her shoulders slumped.

Arlon peered at her, taking in her bedraggled state, then viewed the rest of their motley crew before answering.

"I'd say only a little more than a kilometre. How are you holding up?"

"Cold, hungry and bloody tired. Apart from that, I feel like shit."

Arlon smiled. "Thank you for your help, Clarice. I doubt I could have won that contest. You were...terrific. Really, quite bloody marvellous."

Clarice looked at Arlon with surprise. She had never been the recipient of such extravagant praise from her boss. Though she yearned desperately to please him daily, she had yet to see evidence that she was in any way appreciated or even acknowledged by her handsome mentor.

"Thank you, Arlon, I appreciate that. There's hope for you yet."

"Meaning?"

"You sounded almost human just then. It's a good sign."

"Ms Manning, my condition is incurable. You're delusional if you think I might somehow overcome it given sufficient encouragement or medication."

"Yep, there you go, spoiling it all again. No hope for you, boss, no hope at all."

"I know that. I just finished telling you the same thing."

"Marry me?" suggested Clarice, without humour.

"Beg your pardon?"

"Marry me, Arlon."

"I can't quite believe what I'm hearing. Are you proposing?"

"Wow, nothing gets by you, does it? Yeah, Arlon. I'm asking if you'd like to become my husband. All very acceptable in our enlightened age of supposed equality."

"I get that. I accept that a marriage proposal may come from either gender nowadays. What I don't understand, and I may well be quite dim, is why you would propose in the first place. Isn't there supposed to be some sort of first date involved before a proposal?"

"If I sit around waiting for you to ask me out on a date, Arlon, I'll be an old maid before it happens. Besides, normal rules don't apply in our case. Flirting with you is out of the question. Impressing you with my charm and whatever good looks I might possess is equally useless. So, I am left with my only other option, logic."

Arlon stared in wonder at his secretary. The others in the group looked on in rapt silence while the little drama unfolded. Clarice's genuine smile would melt anyone's heart. Aimed at Arlon, it was met with patient tolerance.

"A marriage proposal based on logic? To what end?"

"A marriage of convenience, if you like. I will have the man I love and adore more than any other man on earth. You will have the knowledge that you can depend on me to be by your side through thick and thin till the end of our days. I know you can't love me in the normal sense of the word, Arlon but it makes no difference to me. I don't expect to be able to *cure* you, as you so indelicately put it. I expect nothing except maybe the promise that you keep yourself for me alone in whatever capacity you can. I love you more than I could ever adequately explain to you, have done since the first moment I set eyes on you at the job interview. I know you must feel...no. Wrong word. You must have some sort of attraction there or else you wouldn't have hired me. There were many applicants far more qualified than me. I looked up the files after you hired me." Clarice smiled and shrugged by way of an explanation.

"I admit that I chose you over the others for a reason, but I wouldn't go so far as to call it an attraction. That implies an emotion."

"What then?"

"I don't know."

"Liar."

"Not knowing does not always qualify as lying, Clarice. I think you're making the story suit your purposes. This might also not be the best time and place...?"

"I know *you* don't get embarrassed, so don't be concerned on my account. We're a good fit, Arlon. We get along well. I can take your strangeness when others are put off by it. I can be your guiding hand when it comes to handling clients and your lack of emotions are causing concerns."

"I hate to be the bearer of bad tidings, but in all likelihood, there won't be a job for you if we ever get out of this. I'm fairly certain the agency will no longer be a viable proposition after this fiasco."

"Oh, I have a few ideas where that's concerned. You give up far too easily."

"No, I think he's right on the money there, missy," argued Travis, who stood a short distance from the pair, holding the rifle that Arlon had laid aside. "Sadly, none of you is going to survive the calamity, as it will be known in the newspapers, when I relate the tale of our plight to the waiting media."

Arlon saw the maniacal glint in Travis' eye as he stood tall in the gloomy light. It appeared he had grossly underestimated the man's determination to make good on his threats. There was something else at play, though, something no one had picked up on yet.

"What on earth are you thinking, Travis? Have you gone completely insane?" asked Gloria.

"Desperate measures for desperate times, I'm afraid," Travis ventured laconically.

"What does that crap mean? You can't expect me to remain silent when we get..."

"There is no 'we', my dear wife. You will be joining this bunch of misfits in the tragedy that befalls the ill-fated expedition to Allies Creek, I'm afraid."

"Why would you even be joking about such a thing? Even you couldn't be that dim-witted to seriously consider doing such a stupid thing, and what for?"

"For the money, of course. It's always about the money. Everything. Life is about making money, and lots of it. I fucked up, babe. I invested where I shouldn't have and we are stony broke. Nothing left, not a brass razoo. In debt up to our eyeballs and lenders breathing down our necks. Allies Creek was meant to be our Hail Mary. A quick purchase, an even quicker basic reno done, then sell the shebang for a nice big profit. That dream went out the window once all this shit started. No one is going to buy it now. We own it, or, rather, the banks own it and are going to demand repayments very shortly. Repayments we are unable to make."

"Oh, for goodness sake, we have credit cards with high limits..."

"All maxed out and no way of paying even the interest."

"Our assets?"

"Mortgaged to the hilt and beyond."

"Then...how is this going to help you? What sort of an idiot are you that you think killing these people is a way out?"

"Not them, *you*."

"Me?"

"Yes, you, dear. Your death by that animal will bring me a tidy little fortune to help me get out of debt and back on my feet. Thankfully, I won't have to put up with your ghastly face while I'm rescuing my company. Your passing will be a huge win-win for me."

"You're finally showing your true colours here, aren't you? I still have no idea how my death, accidental or otherwise, will benefit you"

"Insurance."

"Really?"

"Absolutely."

"So, that was your plan all along? That was the reason you insisted I come out here to inspect this property with you. Even if it turned out that the property was a wise investment, you still needed the insurance money from my death to make good on your debts and to start renovations here."

"See? Not so dumb, huh? Who's the idiot now?" Travis asked as he raised the weapon toward his wife.

TWENTY-ONE

Afterwards, everyone would reveal their individual versions of the events that followed. For Arlon, it played out in slow motion, in vivid colour, repeated for months thereafter in his dreams. As he watched from his seated position, Travis' chest began to expand as if he were inhaling deeply. Blossoming from the expansion, a crimson stain appeared on his shirt front, spreading evenly from a central point, through which emerged a lethally-sharpened steel shovelhead.

Travis looked on in astonishment at the strange object emerging from his chest. Unable to fathom the significance of the mysterious item, he uttered a small whimpering sound and descended gracefully to his knees.

Far from being shocked or traumatised by the tragedy befalling her husband, Gloria walked across the small distance to stand over him.

"Looks like I get it all now, doesn't it?" asked Gloria casually.

"Ha! There's nothing left, I told you," spat Travis, with a hint of blood at the corners of his mouth.

"Did it never occur to you to ask me why my credit card was maxed out each month? Sure, I went shopping occasionally but that was not the bulk of my expenditure. Most of it went on life insurance premiums for *you*, dear. I took out a policy on you over a year ago, knowing how dangerous a game you were playing. Did you think I wouldn't notice the gambling? Did you think I was too stupid to realise you were digging yourself deeper and deeper in debt with hoodlums? Ten million, that's what I get now. With everything in your name alone, something you planned for when you would finally leave me, I have none of those debts you incurred.

"So, to answer your question...you. You are the idiot now and always were. You had a loving, faithful wife by your side and you chose to spurn her for your young trollops, making you think you were far more than you could ever be. "

With that Gloria spat directly into his face, turned on her heel and left the circle of stunned onlookers.

Only Arlon glimpsed the massive shape fleeing the scene from the periphery of their circle after the spear was thrown. Though it was unanimously accepted that the rustic spear could only have been thrown such a long distance by Birrani Nullah Bone, no one else saw him. Neither could anyone publicly offer a reasonable explanation for the act. Arlon believed he knew the reason, but would not reveal his suspicions to anyone at that time. Only a year later did he confess his assumptions to his adoring wife.

The trek back to Allies Creek proved to be relatively uneventful. Rainfall provided vast relief to their parched throats as the heavens opened up again to replenish the land with its life-giving sustenance. The weary travellers did no longer found discomfort in being soaked to the bone. The warm sun soon washed over them to dry their clothes as the clouds dispersed.

Like a desperate desert wanderer happening upon an oasis in the middle of the blistering heat, so did the small group stumble into the township at long last, to find it had escaped the ravages of the fierce fire that had decimated the surrounding countryside. Standing in the middle of the muddy field was a figure whom no one immediately recognised. When the man saw them approaching from the perimeter of the town, he began to wave his hat and lope toward them with an awkward gait.

"Well, I'll be... You know who that is?" Bill asked of no one in particular. "That's Gavin Gaze unless I'm completely mistaken. Somehow he managed to survive, after all."

"I would venture that this unaffected miracle is probably his doing as well," suggested Arlon.

"How do you mean, Arlon?" asked Clarice.

"I'd say he used the ample fire protection equipment here to good use, protecting the entire town from being engulfed in flames.

Have a look, everywhere else is black except here," said Arlon as they approached a happy man, far removed from his usual sombre demeanour.

"Well, you lot are sure a sight for sore eyes," said Gavin. "I didn't hold out a hope in hell for any of you making it out of that alive. Where the heck have you been?"

"Long story, old boy," said Bill jovially. "But what happened to you, more to the point?"

"Roo ran across the road in front of me and I swerved to avoid it. Ended up smashing into a gum tree. My leg got trapped for a while until I managed to grab a branch from the tree that had broken off and was near the window. I used that to lever the steering wheel aside enough to get out, then had a long walk back here."

"We thought he'd gotten you, for sure."

"Who?" asked Gavin.

"Birrani."

"Huh? That thing we heard?"

"Yeah. So, you're all right? No broken bones or other injuries?"

"Nah, a bit of a bruise and a limp, that's all. What happened to that other fella, you know?"

"Mr Henderson got what he had coming to him," offered Gloria with a steely look of determination, before striding past him on her way to the main house.

Gavin gave Bill an enquiring look.

"Yeah, didn't make it."

"She okay, then?"

"Right as rain, I reckon. Arlon here executed a small miracle to rescue the pair of them."

"So, is it, is it dead, then?"

"No. Birrani Nullah Bone lives. How long he lives is another question. Once we tell our stories to the authorities, there's sure to be a manhunt organised for him. Don't like his chances."

"I think he'll surprise us all, Bill. If I'm any judge of character, he will be long gone without so much as a trace when the police come looking for him, and I suspect his grandparents will also be gone, along with the rest of the camp near here. I suspect that he'll finally manage to find some peace in his troubled mind," said Arlon.

The bedraggled crew made their way to the house where it all began, where they gratefully ate some decent food, showered and finally fell into an exhausted sleep. Allies Creek descended into the peaceful atmosphere described in the sales brochures by the optimistic realtors. However, around midnight Arlon was woken gently by a pair of soft, moist lips upon his own. While he was unable to see anything within the dark caravan, he knew instantly who it was by the subtle aroma of an expensive perfume he could not name.

A finger was placed upon his lips just as he was about to remark on the strange event.

"Don't say a word, not a word, Arlon. For once in your life, don't spoil it by talking," whispered Clarice.

Clarice guided the inexperienced man through the intimacies of love-making expertly, delivering them both into the throes of sublime ecstasy. For Arlon, it was as if time had become suspended as his body experienced sensations that he never knew existed. It was as close as he would ever come to feeling something resembling emotion. His heightened physicality forced his emotionality to respond to the sensations assailing his body. While it might never be described by Arlon as being joyous or exhilarating, it was, nonetheless, an entirely satisfactory experience, one he hoped to repeat on many occasions thereafter.

His one word, whispered into Clarice's ear before they both drifted off into a contented sleep, was, 'Yes.'

Clarice smiled as she heard the answer to her question voiced a short time ago in the small clearing, where one man's life ended and another began. She had already begun the machinations of a new business model in her mind. The B.A.M. Detective Agency was born that night. She saw that their lives would take on a completely new direction, one in which she had quite a vast experience on the net. The acronym for the new direction she and her husband would pursue stood for The Bizarre and Mysterious Detective Agency, specialising in just that. Clarice knew from her many midnight jaunts delving into the unexplained and bizarre on the web that she could drum up a load of business for their new partnership.

Arlon had the perfect demeanour to cope with incomprehensible situations avoided by anyone in the mainstream environment. She saw his shortcomings as essential in their new endeavours, where emotional judgements would be considered anathema by the clients. She knew of at least one person who believed her house to be haunted and was in desperate need of their assistance. Her sister spoke of her love for her inherited house and her anguish at the occurrences forcing her to abandon it.

She and many, many others desperately seeking help and finding conventional doors closed to them would finally find some solace and possibly answers with Arlon and the B.A.M. Detective Agency. It was up to her to convince Arlon of the new direction he must take to survive financially.

The End.

B.A.M.
AN ARLON GREY NOVEL
BOOK 2

JOSEF PEETERS

ONE

After a long day of travelling, from the picturesque Shute Harbour on the central Queensland coast to their destination on the equally idyllic Cid Island in the Whitsunday group, Arlon Grey was quite willing to go straight to bed. He did not take well to water of any variety other than a hot shower. He didn't even like having a bath, if truth be told.

Not since being young and spending time in a small seaside village, where he had had an encounter with a rather large shark, had he ventured into or onto water. Though he never showed an emotive response to his aversion of water, because of his condition, he balked at the possibility if it was mentioned or became necessary.

The smallish island did not offer an airstrip or any other means of ingress other than by sea, and so Arlon was forced to accept the bothersome journey. Clarice Manning, the woman whom he had recently agreed to marry, on the other hand enjoyed the experience immensely. Though her café au lait complexion did not tan as readily as she would have liked, she seized the opportunity to bask in the glorious sunshine on the bow of the dual-hulled powerboat as they crossed the Coral Sea, allowing the wind to waft through her golden, curly locks.

Later that day, the 1994 34ft Devil Cat, which the pair had hired from a private operation, lay at anchor within the sheltered bay. After Arlon had been given some basic instructions and was taken through the safety aspects by the elderly owner, they loaded their provisions and personal belongings for the expectant week or so on Cid Island in the home of Gail Sandringham, Clarice's sister. Gail had inherited the island home from her late husband's mother. Ben Sandringham had passed away only a year earlier under strange circumstances.

Gail adored her island sanctuary, despite the tragedy that had taken her husband such a short time ago. Clarice had grieved along with her sister for her charismatic brother-in-law. She had read the long letters her sister had written of the happy times they had shared on the island in the home her mother-in-law owned, but no longer frequented, because of ill-health. Ben was her only son, so, when Patricia Sandringham passed away, the home went to her daughter-in-law.

While it was heart-breaking enough that her husband had passed away prematurely under a cloak of mystery, Gail informed Clarice of other strange occurrences while she stayed at the island home. Events had progressed to such an extent that Gail had decided to move back to Sydney. When Clarice informed her sister of the new direction her employer had taken with his business; namely the newly-formed and renamed Bizarre and Mysterious Detective Agency or B.A.M., as it was shortened to, she leapt at the opportunity to hire the detective to investigate the goings-on at their island home.

It had taken all of Clarice's considerably persuasive powers to convince her husband-to-be to take on a new direction following the semi-successful conclusion of their previous assignment, despite the calamitous events that preceded it. Arlon's unique qualities made it a perfect fit in Clarice's mind. While their previous engagement would have been a spectacular disaster in the eyes of most, it had turned out in their favour financially and fortuitously, as far as Clarice was concerned.

No longer viewed in the conservative light he would have preferred, Arlon came out of the debacle with a completely new reputation and a strange following among the darker, more obscure proponents of the macabre and mysterious who frequent the internet to chat among themselves. Introduced to the underworld of the occult and other happenings in which he was a fledgling virgin, Arlon was convinced by Clarice of the lucrative business to be made from that niche.

The Bizarre and Mysterious Detective Agency was born shortly thereafter, with Arlon accepting their first brief to investigate the suspicious circumstances surrounding the death of his fiancée's brother-in-law. Clarice also saw it as an excellent opportunity to test the waters of their unproven relationship.

Arlon had accepted her proposal at a moment she deemed his weakest; in the afterglow of sex. She had held slim hopes for her chances of ever luring her lover into bed, let alone convincing him of marriage. She was, however, under no illusions as to the reason he accepted. Because of his condition he was unable to respond in a normal sense. Alexithymia prevented him from expressing or experiencing emotions, both a curse and a blessing at times. It was a rare piece of the autism puzzle and Arlon was rated in the highest percentile among the afflicted.

If Arlon were to keep hold of his tongue he could be mistaken for a dashing film star, with his blue-black wavy hair and cobalt-blue eyes that pierced the soul of any female who happened to come under their gaze; until he opened his mouth. That event was usually sufficient to sour the opinion of the most ardent admirer.

"I'm off to bed, then," said Arlon, the moment they entered the stylish beach 'shack'.

"Arlon! No, you can't mean that?" asked Clarice as she followed him through the front door.

"You should know better than that."

"Yeah, I get it, you always say what you mean. I was just voicing my shock, that's all. It's two o'clock in the afternoon and you want to go to bed? Arlon, we've arrived at possibly one of the world's most idyllic destinations for romance and pure tranquillity and all you can think of is going to sleep?" Clarice asked in desperation, as she struggled with some of their luggage.

"I thought we were here to do a job?"

"That, too," she admitted. "Here, take this through to the bedroom, would you? How come you gave me your heavy case while you took mine?"

"I didn't give it to you. You almost shouldered me out of the way to get hold of it, if my memory serves."

"How was I to know you loaded *my* suitcase with *your* gear?"

"You weren't."

"Exactly!"

"Your point?"

"Why did you?"

"Yours is bigger than mine and I needed the space more than you," he explained in a deadpan tone.

"How come?"

"How come, what?"

"Why did you need more space than me?"

"I have more stuff. I would have thought that was obvious."

"Don't tell me you brought all your safari suits and that ridiculous pith helmet thing?"

"Of course," said Arlon, as he proceeded to relieve Clarice of the heavy case, which he transported to the main bedroom of the three-bedroomed house.

"Well, why, for goodness sake?" she asked following him. "Arlon, we're on an island, completely alone, secluded in our very own little bay. Why would you need to bring your Livingstone costume?"

"It's a practical ensemble for venturing into the wilds. I prefer to be covered and protected at all times, Clarice."

"It doesn't bother you that you look like a fool wearing that silly outfit?"

"Of course not. Nothing bothers me, you know that."

"I thought we might have some fresh fish for dinner tonight," suggested Clarice, boldly changing the subject.

"That sounds fine. What's stopping you?"

"You haven't caught it yet."

"Caught what?"

"Dinner!"

"You can't be serious?"

"Why not?"

"Me? Catch a fish?"

"Haven't you ever gone fishing?"

"You know how I am about the water."

"I don't get that. I've seen you face up to some pretty tough dangers without blinking an eye. You say you don't have fear, because that is an emotion, so why are you afraid of the water?"

"I don't *fear* the water. I don't even fear what's in the water. I just don't wish to be on the menu, that's all. The sharks don't come on land where I live and I, in turn, do not enter the water where they live.

"It's the fishing *line* that goes into the water, Arlon, not the fisherperson. Are you saying you've lived on the beach as a child and never went fishing?"

"No."

"Well, then?"

"What?"

"Off you go and catch our dinner. You'll find all the equipment you need in the shed at the back of the house, according to Gail. Bait is in the freezer. Apart from a decent sunhat, I want you out there in some shorts and a T-shirt, Arlon. Thongs on your feet if you must; other than that, nothing. I want you to get some sun onto that magnificent body of yours."

"Is that the shed where...?"

"Yes, but don't even think about starting work yet, mister. I want you all to myself for our first day here. Tomorrow you can begin your investigations."

"I don't think your sister is paying us to have a day off."

"Gail told me we should have some leisure time while we investigate her husband's grisly death. The police haven't gotten any further, and she needs us to bring her some closure, but she expects us to enjoy some of our time together on a pristine island. Besides, she has oodles of dosh coming to her from her mother-in-law's passing. This island home is only the tip of the iceberg."

"Does she own the entire island?"

"No. In fact, she doesn't own anything. She inherited the remains of a ninety-nine-year lease on this bay. It has less than thirty years left on it, with the option to renew once it reaches expiry. The home was built by Patricia Sandringham and her husband in the fifties as a holiday getaway. When her husband, Conrad, fell from the rocks on the point fifteen years ago, she seldom ventured back here. Ben began visiting the island on his own. When his mother became gravely ill, she never returned."

"Then one year ago Ben Sandringham, the son and Gail's husband, dies in... unique circumstances?"

"Uh, uh, not going to happen, Mr Detective. I have to get us squared away in here and you are on strict orders to provide dinner and get some sun. In other words, relax. Shoo!"

Arlon managed to snag hold of a straw hat as he was unceremoniously ushered out the back door. It was only when he placed the hat on his head that Arlon realised it was about three sizes too large. He had to hold his head back at an awkward angle to see where he was going. He walked along the shaded sandy path toward the large shed at the rear of the property housing the diesel generator, miscellaneous machinery and a mechanical workshop. It was where Ben Sandringham's body was discovered. At least, what was left of it.

Lining the pathway on either side were the ubiquitous collections derived from numerous beachcombing expeditions.

Clam shells, driftwood in interesting shapes and sizes, rocks and other items presumably found by the Sandringham family during their frequent visits. Interspersed between the odd assortments were the solar bollards lighting the path at night in differing hues to create a festive atmosphere, so Arlon was told. He did not understand how coloured lights could add anything of value to any situation. Parties, festivities, gatherings...*holidays* (albeit working holidays), were completely lost on him. Arlon's condition deprived him of many normal associations taken for granted by everyone else. He derived no pleasure from the company of others, no enjoyment of his surroundings or all the other emotions of a positive or negative kind.

Arlon recalled his parents' sadness and frustration when they were unable to receive love from their only son. His time spent with them at the seaside residence of his youth did not conjure happy memories, nor even laughter and enjoyment where his parents were concerned. The harder they tried to gain some emotions from their son, the worse it became for them: they sank further and further into depression. Rather than accepting their son's condition and learning to live with it as best they could, they had made it their impossible mission in life to break through to him.

The shell did not crack, the emotions did not flow, and their family fell apart. They provided for him, saw that Arlon had the best schooling they could afford, but grew sullen with their disappointment, eventually blocking him out altogether. They no longer felt guilt that they had somehow contributed to their son's condition. That had been disproved by the diagnosis. However, when they refused to accept that they could not get through to him, it caused them more and more grief.

The large, insulated shed of corrugated-iron exterior and sound-proofing interior, loomed at the end of the path. Gail Sandringham had sent a mechanic to service the generator and ensure that all was in working order before her sister and Arlon arrived. Arlon could hear the dull thrum of the generator, despite all the effort to suppress the noise. He felt the vibrations through the soles of his Dunlop Volleys as he approached the heavy, latched door.

A pair of seagulls in the treetops above him squawked their protest at his intrusion into their midst. Arlon peered up through the dappled light, wondering if the birds had built a nest above him. Then he wondered if seagulls nested in trees at all. He felt sure he had read that they nested on the ground, mainly among the low shrubs and other vegetation adorning the dunes. This was just one of the many useless facts running around Arlon's mind, garnered from a troubling childhood spent almost entirely on his own, reading everything of a factual nature he could lay his hands on.

To either side of the doorway rested a sentinel pair of large, barnacle-encrusted boulders. It would have taken quite some effort to move the rocks there from where they were presumably found on the beach. Arlon pondered the possible reason anyone would go to all the trouble to line the path with debris and to haul huge rocks from the sea. It didn't make any sense to him. As he drew near the door, reaching out to release the latch, Arlon suddenly retracted his outstretched hand.

He peered about him with a look of concern creasing his handsome features. If asked to describe what he was experiencing, he would have had some difficulty. It was as if there was a drop in pressure about him. He wondered if perhaps it was the precursor of an impending earthquake. He had read that some people claim to experience an increase or decrease in seismicity before an earthquake. It was very brief and Arlon dismissed his initial assertions. He unlatched the door, stepping through into the gloomy interior where the deafening sound of the generator pulsed and pounded the senses.

While he was sorely tempted to poke around to get a head start on his investigations, he dismissed the notion in favour of appeasing his wife-to-be. She could get very upset if Arlon chose to ignore her wishes to relax and catch dinner. He found the light switch on the inside of the door frame and flicked it on.

To the left of the entry was a small area given over to housing fishing rods in overhead racks, benches and sinks for cleaning fish and tending to tackle and other assorted paraphernalia. A chest freezer gave off a pungent fishy odour when he lifted the lid. He retrieved a plastic bag of frozen prawns from it. He then chose a suitable beach rod with a side casting reel. He was familiar with the operation of that particular type, which basically resembled a hand-held reel mounted on a rod.

A wicker creel, a small tackle box with sufficient hooks and sinkers, along with a filleting knife and a hook remover, completed his provisioning. He gave one last look around the cavernous interior before switching off the light and closing the door as he exited the shed. Relieved to be away from the imposing noise, Arlon made his way along the path, then veered around the house to head for the beach.

Things had certainly changed for Arlon since his last assignment for a long-time friend and client. The job had not ended well. In fact, it spelled the final days for his conservative detective agency. While he had rescued a woman and been paid handsomely for the effort, the notoriety he gained did not bode well for that kind of business any longer. Once he had agreed to marry Clarice, his secretary and assistant of a couple of years, she nudged their agency into a very new and, to Arlon, totally foreign, direction.

Clarice had been an aficionado of the bizarre and weird for some time as she trawled through the internet for stories that few believed. Her hunger for the obscure involved her in many chat groups with fellow conspirators. When it seemed obvious that Arlon's conservative agency would no longer gain sufficient contracts to keep the business afloat, Clarice threw him in the deep end with his first serious client seeking answers to a grave mystery.

The entrance onto the grand vista once he was over the dunes cut short Arlon's reveries. The sun was high in the sky. The snow-white sand leading down to the mirror-like waters of the tranquil bay would take anyone's breath away. For Arlon, it did nothing more than affirm his wish to be anywhere but there. From under a coconut palm marking the beginning of the path to the house through the dunes, Arlon retrieved a lightweight reclining chair.

He made his way down to the water's edge, where he set up his chair at the appropriate angle to relax while keeping an eye on his fishing rod. He deftly baited the single suicide hook with a decent-sized, sufficiently-thawed prawn, twisted the reel to face the tip of the rod and then let fly with the weighted line to a distance of some thirty metres from the shoreline. From one of his shirt pockets he retrieved a tube of zinc cream to spread onto his nose.

He placed the handle of the rod into the metal rod holder he had spiked into the soft sand beside his chair, then reclined comfortably. The boredom hit him almost the moment he sat down, with his eyelids beginning to sag. The warm sun lulled his body into an immediate snooze. Fortunately, he had had the foresight to set the drag on his reel correctly, for, moments after he subsided into slumber, the reel began to scream as the line ran out.

Reflexively, Arlon's hand shot out to the rod and reel, which he removed quickly from the holder. Before he had time to consciously decide upon a course of action, he reared back on the rod to set the hook firmly into the mouth of the fish. Rising from the recliner, Arlon began the process of raising the rod to drag the large fish in by a metre before winding up the gain as he dropped the tip once more. This action was repeated many times as the large pelagic was brought slowly to the shore.

The GT, or giant trevally, weighed about fifteen kilos and Arlon was feeling the strain on his muscles after landing the fish. Satisfied that he had caught dinner, he set about returning to the house. The heavy fish and the other fishing gear made the trip back a slower one with a few rest stops.

At the shed, he placed the fish on the stainless steel sink, ready for cleaning, filleting and deboning. Unlike their non-pelagic cousins from which a nice clean, boneless slab of flesh was possible, a pelagic had to have a centre, lateral line of bones removed.

Arlon placed the rod and reel back into its rack, then distributed the remaining gear to the places they belonged. He then washed down the fish with fresh water. He decided that Clarice would have the honour of dressing the fish, as he had done all the hard work in catching it. As he left the shed he once more felt that WHUMP he had experienced earlier. It was a gut-somersaulting feeling almost like the experience on a roller-coaster. It lasted only milliseconds, yet made him look about uncertainly, wondering if he was imagining it.

Glad to be out of the noisy shed once more, Arlon made his way back to the house, where Clarice was still packing clothes into a chest of drawers.

"Back so soon?"

"You asked me to catch dinner; I did. You didn't say anything about staying out there a certain length of time."

Clarice stared at him to ascertain if he was telling the truth.

"You telling me you already caught our dinner?"

"Yep."

"Well?"

"Well, what?"

"Where is it?"

"In the shed, waiting for you to clean and fillet it."

"I don't believe it."

"Why would I lie?"

"I can't believe you would leave it to me to clean and fillet the fish. Why wouldn't you do it and bring in for me to cook?"

"Surely I don't have to do everything?"

"Ooh, you're sounding more like a husband every day," she sighed. "Go on then, wipe that silly cream off your nose and I'll go out and slave over *your* fish."

"Aren't *you* eating any, then?"

"Arlon, I swear..."

"You do not."

"I bloody do!" she admonished, before stomping off through the rear door to the shed.

When Arlon returned from the bathroom after cleaning his face, Clarice was in the living room.

"Well, that was quick. See? I was right to let you clean and fillet the fish if you were that quick," suggested Arlon, as he sat heavily on the cane sofa with coastal pattern print cushions.

"Very funny. Why don't you take up comedy as your next gig?"

Arlon looked at her with surprise, "I don't get it. Why would I want to take up comedy? I have a perfectly good job..."

"Give it up, Mr Funny Man. I knew it was too quick for you to be back. Did you decide against fish for dinner?"

"What are you talking about, Clarice? I caught..."

"Hey, enough with the jokes already. I'm not amused, Arlon, okay? I was hoping we could have a lovely fresh fish dinner out there under the stars tonight. I think there's even a full moon tonight."

"Well?"

"Well, what?" said Clarice, with an angry face and her hands on her ample hips.

"What's wrong with the fish I caught?"

"Where is this mysterious fish you caught?"

"Clarice, have you been drinking? I left it on the sink in the shed. If you really don't want to clean it up, then just say so."

"On the sink?"

"Clarice, are you getting hard of hearing? Yes, on the sink."

ABOUT THE AUTHOR

Josef arrived in Australia with his parents and siblings in 1964. A near lifetime of creative pursuits has culminated in his desire to produce entertaining stories. Josef lives with his wife in the tiny outback town of Moulamein, NSW Australia where they own and manage a small caravan park, while they each indulge in their artistic endeavours. Josef chooses to base his stories in Australian settings, populating them with authentic-sounding Aussie characters. While this approach will not appeal to everyone, he stays true to the country he has grown to love.

If you would like to follow the author and keep up with his latest books, please visit his website;
http://lakesidecaravanpark.wixsite.com/josef

If you enjoyed reading Josef's book please leave a review on either Amazon or Goodreads.